Paint the Librarian Dead

A Booker Falls Mystery

by

Kenn Grim

Copyright 2018 © by Kenn Grimes

For information, email Cozy Cat Press, cozycatpress@aol.com or visit our website at: www.cozycatpress.com

COZY CAT
P R E S S

ISBN: 978-1-946063-55-7
Printed in the United States of America

Cover design by Paula Ellenberger
www.paulaellenberger.com

10 9 8 7 6 5 4 3 2 1

For Beth, Harriet, Monica and Sarah,
outstanding librarians with whom I have had
the great pleasure of working.

Thanks to my readers, *Judy Grimes, Madge Walls,* and *Linda Miller*

To *Dave and Julie Sprenger*, owners/operators of the Laurium Manor Inn (the Hoatson Mansion) and the Victorian Hall B&B (the McDonald House), Laurium, Michigan

To *Bill and Vic,* volunteers at the Vintage Fire Museum, Jeffersonville, Indiana

Other books by

KENN GRIMES

*Camptown . . . one hundred and fifty years of stories
from Camptown, Kentucky*

The Other Side of Yesterday

Strangled in the Stacks

Trifecta of Murder

CHAPTER ONE

"Frank Mitchell?"

Frank turned to find a large man standing in front of him, a man he remembered seeing once before. Before he could say or do anything, he felt the sharp stab of the knife as it slid in between the fourth and fifth ribs of his left side.

The man pulled the knife back out and stood for a minute, watching as Frank doubled over and dropped onto the snow-covered sidewalk.

"Don't be messing around with that nigger no more," the man said.

He removed a handkerchief from his pocket, wiped Frank's blood off the knife, turned and walked quickly back to his car parked across the street in front of J. P. Finnegan's Fancy Groceries and Fresh Meats.

Minutes later he was headed out of town.

*****

Snow and sub-freezing temperatures had gripped the town of Booker Falls for the past five days.

The college library had been closed on Monday, the result of a broken boiler. It wasn't scheduled to be repaired until tomorrow.

As a result, Myrtle Tully, who held the position of assistant librarian, was on a paid holiday and making the most of it.

She'd spent the morning at Paige Turner's New, Used and Rare Books Store, then met Daisy O'Hearn, her best friend and fellow boarder at Mrs. Darling's Boarding House, for lunch at Miss Madeline's Eatery.

It was a rare treat for both of them, as their rent included all their meals, and neither was in a position to spend money they didn't have to.

Later, Myrtle had ridden with another fellow boarder, Henri de la Cruz, out to the old logging camp northeast of town.

At first, she had declined Henri's invitation.

"Henri, it's cold outside. I'd much prefer to sit here by the fire and read this new book Paige got in at the store yesterday."

"What's it called?" asked Henri, taking the book from Myrtle's hand. "*The Mysterious Affair at Styles*? And who's Agatha Christie?"

"It's a murder mystery. You know how I love murder mysteries," said Myrtle, giving him a wink. "And this is Miss Christie's first book. But from what I've read so far, it won't be her last."

"We'd be taking the sleigh."

"The sleigh?"

Myrtle loved the sleigh!

She'd had the pleasure of riding in Henri's sleigh twice before, the first time a year ago when she'd gone with him to interview Paul Momet about the unsolved death of a young woman who had been murdered some twenty-eight-years before, in 1895, and whose case had been reopened; and later that same month when he gave her a lift to St. Barbara's Catholic Church to attend Christmas Eve Mass.

"Did you put the Packard away?" asked Myrtle.

Several months earlier, Henri had become the owner of the third automobile to call Booker Falls home, a 1920 Packard Town Car.

At Henri's urging, Myrtle had reluctantly put her own car, a thirteen-year-old Model N Ford, away for the winter in the big barn out behind the boarding house, where it shared space with two carriages, one belonging to Mrs. Darling and the other to Henri, as well as the sleigh.

Jessie and Hank, the two horses who provided the horsepower for all of the non-motorized conveyances, also called the barn home.

As County Constable, Henri had decided to keep his car out a while longer, in case it was needed for police business.

"No, I thought a sleigh ride might be fun, eh? Besides, the roads out there will probably be unpassable in a car. There must be a good three feet on the ground."

So Myrtle found herself at the logging camp, where Henri was giving her the grand tour.

"You've been here before?" asked Myrtle.

"Yah. A couple times with old Mr. Koskinen."

"Mr. Koskinen? The one who's ninety-four?"

"Do you know him?"

Myrtle shook her head. "No, George told me about him when we visited the falls, and I asked how they got their name."

"I see." Henri's tone had an unmistakable frostiness to it. He knew about the picnic George had taken Myrtle on to the falls. And though he knew he had no claim on her, even if they *had* gone out several times— shared a few kisses, maybe more—he wasn't all that keen she was also seeing George Salmon, the town mayor.

"What's that building over there?" asked Myrtle. She pointed to a large structure leaning precariously to one side. She hadn't missed Henri's annoyance and thought it best to change the subject.

"According to Mr. Koskinen, that was the camp office and store. The foreman and the log scaler lived on the top floor. At the store, the loggers bought things like socks, and tobacco and some clothes—and sewing material. They didn't have anybody around but themselves to mend something when they tore it."

"What's a log scaler?"

"He's the fellow who measured the cut timber for volume and determined its quality. Then he figured out how much it would be worth."

"Is that bigger building the barn?" asked Myrtle.

"No, that was the bunkhouse. It held over seventy men. The cook shanty was attached to it. That's where the meals were prepared and eaten. As you can see, it's fallen over now. The barn is over there." Henri pointed to the far side of the camp. "They kept the horses and oxen and hay and some equipment there. Next to it was the blacksmith shop."

"I imagine logging was hot, sweaty work," said Myrtle.

"I suppose to some extent. But all the work was done during the winter months, so they sure didn't have to worry about summer heat."

"The winter? But that's the worst weather. Why would they work only in the winter?"

"That way they could drag the logs on sleds—the horses and oxen would—they'd drag them over the snow to the river banks. They'd leave them there 'til spring when they'd float them downstream."

Myrtle looked up at the towering trees that stretched above them, their branches heavy with snow.

"I suppose these have all grown back since they quit taking the lumber out," she said.

"Yes and no," said Henri. "These trees *have* grown up since then, but they aren't the same kind of trees that were here when logging was going on."

"What do you mean?"

"When logging was at its peak, all the trees were white pine. That's what they were harvesting. But when those were all gone, that allowed the trees you see here now—aspen, sugar maple, jack pine—to come up in their place."

Henri looked up at the sky. "It's getting dark. We'd better be getting back, eh?"

*****

The snow, which had let up while Myrtle and Henri explored the logging camp, started up again. By the time they arrived back at the main road, it was coming down harder, the temperature had dropped considerably, and night was coming on fast.

"I really appreciate this foot warmer," said Myrtle as she pulled the collar of the skunk fur coat up around her neck. On her head, she wore a full fur Russian hat she'd purchased a few days before at de Première Qualité Women's Wear Shop.

Henri had remembered from their previous sleigh rides together that Myrtle found the foot warmer, a small metal box with hot coals placed inside, to be especially welcome. By now, the coals were almost out, but the container still provided a modicum of warmth.

The moon was eighty percent visible and, with no clouds to hide them, myriad stars filled the night sky.

"Henri, it is so beautiful out here," said Myrtle, as she snuggled down under the lap robe Henri had also thoughtfully brought along.

Brightly colored flowers—red, yellow, white, purple—spilled forth from a cornucopia set on a dark background. She remembered Henri said it belonged to his mother.

Myrtle leaned her head back. "Look at those stars," she said. "I've never seen so many."

"You know what Mrs. Darling would say, don't you?" asked Henri.

Myrtle turned to him. "No. What would Mrs. Darling say?"

"You see one star, you've seen dem all."

Almost seventy years of age, Mrs. Darling, while pleasant, kind and considerate, was not one to mince words.

Myrtle remembered on two occasions hearing her utter words to the effect of what Henri had just quoted. The first was the previous summer's Fourth of July parade, which the old lady chose to forego—"*You see one parade, you've seen dem all*"—and the second time on their trip a few months ago when the two of them traveled to Marquette to visit a former boarder at Mrs. Darling's boarding house, now in prison there.

Myrtle had attempted to get her landlady to look at Lake Superior as they drove past it.

"*You see one lake, you've seen dem all,*" her landlady had replied.

"I'm sure you're right," said Myrtle. "That's exactly what she would have said. But I think they're wonderful."

The trip from the logging camp back to the boarding house took them past the library. A solitary light above the front entrance provided the only illumination.

They were within fifty yards of the building when, suddenly, the front door burst open and a man ran out, carrying a flat square object. Within seconds he disappeared around the corner of the library, toward a garden area that held a pond and a grotto.

Myrtle grabbed Henri's arm. "Henri, did you see that?" she asked.

"Yah," said Henri, as he urged Jessie to a faster gait. When they reached the library, both of them sprang from the sleigh, following the tracks left by the man on the snow-covered ground. The only light there was that provided by the moon, which proved to be more than sufficient to allow them to spot tracks leading to the edge of the pond, now frozen over.

"He must have gone across the pond and run into the woods," said Henri.

But when they reached the far side, there was no sign of any tracks.

"Where did he go?" asked Myrtle, looking around.

"I don't know," said Henri. He walked around the pond, first to the point where it ended at the grotto, then back to the other side.

No tracks.

"He couldn't have just disappeared," said Myrtle.

"I sure don't know where he went," said Henri as he walked over to the woods. He didn't expect to find tracks there either, but he didn't know where else to look.

"Nothing there," he said, returning to Myrtle's side. "That *was* a painting he was carrying, wasn't it?"

"It must have been. I don't know what else it could have been."

"We should go inside and see what's missing, eh?" said Henri. "You have keys?"

Myrtle nodded.

The Adelaide College Library was the repository for a dozen paintings bequeathed by the founder of the college, Louis Amyx, upon his death in 1888. All the works were by French artists, including one each by Pierre-Auguste Renoir and Paul Cézanne.

Six of the works hung on the library's west wall, with the east wall containing the rest.

Once inside, Myrtle turned on the lights and quickly scanned both walls. Nothing appeared to be missing.

"They're all here," she said.

"Are there any other paintings?" asked Henri. "Any worth stealing?"

"No, this is all . . . except . . . ."

"Except?"

"There is one more piece, upstairs. It's a portrait of Mrs. Amyx. Her brother built the library."

Myrtle climbed the spiral staircase, Henri trailing behind her. When they reached the top, they stopped.

"Looks like it's still here," said Henri.

The portrait of Betsy Hutchinson Amyx, a magnificent piece that measured some six feet in height and five feet across, looked down upon them.

"Besides," he continued, "what the fellow had under his arm wasn't anywhere near this big." He turned to Myrtle. "You're sure there are no other pieces of art in the library?"

Myrtle shook her head. "Not that I'm aware of. Oh, wait, Mr. Mitchell has one in his office, one he painted."

"I've seen that painting," said Henri. "Pretty much like the one I have in my office. I can't see anyone wanting to steal it. All of his stuff is always so dark— browns and greens and black. He never has any bright color in his paintings, like yellow or red."

"I can't speak to the yellow," said Myrtle, "but George told me once Mr. Mitchell never uses red because he thinks it somehow is connected to the devil."

Henri rolled his eyes.

Back downstairs they peered through the windows of the office of Frank Mitchell, the head librarian and Myrtle's boss.

The painting still hung on the wall.

"Well, okay, then, we have a mystery, don't we?" said Henri. "If it wasn't a painting the fellow was carrying, what was it?"

"That's not the only mystery," said Myrtle.

"What do you mean?"

"Where did he disappear to?"

CHAPTER TWO

Gus Oosterman looked up when he heard the tinkle of the bell above the front door. His eyes widened when he saw Frank Mitchell stagger in, clutching his side, his face showing not much more color than the snow on the wooden sidewalk outside.

"Holy Whaa!" exclaimed Gus. "Vhat happened vit you?"

"I been stabbed," said Frank, draping himself across one of the counters that displayed men's shirts. "Get Doc Sherman—please!"

"What's all the commotion?" asked Gus's wife, Ebba, as she emerged from the back of the store.

"It's Mr. Mitchell—somebody done stabbed him," said Gus.

Ebba brushed past her seemingly frozen husband and raced to Frank's side. Gently, she helped him as he crumpled to the floor.

"Well, don't just stand dere like a poop!" said Ebba. "Run across da street to Doc Sherman's office. See if he's dere and if he is, bring him over."

Finally galvanized into action, Gus hurried out the door.

Ebba unbuttoned Frank's greatcoat and saw the splash of blood as it oozed through his shirt.

"Mr. Mitchell, you stay put right dere," said Ebba. I'm a'gonna go to da back and get a towel to put on dere 'til da doc gets here."

Ebba scurried to the back room, but before she could return, Ambrose Sherman burst through the door, almost tripping over Frank.

"Frank, you okay?" asked Ambrose, as he knelt beside him.

"It hurts," said Frank, through clenched teeth.

"Well, okay, then, let's have a look."

Ambrose unbuttoned Frank's shirt and moved him onto his side, exposing the wound entry.

"Doesn't look too deep," said the doctor. "I think your coat kept it from getting any deeper." He removed a pad from his bag and carefully dabbed Frank's wound, soaking up what little blood remained.

"Who did this?" asked Doctor Sherman.

"I don't know his name," said Frank, "but I know what he is."

"*What* he is?" asked Ebba, watching the doctor apply a bandage to the laceration.

"A Klansman," said Frank. He winced as Doctor Sherman pressed a little too hard. "He's with the Klan."

"Sorry," said Ambrose. "So, Frank, what makes you think it was a Klansman?"

"I had a run-in with them last month," said Frank. "Four men. It's about this woman I'm seeing."

Ambrose nodded. It had become common knowledge that Frank, though in his sixties, was seeing one of the students at the college, a young woman not yet twenty. Compounding the situation was the fact the girl was a Negro, and Frank was white.

Ambrose had even heard that the girl's father had confronted Frank at the library and made threats on his life.

"Okay," said Ambrose, getting to his feet. "Like I said, the wound isn't too deep. You'll hurt for a few days, but nothing to worry about. Go home and get some rest."

"Gus will help you home," said Ebba. She took her husband by the elbow and moved him toward Frank, who by now had gotten to his feet and was buttoning up his shirt.

"Oh, sure, yah," said Gus. "Come on; I'll valk you home, make sure you get dere okay, eh?"

*****

It was almost ten o'clock by the time Henri and Myrtle arrived back at the boarding house. While Henri secured the carriage and Jessie in the barn, Myrtle went in through the back door to the kitchen. She found Mrs. Darling sitting at the table, a cup of tea in front of her.

She had a worried look on her face.

"Mrs. Darling, you okay?" asked Myrtle, as she removed her hat and coat.

"No, dearie, I ain't," said the old lady without looking up.

"Why, what's wrong?"

Myrtle got a cup from the cupboard and a sachet of thimbleberry tea off the shelf and placed it in the cup, which she filled with water from the still-hot teakettle. She joined her landlady at the table.

"It's your boss, dat poor Mr. Mitchell," said Mrs. Darling.

Myrtle's eyes widened. "Mr. Mitchell? Why? What happened?"

"He got attacked again."

"What?" Now Myrtle was *really* concerned.

"Yah, some man stabbed him downtown, in front of Mr. Oosterman's store."

"Is he okay? Is he . . ?"

"Oh, he ain't dead. Fact is, he wasn't even hurt bad. But, ya know, dis is da second time now, in a little over two months."

At that moment, Henri came in, and Mrs. Darling repeated the whole story.

"Doc Sherman called," she said. "Wanted to make sure you knew."

"I should go over there," said Henri.

"Doc says he's okay for tonight. But you might want to stop by tomorrow, eh?"

Henri nodded. "That's what I'll do, then. Is there any more tea?"

Mrs. Darling started to get up. "I'll get it for you."

Myrtle laid her hand on her landlady's. "You sit right there. I'll take care of it."

*****

Frank Mitchell's stabbing was the topic of conversation at the breakfast table the next morning.

"Who could do such a thing?" asked Daisy, as she spread a generous dollop of thimbleberry jam on her English muffin.

"I talked with Doc Sherman a little bit ago," said Henri. "He said Frank told him it was a Klansman who stabbed him."

"A Klansman?" said Pierre, Mrs. Darling's fourth boarder. "That's what happened to him . . . when? Back in October?"

"That's right," said Myrtle, "right in front of the library. A band of five men attacked him." She turned to Henri. "They never found out who they were?" she asked. "The state police over in Marquette?"

Henri shook his head. "Nah. According to Captain Wysocki, they're still looking into it, but they don't have much to go on."

"Might this have been one of those men?" asked Daisy.

Henri shrugged. "Maybe."

"How is Mr. Mitchell doing?" asked Pierre.

"Doc says he'll be fine. He didn't lose much blood—just shaken up."

"I should think so," said Daisy.

CHAPTER THREE

The day had not gone well for Myrtle.

It started off badly at breakfast when she spilled coffee on her white blouse and had to quickly change. She appreciated Mrs. Darling's offer to wash it straightaway so that it wouldn't stain.

She had mixed feelings when she arrived at the library to find that Claude Amyx, the diminutive janitor and sometimes handyman, had, indeed, gotten the boiler fixed, though it had not yet had time to warm up the building. Consequently, she spent the day wrapped up in her coat, trying to keep warm, at the same time attempting to catch up on work that had gone undone since the boiler had died three days before.

The final straw was when the strap on her snowshoes broke fifteen minutes after she left the library, heading home.

She shuddered, remembering when the same thing happened a year ago. Except then she got caught in a blizzard and would have died if Daisy and Henri hadn't found her. Thankfully, there was no blizzard today. The sky was clear, and only a few flakes flew about.

She'd walked the two miles from the library before in the snow; she could do it again.

Two hours later, when she reached home, she was hardly able to drag herself up the front steps onto the porch and into the house. She thought—briefly—of plopping down in one of the rockers, though the temperature was barely above freezing. But her need to get out of her work clothes overcame that idea.

Once inside, she picked up the pile of mail from the little table in the hall placed there for that purpose and rifled through it, looking for anything that might have her name on it.

Then she smiled.

And everything bad that had happened since breakfast that morning no longer mattered.

It was a letter from Thomas.

Seeing his name made her feel better. She thought back to that night two years ago, in Paris, when she first met him.

She had been on her way home, back to America, after serving as a "Hello Girl" for the Allied Expeditionary Force, when she and two of her friends decided to celebrate their last night. She never knew what became of the other two girls.

Thomas was a student at École des Beaux-Arts—or so she thought at the time—and gone with him to his apartment on the Boulevard de Clichy. Ten years earlier the place had been home to Pablo Picasso. One of his sketches was still on the wall.

She'd spent the night there and in the morning left without saying goodbye. She'd returned to her boarding house and thought that was the end of it.

Then, a few months ago he'd appeared unexpectedly, literally on her doorstep. He had come to Booker Falls, specifically to the library, to see the collection of paintings the library held.

They'd sat in the garden outside by the grotto, where she discovered he hadn't been a student, but a professor, at the university, and now worked for Chapellier Galleries, a prestigious art gallery located in London.

Born in England, in his early thirties, and educated at Oxford, at the Ruskin School of Art and, later, at the Leeds School of Art, Thomas was not only an accomplished artist in his own right but possessed connoisseurship, a quality that served him well as a purchasing agent for his employer.

On that previous trip, he had remarked that one of the paintings hanging in the library was a forgery. When Myrtle later asked Mr. Mitchell about it, he was enraged, asserting he knew it was not, as he had been present when the piece was given to the library.

Thomas had promised to return to Booker Falls on one condition: that Myrtle would allow him to paint her portrait, although just how revealing the work would be had never been confirmed—whether it was to be a nude portraiture or not.

Myrtle ripped open the envelope, read the letter, and bounded up the stairs.

*****

Myrtle knocked on Daisy's door. "Daisy," she said.

"Come in," came Daisy's voice from inside the room. "It's not locked."

Daisy looked up from her typewriter as Myrtle entered. "You know, if it's not locked, you can always come on in. I've got nothing to hide."

"I want to make sure I don't interrupt if you should have a lover in here," said Myrtle, as she plopped down on the bed.

"A lover, huh? Well, first of all, I would have to *find* a lover. Though I doubt seriously Mrs. Darling would tolerate such shenanigans under her roof."

"I know—I was kidding. Guess what?"

Daisy shook her head. "A long lost uncle died and left you his fortune."

"Even better. I got a letter from Thomas."

Daisy's eyes got big. "Thomas? Your lover from Paris?"

"It was one night, Daisy. I'd hardly call him my lover."

"But you did . . . you know, *do it*. You told me so yourself."

Myrtle felt her cheeks get red. "Yes, and I never should have told you. Anyway, it was just that one time."

"What did the letter say?" asked Daisy.

"He'll be here next month," said Myrtle, a big grin covering her face.

"So, are you going to let him?"

"Let him what?"

"Paint you. You said he wanted to paint you; in the nude, maybe. Are you going to let him?"

Myrtle blushed again. "I haven't even thought about it."

Daisy chuckled. "If you can't say 'no' then, believe me, you've thought about it."

CHAPTER FOUR

Six-twenty-five. Five minutes until the library closed.

In her mind, Myrtle had her coat half-way on, and she was ready to go. She always looked forward to closing time on Saturday because she wouldn't have to be back to work until Tuesday. She liked her job— loved it, actually—but sometimes the routine got downright boring.

Add to that the fact that Mr. Mitchell had not been in since he'd been stabbed three days earlier and she'd had to handle both his duties and hers; though the duties he assumed for himself were minimal at best.

She'd be happy to leave the library behind for two days.

When she heard the front door open and shut, her first thought was that it better not be a student because they knew darned well what the hours were.

It wasn't. It was Thomas.

"Thomas!" Myrtle cried. "What are you doing here?"

"I wanted to see you. I wrote you I was coming. I just arrived in town, and after I got settled in, I took off for here."

"But when you left before you said you wouldn't be back until next year; and your letter said next month."

"A change of plans: I'll tell you all about it."

"Did you drive?"

"No, I walked from Miss Wasserman's," said Thomas. "I didn't drive this trip. It's all by rail. I had a man drive me here—to Booker Falls—from Houghton. I walked here, to the library."

"Well, I'm glad to see you," said Myrtle. She hugged him and gave him a peck on the cheek. "I'm closing up the library. Why don't we go back into town to Miss Madeline's and we'll get a bite? And you can catch me up on what's been happening with you."

*****

"So you're staying at Miss Wasserman's," said Myrtle after they had gotten their table and placed their order with Mona, the waitress, who was also Miss Madeline's granddaughter.

"Yes, she seems nice. And it's a magnificent house. I'm amazed at how grand many of the homes are here."

"Well, we're not Paris—or New York, or London, or New Orleans. But we're not exactly country bumpkins, either."

"I didn't mean to imply . . . ."

"No, it's fine," said Myrtle. She laid her hand on Thomas's. "I was astonished myself when I first arrived in town at how civilized it was. I thought I would find wolves roaming the streets."

Thomas laughed.

Myrtle liked his laugh—it was sincere and full of life.

"And my room is delightful," said Thomas. "Apparently at one time, it belonged to the daughter of the man who owned the place."

Myrtle stared at him.

"Rachel's room?" she said.

"Why, yes, I believe that's what Miss Wasserman said: the room had belonged to her charge, Rachel."

This time it was Myrtle's turn to laugh.

Thomas's brow furrowed. "Did I say something humorous?"

"Miss Wasserman didn't tell you about the room?"

"Here you go," said Mona, setting their plates down.

"What is this again?" asked Thomas, eyeing the bowl in front of him.

"Mojakka. It's Finnish—fish soup. You'll like it."

Thomas took a spoonful and tasted it. "Yes, you're right," he said, looking up at Myrtle. "It is excellent. Now, what about the room?"

"That was the room she was killed in;" said Myrtle, sipping her sweet thimbleberry tea. "Rachel."

Thomas had just taken another spoonful of soup. This time it stopped part way to his lips. "What? She was killed in that room? When? How?"

Myrtle explained that a few months earlier there had been three murders in Booker Falls in four days, two in the house in which he was now staying.

"My goodness!" exclaimed Thomas. "Was the culprit apprehended?"

"Oh, yes," said Myrtle. "He's now behind bars over in Marquette."

Thomas shook his head. "I wish she would have told me."

"Would you have gone elsewhere?"

Thomas thought for a minute. "I suppose not. There's no blood on the floor or the walls or anywhere that I can see, so I guess there's no reason to be alarmed. But I do wish she would have told me," he said, taking a drink of his tea.

"How long are you here for?" asked Myrtle.

"I have to head back the day after tomorrow."

"Then you must come to the boarding house tomorrow evening for dinner."

"Am I still invited?"

"Oh, yes. Mrs. Darling said whenever you showed up she would set an extra place."

"I've been looking for a place to set up my studio," said Thomas, staring at Myrtle over his cup.

"Your studio?"

"For when I paint your portrait."

Myrtle's eyebrows raised. "I wasn't aware we confirmed that," she said.

"Oh, yes," said Thomas, grinning, "we confirmed it all right. What we *hadn't* confirmed was how it would be done."

"You mean . . . ."

"Yes, that is what I mean."

Myrtle's face grew red. "We shall have to discuss the whole thing," she said. "And did you find a place; assuming I say yes?"

"I had hoped to use the space above Miss Wasserman's carriage house; it would have been perfect. Unfortunately, one of the other boarders, Mr. Hutchinson, a very nice man, already has rented it for his studio."

"He's an artist?"

"Yes, and quite good, I dare say. He showed me some of his work. His style is similar to the old masters: you know, Rembrandt and Vermeer and Claesz? He works in oil, which I feel is the best medium. That's why I use it. He said he was a friend of your boss."

"Mr. Mitchell?"

"Yes. Said they were in school together."

"Strange Mr. Mitchell has never mentioned him. How long has he been here?"

"Moved in a little while ago. He was Miss Wasserman's first tenant. Since that space wasn't available, I looked elsewhere and found another site for when I return next month."

"So you're coming back next month?"

"That's the plan. Then I'll have a whole week."

"Where is this new place you found?"

"I'll take you there when we leave here," said Thomas.

"You told me when you left in October you were heading for Minneapolis, and then back to Chicago and eventually back to New York."

"As I said, there was a change of plans. The fellow scheduled to go to the west coast took ill, so my employer asked me to go instead."

"To the west coast? California?"

"When I left here I did go to Minneapolis first, as planned. I found some nice pieces of early American art there, works by Alexis Jean Fournier and Elisabeth Chant. Oh, and a few by a fellow named Grafton Tyler Brown. I was surprised when I found he was colored."

"Really? Why? Did you not think negroes talented enough to produce works of art?"

"Why . . . why I didn't mean to imply; no, not at all. I know some very good colored artists. I was merely surprised to find an American one who was—I think perhaps I should stop talking."

"That's all right," said Myrtle, chuckling. "I'll let you get by on one—but just one."

"While I was in Minneapolis I attended what you Yanks call a football game."

"Really? You went to a football game? Who was playing?"

"It seems your universities have these teams that travel from place to place to play one another. Assault one another is more like it. Anyway, some team from Indiana was playing the Minnesota team. I believe the Indiana team won. I couldn't believe the crowd that came out to watch these blokes bludgeon one another; must have been ten thousand people or more."

"I suppose you think your rugby games are so much more refined," said Myrtle.

"Well, they are. They're played by gentlemen, not thugs."

"Okay, I'll let you by on that one, too," said Myrtle, trying to hide her amusement. "And, then, you went to California?"

"First I was in Denver for a week and then on to California."

"Only one week in Denver?"

Thomas shook his head. "I must say, as hard as I tried I found little in the way of saleable art there. It's as though it's a wasteland as far as talent is concerned."

"And California?"

"Ah," said Thomas, "much more rewarding. Not only does the state produce some marvelous artists, but I also found many works of your American West there done by men who lived elsewhere. I was able to send back to New York pieces by Thomas Ayers and John Englehart. Oddly enough, they both seemed to be obsessed with your Yosemite Valley. And William Keith; amazing work. Unfortunately, all of those men have passed on now. But I did get to visit one fellow, Thomas Moran, who lives in Santa Barbara. His landscapes are magnificent."

"It seems it was a productive trip."

"Quite so. Oh, and in Hollywood, I met someone who knew you."

"Knew me? Who knows me in Hollywood?"

"He said his name was Jelly Roll Morton. But he said you knew him as Ferd Morton."

"Ferd!" exclaimed Myrtle. "Of course! His mother did housework for us. Sometimes she brought Ferd with her. He was a few years older than me. We'd play together in the parlor. We owned a piano, an upright, and Ferd enjoyed fooling around on it. He got to be pretty good.

"We were so sad when his mother passed away unexpectedly. I think he went to live with his grandmother. Wait a minute—you say he's 'Jelly Roll?' Is he the one who wrote 'Jelly Roll Blues?'"

"That's what he told me. You know the song?"

"Know it? It's one of the best jazz pieces ever written. I even heard it in some of the places the girls and I went to in Paris. How did he know you knew me?"

"We were having drinks in this speakeasy. He was in town—he lives in British Columbia now—and he was in town visiting a friend; he started talking about his wife, Rosa, and I got to talking about . . . well, about you. I told him you were from New Orleans and he put two and two together."

"Ferd Morton. I'll be darned," said Myrtle.

"Come on, let's go," said Thomas. He laid a few bills on the table. "I'll show you what I found."

CHAPTER FIVE

They walked down the street and stopped in front of the grocery store. Thomas took out a key and unlocked a door set off to one side, which opened onto a stairway leading to the second floor. Myrtle followed him up the stairs. At the landing three doors led to three different rooms. Thomas pulled out a second key, unlocked one of the doors and swung it open.

"Come in," he said. "I'm renting the space from Mr. Finnegan. This is where I shall paint your portrait."

An easel holding a large canvas stood facing the windows that looked out onto the street. A Pochade box sat on a table next to the easel, along with tubes of paint, brushes, a bottle of turpentine, a palette, rags and a collection of palette knives.

Underneath all of it was an outsized canvas drop cloth designed to prevent any paint from getting on the wooden floor, though the floor's condition was less than pristine to begin with.

"That is really big," said Myrtle, eyeing the five by four-foot canvas. "And you're going to do this in oil."

"Only oil can capture the beauty of your face . . . and your body."

Myrtle turned and looked at Thomas. "You're still intent on painting me . . . you know?"

"That would be my preference. But only if you agree."

"How . . . how much of me would be exposed?" asked Myrtle, a tinge of concern in her voice.

"Come, let me show you something."

Thomas walked over to the table that held the books. He picked up the largest one that contained photographs of paintings. Flipping through the pages, he stopped at one and handed the book to Myrtle.

"This is a painting by an acquaintance of mine, John William Godward. He and I come from the same area in London, Wilton Grove in Wimbledon. He's older than me. He's the one who encouraged me to become interested in art. The piece is titled, *Athenais*. He painted it back in 1908."

Myrtle took the book and studied the photograph. It was a young woman, about the same age as she, but with dark hair and a considerably fuller figure. Facing forward, her arm was perched on the wall running behind her. She was draped in gossamery red material that fell to the ground at her feet, concealing her private area and her left breast, but leaving her right breast visible under the diaphanous garment.

Myrtle looked at Thomas, her eyes wide open.

"Really?" she said.

Thomas nodded. "You will look beautiful."

"What about this?" Myrtle pointed to the woman's exposed breast.

"What about it?"

"Are you planning on doing this with me?"

"Well, it wouldn't really be a nude if *something* weren't showing, now would it?"

"I don't know," said Myrtle, laying the book on the table. "I'm not sure . . . ."

"Tell you what," said Thomas. "Let's do it that way. Then, when it's finished, if you truly don't like it, I'll cover it."

Myrtle chewed on her lip. Finally, she said, "Well, okay, I guess we could try that. But you *promise* if I don't like it you'll cover it?"

"On my mother's grave."

"I thought you said your mother was still alive."

Thomas grinned. "You caught me there."

Myrtle shook her finger at him. "I'm holding you to it," she said.

Myrtle looked back at the *Athenais* painting.

"I don't believe I have anything like that gown in my closet."

"That's no problem. You provide the body: I'll paint the gown on."

Myrtle walked over to the table that held the equipment.

"What is this?" she asked, picking up the largest palette knife, almost nine inches in length.

"That is a palette knife. I use it to apply paint onto the canvas."

"You don't use a brush?" asked Myrtle.

"Oh, yes," said Thomas, "I use both. Sometimes I even use my thumb."

They both laughed.

Myrtle held the knife up. "I venture you could kill someone with this."

*****

"I'm looking forward to meeting Thomas," said Daisy.

Back on the street, Thomas had given Myrtle a peck on the cheek, then headed back to Miss Wasserman's, while she started for the boarding house.

Her first stop when she arrived there was Daisy's room, to announce that Thomas was in town.

"Tomorrow evening;" said Myrtle, "he'll be here for dinner. I have to let Mrs. Darling know first thing in the morning."

"So, you're going to let him paint you, right?"

Myrtle sighed. "I suppose so."

"Come on," said Daisy, giving her housemate a light jab on the shoulder. "You know you're looking forward to it. Now—clothed or in your birthday suit?"

Myrtle shook her head. "Who could I ever let see it if I were nude?"

"I bet Mr. Mitchell would let you hang it in the library," said Daisy, a devilish grin spreading across her face.

CHAPTER SIX

Mrs. Darling treated Thomas as if he were a visiting dignitary—or a long lost son.

"Now, Mr. Wickersham, you sit right here," she said, pointing to the seat usually occupied by Henri. Myrtle, Daisy, and Pierre were already seated.

"Where is Henri?" asked Myrtle.

"He said he couldn't make it dis evening," said Mrs. Darling. She picked up Thomas's napkin and arranged it on his lap.

He smiled, blushing.

Daisy noticed the plain cotton napkins that were usually on the table had been replaced with fine linen ones. The tablecloth was a lot nicer than she remembered, too.

"Mr. Wickersham," said Mrs. Darling, "we are so happy to have you wit us dis evening. How long will you be in town?"

"Only until tomorrow, I'm afraid," said Thomas. "But I will be returning after the new year sometime, for a week."

"Den we will have you back den, too," said Mrs. Darling. "I hope you like tea. But of course, you like tea—you're English. Let me go get da pot, and I'll be right back. Dinner will be ready in five minutes."

"You're getting the royal treatment tonight," said Myrtle as she placed her napkin on her lap.

"I've not seen these napkins before," said Pierre.

"Neither have I," said Myrtle.

"I've been living here for four years," added Daisy, "and I've never seen either them *or* the tablecloth."

"I thought you told me once you came to Booker Falls in 1915," said Myrtle.

"Yes, I did. But I didn't come here to Mrs. Darling's until a year later; my first year in town I lived at the Walther."

"The Walther?" said Myrtle. "That must not have been too pleasant."

"No, it wasn't," said Daisy. "All the other places in town were too expensive. I'd come here and talked with Mrs. Darling, but she already had four boarders. A year later, Mrs. Warner left to join her daughter in Kalamazoo, so I moved in. Just before you arrived poor Mrs. Armstrong passed away."

"Not in my room, I hope," said Myrtle, feigning horror.

"No, in the hospital over in Houghton."

Myrtle told Daisy and Pierre about Thomas's room at Miss Wasserman's.

"Wow, that must be creepy;" said Daisy. "sleeping in a room where someone got killed."

"It was a bit unsettling when Myrtle told me about it;" said Thomas, "but I made it through the night last night with not one visit from the young lady's ghost."

Everyone laughed.

Mrs. Darling returned with a large bowl, which she placed in the middle of the table.

Thomas looked at the dish, sniffed it, and grinned.

"Is that what I think it is?" he asked.

"Bubble and Squeak," said Mrs. Darling, puffing out her chest. "A proper English dish I am told."

"I love it!" said Thomas.

"What in the world is 'Bubble and Squeak?'" asked Myrtle. "You've never served this before, at least not when I was present."

"Nah, first time," said Mrs. Darling. "I got da recipe from Mrs. Ainsworth—she's English, ya know."

"What's in it?" asked Daisy.

"Oh, a little a dis and a little a dat;" said Mrs. Darling. "mostly cabbage. I'll go get da rest. You all go ahead and serve yourselves now."

One by one, each of them dished out a portion onto their plates.

"And here's da rest," said Mrs. Darling, coming back into the room. She set down two more serving plates, one containing poached eggs and the other, strips of cold roast beef. "Okay, eat up. We got thimbleberry pie for dessert."

The next twenty minutes were taken up amidst minimal conversation with the enjoyable task of devouring the repast Mrs. Darling had prepared.

Finally, Pierre, finished, sat back and dabbed at his mouth with his napkin.

"I almost hate to use this," he said, "it's so nice."

"I know what you mean," said Daisy, following suit.

"Ah, all finished, are we?" asked Mrs. Darling entering the room.

"Mrs. Darling, that was absolutely delicious," said Thomas. "As fine as I ever tasted in London."

"I'm glad you liked it," said Mrs. Darling as she gathered up the empty plates. "Anybody ready for dessert?"

"Yes," said everyone in unison.

"I understand you're from Boston," said Thomas, turning to Pierre.

"I am. I rather miss it. Booker Falls is considerably different."

"Yes, it certainly is," said Thomas.

"And where do you reside, Mr. Wickersham?" asked Pierre. "That is, when you're not traversing the country."

"London is my home. But I spend considerable time in New York."

"One of my favorite cities," said Pierre.

"You got there often?"

"Every chance I had."

"I was there in September when the bomb exploded," said Thomas.

"Bomb?" said Myrtle. "What bomb?"

"On Wall Street. Thirty-eight people were killed, hundreds more injured. I was in town that day but, fortunately, not in that part of the city."

"I understand it's believed to be the work of the Galleanists," said Pierre.

"That is what I heard also," said Thomas, "though there has been nothing substantial to support that supposition."

"What are Galleanists?" asked Myrtle.

"Italian anarchists," said Pierre. "Ah, now here's a more pleasant topic: Mrs. Darling has brought our dessert."

Thomas turned to Daisy. "Miss O'Hearn, Myrtle tells me you're a reporter for the local newspaper."

"I am," said Daisy. "And it's Daisy, not Miss O'Hearn."

"Are you from here, then?" asked Thomas.

"No, I was born in Chicago."

"And what brought you to Booker Falls?"

Daisy hesitated. She wasn't going to tell him she'd been running away from the brother of the husband she'd thought she'd killed, though she'd found out later he hadn't died. No, she wasn't about to tell him that.

"Wanderlust," said Daisy. "I felt like I needed to get out of Chicago." That much was true.

"I see. And so you wandered all the way up here to Michigan's Upper Peninsula."

"Traverse City, first; then Booker Falls."

Thomas turned to Pierre. "And you, Pierre, what is your line of work?"

"I teach here at the college; literature, and French."

"Tell me more about Boston," said Thomas. "All I know is that's where you blokes threw the tea into the bay because you didn't like our king."

"I do not feel I can be blamed for that," said Pierre. "I am Canadian, you see."

"Ah! A fellow compatriot of sorts!"

For the next forty-five minutes, Thomas and Pierre talked about the cities they had in common which they had visited.

Thomas looked up when the Grandfather clock in the corner struck seven.

"I must be going," he said. "The man who will drive me back to Houghton is picking me up first thing tomorrow."

"You'll catch your train there?" asked Daisy.

"Yes."

"Perhaps the next time you come you will be able to take the train all the way to Booker Falls," said Pierre.

"Oh?" said Thomas.

"Yes," said Myrtle. "We're supposed to start getting passenger service here the first of the year."

"That certainly would be more convenient," said Thomas.

*****

Myrtle and Daisy sat together on the sofa in the parlor after Thomas left and Pierre had retired for the night. Mrs. Darling entered with two cups of tea.

"That Mr. Wickersham, he is a fine gentleman," she said, setting the cups down on the table in front of the women. She looked at Myrtle. "I bet he'd make someone a mighty fine husband someday."

She turned and left the room.

Daisy giggled. "You think she's trying to tell you something?"

Myrtle nodded and sipped her tea. "Could be."

"She's right, though," said Daisy. "And not only is he a fine gentleman, as Mrs. Darling says, he is mighty fine looking, too."

"Do you know where Henri was tonight?" asked Myrtle.

"Mrs. Darling said he was having supper with his mother. But I think that was an excuse."

"Excuse for what?"

"He didn't want to be here when Thomas was here," said Daisy.

"Why? You think he's jealous?"

"You are naïve. You know that?"

Myrtle didn't answer.

"You still haven't told me about the painting," said Daisy. "Are you going to be . . . you know . . . ?"

Myrtle smiled. "You'll just have to wait and see."

CHAPTER SEVEN

Nick Clearmont lay on the bed in his room at the Douglas House in downtown Houghton.

His trip had been successful; he'd closed the deal to purchase equipment for the new smelter he and his brother were having built back home.

An added bonus had been coming across that fellow in Booker Falls. He'd been easy enough to recognize there on the street, with his bright red horseshoe mustache.

And that gold tooth: Nick had wanted to yank it out of the man's mouth when he and the other members of the Klan made a special trip to Booker Falls a few months earlier, but his brother had stopped him.

They'd driven over from Marquette when they heard about some old geezer who was involved with a nigger—a teenage nigger at that. They had let him know in no uncertain terms it wasn't right for a white man to be fooling around with no nigger. As Klan members, they had a responsibility to keep things straight between the races.

They hadn't killed him. Just beat him up enough for him to get the message.

Nick pulled a handkerchief from his pocket and stared at the blood.

I'll keep this as a little trophy. Show it to the fellas when I get back to Marquette.

And just maybe, on his way back through Booker Falls, he thought, he'd finish the job.

CHAPTER EIGHT

Myrtle glanced at the clock for the fifth time in ten minutes.

Although it was only a few minutes past eleven, the hunger pangs she felt told her it was definitely time to get out the meatloaf sandwich Mrs. Darling had sent with her for lunch.

The problem was, she wasn't supposed to eat at the desk; Mr. Mitchell usually relieved her for a half hour so she could go out into the garden when the weather was nice, or upstairs into one of the storage rooms when it wasn't.

But he was nowhere to be seen.

In fact, he hadn't even come in that morning or called to say he'd be late.

Yesterday had been his first day back to work after having been attacked last week. Myrtle wondered if he'd suffered a setback.

She went into his office and tried to call either Henri or George by phone to have them check on him, but Maribel, the town operator, wasn't able to reach either one.

She was about to say the heck with it, forget the rules and break out her sandwich, when Mr. Mitchell came through the front door. He was accompanied by a distinguished looking gentleman in his mid-sixties, about the same age as Frank.

The man wore a fawn-colored beret and a long, flowing Victorian cape of the same color.

"Miss Tully," said Frank, "I'd like you to meet my oldest friend, Herman Hutchinson."

Fve-foot-nine, Frank towered over his companion by a good seven inches.

"Mr. Hutchinson, nice to meet you," said Myrtle. "I heard you had moved to town."

She stuck out her hand and immediately regretted she didn't always follow the social nicety of waiting for the gentleman to make the first move.

Herman had held up his right arm to reveal a missing hand, at the same time extending his left hand with which he grasped Myrtle's.

"Oh, I'm so sorry," Myrtle managed to get out. "A war injury?"

"As a matter of fact, yes," said Herman. "Corporal— U. S. Seventh Cavalry. How did you know?"

"Your greatcoat—my Uncle Philpot had one very similar to it."

"I thought you were from the South," said Frank.

"I am. But Uncle Philpot was from Massachusetts."

"Herman was at the Battle of Wounded Knee," said Frank. "That's where he lost his hand."

"The Lakota Pine Ridge Indian Reservation in North Dakota," said Myrtle.

Herman's eyebrows arched. "You're familiar with it?" he asked.

"It was a few years before I was born," said Myrtle, "but I remember studying it in school. And I recall my father thought it was a terrible blight on our nation what we did there."

Herman grimaced. "I fear I must agree with your father. I am not proud of what happened: it's something I live with every day of my life. You were wrong about one thing though: it was South Dakota, not North Dakota."

"Ah," said Myrtle. "You're right."

"Enough of war talk," said Frank. "Herman and I attended school here together and were both in the first graduating class. In fact, it was his father who built the library."

"Oh, I see," said Myrtle. "So it is your aunt's portrait that hangs at the top of the stairs."

"It is. She was a beautiful woman, eh?"

"She was," agreed Myrtle.

"And Herman is also an artist, like me."

Only better, one could hope, thought Myrtle.

"Yah," said Herman, "Frank and I both graduated with art degrees . . . ."

"And we both discovered they were pretty useless as far as making a living," said Frank.

"So Frank became a librarian," said Herman, "and I became a soldier; at least until I lost my hand. Now I get a pension from the government."

"And so you still paint," said Myrtle.

"Yah. Of course, I had to learn all over to use my left hand, but sometimes something worthwhile emerges on the canvas."

"Nonsense," said Frank. "Herman is an outstanding talent. Unlike me, he works in oil."

"I find it easier to deal with," said Herman.

"Herman, let's adjourn to my office, shall we?" said Frank. "Have you had lunch yet, Miss Tully?"

Thank you for asking! thought Myrtle.

"Why don't you go ahead and eat," said Frank. "I will watch the desk from the office."

CHAPTER NINE

"Don't forget tonight," said Mrs. Darling, entering the room with a pot of steaming coffee.

Since opening the boarding house in 1885, it had been her tradition to host a Christmas party for her boarders every year on December 23rd. That first year she had planned to do it on Christmas Eve, but her two boarders, Faddey and Taavetti Paananen, told her it would not be possible for them to be there.

Brothers who had immigrated to America from Finland to work in the copper mines, they were devout Lutherans who made the sixty-mile round trip every Sunday by horseback from Booker Falls to Red Jacket to attend the Laestadian church located there. They couldn't miss the Christmas Eve Service, they said.

To accommodate them, Mrs. Darling had moved the party up a day to the twenty-third, where it had remained ever since.

Since that first Christmas thirty-five years ago, over fifty people had called Mrs. Darling's Boarding House home, ranging from stays of a month or two to that of Mr. Pfrommer, who arrived in 1891 from Montreal and had left just a few months previous.

*****

That evening they all gathered in the parlor to admire the tree Henri and Pierre had brought in from the woods the day before. A magnificent Balsam Fir, it was so tall the halo of the angel perched at its crown came within a foot of the twelve-foot-high ceiling.

Daisy and Myrtle had spent the morning threading the popcorn Mrs. Darling popped the night before into twelve-foot lengths, and now it was time to decorate. The two of them took on the job of wrapping the strands around the tree, while Henri, Pierre, and Mrs. Darling watched and supervised.

"Right there," said Henri, "I think . . . ."

He stopped when Myrtle gave him a scathing look.

"Looks great to me," said Pierre, not wishing to get the same result.

"I think we're ready for the ornaments now," said Myrtle, when the last strand of popcorn was in place.

"And then the tinsel and then the candy canes!" added Daisy, as excited as a five-year-old.

"No, no," said Mrs. Darling. "Mr. Longet has someting to be added first."

Pierre Longet was the newest of Mrs. Darling's boarders. This was his first Christmas in Booker Falls, having arrived there the past September.

"What is it?" asked Myrtle, getting as excited as Daisy.

Pierre pulled out two boxes from a brown paper sack and handed one each to Myrtle and Daisy.

"Oooh," exclaimed Daisy. "Christmas tree lights!"

"Where did you get them?" asked Myrtle, as she pulled the string of lights from the box.

"I have a friend in Boston who obtained them for me from his brother in Germany."

"They're beautiful," said Myrtle. "Henri, come help me put them up higher on the tree."

"I'll put them around the bottom," said Daisy.

"*Now* we're ready for da ornaments," said Mrs. Darling when the lights had all been placed and turned on.

Myrtle remembered the ornaments from last Christmas, her first in Booker Falls: cotton-pressed and spun fruits and vegetables, elves and snowmen, donkeys, cows, and sheep; brightly colored balls, spheres, crosses, angels and a miniature harp.

Once everything was in place, Henri and Pierre strew the tree with tinsel until it was almost covered.

"Not too much," said Mrs. Darling. "We want to see all da udder stuff."

The last items to be added were two dozen large red and white striped candy canes.

"Hang dose high enough, so's da dog don't get dem, eh?" admonished Mrs. Darling, coming back into the room carrying a tray filled with cups of hot eggnog.

"Henri," said Mrs. Darling, "you be a dear and go get da stollen, will you? And don't you dare eat it all 'fore it gets here," she yelled at him as he headed for the kitchen.

"I'm going to go get my camera," said Daisy, hurrying from the room.

Minutes later, both Henri and Daisy were back. Mrs. Darling served the stollen while Daisy took pictures of the tree.

"When will we be able to see those?" asked Pierre.

"Tomorrow," replied Daisy, setting the camera down. "I have five more frames, and I'll shoot those tonight. Are we going to sing carols when we're finished?" she asked, stuffing a large piece of stollen into her mouth.

Henri took a sip of his eggnog. "It's too bad we don't have Mr. Pfrommer here this year to accompany us on his violin," he said.

Mrs. Darling dropped the bite of bread she was ready to put into her mouth. Large tears began streaming down her cheeks.

"I'm sorry," said Henri. "What did I say?"

"You goose!" said Myrtle. "Mr. Pfrommer. He's not with us because he's in prison . . . where I put him." Myrtle started to cry as well.

Daisy moved to get up, her gaze going first to Mrs. Darling, then to Myrtle, then back. She didn't know who to console first.

Myrtle grabbed her napkin and wiped her eyes. "Well, enough of that," she said. "We're here to celebrate and be happy, not be sad. Now it's out of our system. Besides, we don't need accompaniment," she added, looking at Mrs. Darling who was wiping away the last of her tears with her napkin. "We can sing a cappella."

"We have a piano," said Pierre. "Don't any of you play the piano? Mrs. Darling?"

Pierre had been admiring the piano while Myrtle and Daisy had been looping the popcorn strands around the tree. An 1894 Chickering and Sons Rococo upright Victorian with a black lacquer finish, it appeared to be practically brand new, helped maintained that way in large part by Mrs. Darling's daily dusting and regular polishing. On each side of the keyboard was a music lyre motif set in holly leaves and berries. The front panels featured graceful filigree grill work. Dark burgundy fabric behind the panels gave it a splash of color.

"Oh, no," said Mrs. Darling. "I don't play. Dat was my Eugene's piano."

"Eugene?" said Pierre.

Mrs. Darling looked up and crossed herself. "My late husband, God rest his soul. I lost him in '84, not even a year after we got da piece. I couldn't bear to get rid of it after he was gone, so I brought it along wit me when I bought dis place. I've had a couple of boarders over da years who played, 'specially dat Mrs. Tornton—she taught at da school back in da nineties—

not da college, da young kids school. But I never learnt how."

"Do you mind?" asked Pierre, sitting down on the bench.

As the strains of *O Holy Night* sprang forth from the upright, Pierre's sonorous baritone voice filled the room.

Myrtle, Daisy, Henri and Mrs. Darling, entranced by the magic of the moment, listened raptly as Pierre sang, first in French, then in English, ending with the familiar words:

Christ is the Lord! O praise His Name forever,
His power and glory evermore proclaim.
His power and glory evermore proclaim.

For a brief moment, no one spoke. Then Myrtle began to applaud. Mrs. Darling and Daisy, both of whom had been seated, stood and joined Henri and Myrtle and all four continued clapping while Pierre, obviously embarrassed, acknowledged their appreciation.

"Please," he said, his face flushing.

"My goodness that was marvelous!" exclaimed Myrtle. "*You* are marvelous!"

"Mr. Longet, will you play for us while we sing some carols?" asked Mrs. Darling.

For the next hour, Pierre played while the others joined in on all the old familiar Christmas hymns and Daisy took more pictures.

"Oh, my, look at da time," said Mrs. Darling, as they finished *Silent Night*. "I got to get to bed. Lots of bakin' and cookin' to do tomorrow."

"Not before we give you your gift," said Henri.

"Oh, no, I ain't . . ." Mrs. Darling started to say.

"Shush," said Daisy. "We have a gift for you, and that's that."

Myrtle, who had left the room during the conversation, returned, holding a box, gaily wrapped with Christmas paper displaying angels and shepherds. She handed it to Mrs. Darling.

"Merry Christmas, Mrs. Darling. This is from all of us."

"Oh, such beautiful paper," said Mrs. Darling, her eyes filling with tears.

Carefully, she unwrapped the present and neatly folded the paper. It would do for another present one day.

She opened the box and took out a robe, holding it up for all to see. Daisy took the final picture on her roll.

"Oh, it's beautiful," said Mrs. Darling. "And my favorite color, too."

Myrtle knew Mrs. Darling was partial to Royal Blue and was ecstatic when she was able to have Isabell Dougherty, the owner of de Première Qualité Women's Wear shop, order the robe for her in that color.

The belt, trimmed in powder blue, like the robe, contained long fringe on each end.

"I love it," said Mrs. Darling.

"Yes, we thought your old robe was beginning to look a bit shabby," said Henri.

"I said it looked ratty," added Daisy.

Mrs. Darling looked down at the robe that had served her well for almost two decades.

"You're right," she said. "It does look shabby. I'll wear dis new one from now on. Okay, *now* I'm off to bed if dat's all right wit all youse."

"I'm off to," said Myrtle. "I'm tired."

"Me, too," added Daisy. "See you all tomorrow."

"How about you, Pierre?" asked Henri, after the women had left the room. "You calling it a night, or would you care to join me for a drink?"

"A drink sounds good," said Pierre.

A few minutes later both men were seated in the parlor, each with a glass of Mrs. Darling's company sherry.

"Henri," said Pierre, "I've been wondering—I know Mr. Pfrommer was a boarder here before I came and now he's in prison. And Miss Tully somehow seems to feel responsible for that?"

"Mr. Pfrommer lived here for almost thirty years," said Henri. "Shortly after Myrtle arrived in town she found some letters at the library having to do with a murder that had taken place twenty-eight years earlier, a young woman who had been strangled in the stacks. No one was ever convicted of the crime.

"Naturally Myrtle had to set out to solve the crime— she is pretty, well, I'll say inquisitive, though 'nosey' is the word I'd prefer. Anyway, it turned out Mr. Pfrommer had committed the crime, to cover up a murder he'd done in Montreal before he came to Booker Falls. He almost killed Myrtle, too, if George hadn't intervened."

"He sounds like a horrible man."

"Not at all. He was very kind, very private. He just made some mistakes that ultimately caught up with him. He even apologized to Myrtle for trying to kill her."

"So she solved that crime as well as the three murders that happened soon after I came to town."

"I suppose you could say that," said Henri. "I know Miss Tully would. She seems to attract murders to her like bugs to a light."

CHAPTER TEN

Myrtle looked down at the dress Isabell Dougherty had insisted she slip into—a floor-length black, sequined party dress. A modest boat neckline enhanced by short capped sleeves ensured the dress would not be seen as risqué. The basic fabric, a soft, shimmery silk, had scrolled, sequin patterns that ran from the shoulders of the bodice to mid-thigh. The dress fit perfectly and was accentuated by a short train that swirled whenever she took a step or shifted her weight.

"I like that one!" said Daisy. "And you look gorgeous in it."

Myrtle had spent most of Monday morning at de Première Qualité Women's Wear Shop trying on evening dresses. No corduroy slacks for this event!

Yesterday George had stopped by the boarding house with an invitation to a New Year's Eve party at the Hoatson Mansion in Laurium. Built twelve years before, the four-story, thirteen-thousand square foot home boasted forty-five rooms, including seven bedrooms for the family and guests and three for the maids.

The party—a formal dance—was to take place in the thirteen-hundred square foot ballroom on the top floor.

"Oh, I don't know," said Myrtle, dismissively. Inside, though, she had to agree with Daisy: she *did* look gorgeous!

"And look at the price," said Myrtle, pulling up a tag. "Twenty-five dollars. That's a lot of money."

Daisy cocked her ear. "You hear that?" she asked.

"Hear what? I don't hear anything."

"You. I hear you. You're so tight you squeak."

"Oh, shut up. I am not tight. I'm . . . I'm *frugal.*"

"No," said Daisy, shaking her head. "You're tight. Twenty-five dollars—how often do you get an invitation to the most talked about event in the whole area?"

"You're right," said Myrtle, shrugging. "Why not? I only live once, right? Isabell!"

Isabell hurried out from the back room where she'd been listening to the two women's banter.

"I'll take it," said Myrtle. "Wrap it up!"

"Wait," said Isabell, "it needs one more thing. Here." She held out a black, beaded headband.

Myrtle hesitated. "I . . . I don't think I can afford any more. The dress is . . . ."

"The headband's a loan," said Isabell, placing it in Myrtle's hand. "You'll look beautiful. Just bring it back after the party."

Myrtle smiled. "Thank you."

*****

"Myrtle, look there," said Daisy, as she and Myrtle left the store.

Myrtle looked to where Daisy had pointed and saw what, at first, she thought was just a bicycle. Then she looked again: parked on the street in front of the courthouse was a motorcycle, covered in dust as though it had been ridden a long way.

She spotted a woman coming around the corner of the courthouse.

In her late twenties or early thirties, the woman wore a beige duster that almost covered a pair of boots that looked as though they would be more at home in Texas than Northern Michigan. Long, black hair spilled out from under the brown Stetson she wore.

She was tall, at least five foot ten, Myrtle surmised, and stunningly beautiful.

Myrtle and Daisy watched as the woman stopped at the motorcycle, removed her hat and stuffed it into a bag attached to the back. From the same bag, she took out a leather helmet with goggles, fastened it around her head, adjusted the goggles, and mounted the vehicle.

A few furious pumps and the motorcycle raced off down the street.

"Holy . . . !" exclaimed Daisy. "Did you see that?"

Myrtle was dumbfounded. "Huh?" she managed to get out.

"Did you see that woman who just left on the motorcycle?" asked Daisy.

Myrtle nodded. "Uh, huh," she said.

"Do you know who she is?" asked Daisy.

Myrtle shook her head. "No idea."

"You think she came from Henri's office?"

"I don't know," said Myrtle. "Come on; let's get back home."

*****

"Tell me all about this big event you're going to," said Daisy, as they walked back to the boarding house. "You didn't have much to say at dinner last night or breakfast this morning, other than you wanted me to come with you to pick out a dress."

"I didn't want to say anything in front of Henri," said Myrtle. "And you were gone all afternoon and took off right after dinner."

"Yeah, my boss has me working on a big article about all the robberies that have been happening all over the place."

"Henri mentioned that to me. What's going on?"

"It seems to have begun a couple of months ago," said Daisy. "Someone's been breaking into people's homes and stealing paintings."

"Paintings? Just paintings?"

"Oh, I think a few other things, but mostly paintings. And it looks like it's not only here in Booker Falls, either. There've been reports of burglaries from about five other towns around. But, anyway, what about the party?"

"As I said, it's at this big mansion in Laurium. George's father was a good friend of the man who owns it, and George is still good friends with the two oldest sons."

"And you're staying overnight?" asked Daisy.

"Yes. George's father was also friends with the couple who live right down the street. They'll be at the party, and they offered to put us up for the night. We'll be returning the next day. Mr. Mitchell wants me to come in and do the end of the year inventory on Saturday. He said I've had enough paid time off."

"New Year's Day? What an ogre! So, separate rooms?"

"Excuse me?"

"Where you'll be staying there in Laurium—separate rooms?"

Myrtle gave Daisy a withering glance. "You have some mind, Miss O'Hearn. Of course, separate rooms."

"Maybe they'll have connecting doors," said Daisy, quickening her pace.

"No, I'm sure they won't," said Myrtle, hurrying to catch up with her. "And even if they did, we wouldn't use them."

Daisy turned to Myrtle and smiled. "Opportunities lost," she said, shaking her head.

*****

Myrtle slid into her place at the dinner table as the grandfather clock struck its last chime at five.

"You know, we don't have to be as punctual as we used to be when Mr. Pfrommer lived here," Daisy whispered in her ear.

Myrtle shrugged. "I guess it's a habit now. Besides, I don't like to keep the rest of you waiting."

"Apparently Henri doesn't share your sense of responsibility," said Daisy, as Henri sauntered into the room.

"Sorry," said Henri, taking his place at the table, just as Mrs. Darling entered carrying a large bowl of mashed potatoes.

"Henri, Myrtle has something to ask you," said Daisy, before sliding a forkful of peas into her mouth.

"I do?" said Myrtle. She looked at Daisy, a confused look on her face.

"You know," said Daisy.

"I'm sure I don't know what you're talking about," said Myrtle.

"Okay," said Daisy. "I'll ask. Henri, who was that gorgeous woman we saw coming from the direction of your office this morning?"

Myrtle's mouth fell open. "Why, I didn't . . . ."

"At least we thought she might have come from your office," Daisy interrupted.

"That would be Miss Vanderliet," said Henri. "Katherine—Kitty—Vanderliet."

Daisy's eyebrows arched. "Kitty, huh? You must know her pretty well."

"She arrived in town yesterday," said Henri. "She's a journalist, a reporter. She's here to write a story for a magazine."

"What magazine?" asked Myrtle.

"*Argosy All-Story Weekly*? At least, that's what she said. I've never heard of it, but she said it's been around since 1882."

"What kind of story?" asked Daisy.

"The Steinmyer murders. And Rudolph Foger."

"What!" exclaimed Daisy. "Wait a minute—*I'm* a reporter: *I* should be writing that story!"

"I don't know," said Henri, as he took a bite of mashed potatoes. "I'm only telling you what she told me."

CHAPTER ELEVEN

George had called for Myrtle shortly after lunch. Like Henri, he also had not put away his automobile, a 1920 Briscoe he'd purchased the past summer.

Myrtle was thankful when they arrived at the home of George's friends. A trip that normally took a little over an hour had been twice as long, as they'd been forced to travel over treacherous, snow-covered roads.

George had said their home, while grand, was no match for the Hoatson Mansion down the street, where the party was to be held. Myrtle wondered how much more magnificent that house could be than this one.

As the car pulled into the driveway, Margaret MacDonald ran out to meet them.

"Oh, I'm so happy you're here!" she exclaimed. "Norman and I have been so worried you were lost or had had an accident or . . . or I don't know what!"

"No," said George, getting out of the car. "We're perfectly fine." He wrapped his arms around Margaret in a hug, then released her, turned and opened the car door.

"And this is Myrtle," he said, as she stepped down.

"My dear," said Margaret. "We are delighted to have you with us. You had a good trip, eh?"

"Other than nearly sliding off the road once, it was a beautiful drive," said Myrtle. "Mrs. MacDonald, it is very nice to meet you. George has told me all about you and your beautiful home."

"Minnie, dear. Please call me Minnie. Come, let us get you in out of this horrible weather."

The MacDonald home, a seven thousand square foot, two and a half-story Victorian, constructed of brown brick and red mortar with sandstone trim, boasted a wraparound porch with fluted Corinthian columns.

"My, this is a large house," said Myrtle, staring up at the second and third-floor oriel.

"Wait until you see the Hoatson mansion," said Margaret.

"That's what George told me," said Myrtle.

As the three of them entered through the front door, a young girl of about ten came running to meet them. "George!" she cried out.

George scooped her up in his arms.

"Mary Elizabeth! My, how you have grown. I can hardly lift you anymore."

George turned to Myrtle. "Mary Elizabeth, this is my friend, Miss Myrtle Tully. Miss Tully is a librarian and very well read."

"Assistant librarian," said Myrtle. "Mary Elizabeth, it is very nice to meet you. And please, call me Myrtle."

"Come with me," said Mary Elizabeth, as George set her down. "I'll show you to your room. You get the guest room, Miss . . . Myrtle."

Just then a man entered the room. "George, good to see you again."

"And you, Norman. And this is Miss Myrtle Tully."

"Welcome to our home, Miss Tully. George, we're putting you up in the room above the carriage house. I hope that meets with your approval."

George nodded and picked up his valise. He and Norman headed toward the back of the house, while Mary Elizabeth, Margaret, and Myrtle started up the stairs.

At the landing, Myrtle stopped and gaped at the tripartite stained-glass window of a landscape scene.

"Oh, my, that is exquisite!" she exclaimed.

"It is, isn't it?" said Margaret. "I insisted Norman allow me to have it there."

When they reached the bedroom, Myrtle stopped in the doorway and looked around.

The room was large, half again the size of her own bedroom. A large four-poster bed stood against one wall. Next to it, a small bookcase held a Tiffany lead, stained-glass lamp, and several books. In one corner sat an armoire, similar to those in the four bedrooms at Mrs. Darling's, but made of mahogany, not white oak. A chaise lounge, a chiffonier, and a pier glass completed the furnishings.

"Oh, this is lovely!" exclaimed Myrtle.

"I trust you'll be comfortable," said Margaret. "Once you've settled in, come back downstairs. There's a fire in the library, and Norman will have some hot toddy waiting."

*****

Myrtle entered the library to find George and the MacDonalds already there.

"I'm sorry," she said. "Did I keep you waiting?"

"Not at all, Miss Tully," said Norman. "We've already begun with the hot toddy, and Mary Elizabeth baked some sweetbread cookies for the occasion. Lucinda," he continued, turning to a young girl standing near the door, "would you go to the kitchen, please, and bring Miss Tully's hot toddy?"

Lucinda nodded and hurried off.

"Lucinda came to us last month," said Margaret. "She's from Finland. Our other maid, Rosemarie, has been with us six years, but she's a bit under the weather, so I doubt you'll meet her while you're here."

"Have you lived here long?" asked Myrtle.

"A while," said Norman. "The house was built in 1905. Before that, we lived in the apartment over our store."

"Your store?" said Myrtle.

"We owned a drug store in Red Jacket," said Margaret. "When Norman retired we had this home built. Oh, my! Look at the time. We had best start getting dressed for the party. Myrtle, dear, wait until you see Thomas and Cornelia's home."

Forty-five minutes later, as Myrtle descended the stairs to the hallway, she found George and the MacDonalds waiting for her. She thought Mr. MacDonald looked exceptionally distinguished in his tailcoat suit, white waistcoat, white tie, and white gloves. A top hat and cane made him appear even more so.

George, attired in a double-breasted dinner jacket, also had a cane, though his was more utilitarian.

Margaret McDonald looked stunning in a flattering floor-length dress with three-quarter length sleeves and a modest—but alluring—bodice. Over what appeared to be a shimmering skirt, the overdress, made of soft blue velvet with a complementary jeweled border, matched her headpiece.

But it was Myrtle who was the star of the show in the dress Daisy had convinced her to buy.

"My dear," exclaimed Margaret, "you look positively dazzling. Doesn't she look dazzling, Norman?"

Norman nodded appreciatively.

Myrtle looked at George and raised her eyebrows.

"Dazzling," he said.

"We have a few hors-d'oeuvres in the library," said Margaret. "There will be food at the party, of course, but we have a little time before we head over there."

CHAPTER TWELVE

Otis Blanchard sat on his bed in his rented room at the Walther Building, hands folded on his lap. He stared at a painting on the opposite wall, a mediocre rendering of a vase with four non-descript flowers placed on a cloth-covered table.

He had arrived in town forty minutes earlier, after a four-hour drive over snow-covered roads from his home in Iron Mountain. His daughter, Eloise, had come the day before and was now in her dormitory at Adelaide College.

When he'd discovered several months earlier that she was involved with the school librarian, a man—a white man—old enough to be her grandfather, he'd become livid. He'd driven the hundred miles to Booker Falls where he'd confronted the man in his office and threatened to kill him if he didn't stop seeing his daughter.

But the private detective Otis hired to ensure his demand had been met had reported back that the librarian had not heeded his warning.

When the time came for Christmas break, Otis had returned to the college and brought Eloise back home where he told her she would not be returning to the school. He'd thought that was the end of it until his wife discovered their daughter missing three days after Christmas.

From one of her friends, they found out she'd gotten another friend to drive her back to school.

Sally had implored Otis not to go after her.

"She's eighteen. She's legal. You can't make her do what you want. Da only ting dat will happen if you go up dere is you'll get in trouble."

But Otis had ignored her.

After arranging for his brother to take care of the bakery he owned, Otis had taken off.

Now, here he was.

He thought of the stories his grandpa Willie told him about when he was a slave in Georgia, the account of how Willie's wife, Lulu, Otis's grandmother, had been raped by their owner. She would never talk about it. But Willie knew it to be true because he'd been forced to stand and watch while it happened.

"Don't nevah trust no white man," Willie had told Otis. "Nevah."

There was no way Otis was going to let a white man defile his little girl.

But what could he do?

He'd had a lot of time to think on the road. Just taking Eloise back home did not seem like an option— he knew she'd only leave again. What he needed was a permanent solution.

Otis stood and walked over to the one window in the room overlooking Main Street. Under the glow of the street lights, he watched as myriad people milled about, in a joyous, party mood.

That's when Otis remembered: it was New Year's Eve.

*****

Joker Mulhearn looked up from the whiskey glass he was polishing to see Frank Mitchell and another man enter the room from the barbershop up front. He'd seen the other man around town, but this was his first time in Joker's establishment.

"Well, if it ain't the liberry man. Who's your friend?"

"This is Herman Hutchinson, a friend of mine. And business partner."

"Well, okay, then," said Joker, "What's your poison, friend?"

"Whiskey, please."

"Regular for you, Frank?"

Frank nodded.

"Business partner, huh? What kind of . . . never mind—you got some money for me?"

Frank's face turned red.

"Next week," said Frank. "I promise."

Joker put both hands on the counter and leaned close in to Frank.

"No money? Why are you here? Surely not just to drink."

"To let you know I'm not reneging. I'm going to pay you what I owe."

"You'll have the whole two thousand next week, then, eh?"

Frank grimaced. "Uh . . . probably not the whole amount."

"How much?" asked Joker, narrowing his eyes.

"Two hundred—I think. My friend here and I have something in the works."

Joker looked at the man. "Something, huh?"

He looked back at Frank, nodded, then shook his head. "Two hundred. I told you, you couldn't afford to play poker with all those hoity-toity guys—the mayor, the judge. You're not that good a player. In fact, you stink."

"I know," said Frank, staring down at the floor.

"I've waited long enough," said Joker, straightening up to his full height. "I want the whole two thousand, and I want it by next Wednesday."

"I can't do that!" wailed Frank. "There's no way I can come up with the whole amount."

"If you want to keep breathing you will."

"What? You'd kill me? Then you wouldn't get any money at all."

"I ain't getting none now, am I?" said Joker, loudly. He pulled his vest back to reveal the gun strapped to his hip. "So what's the difference?"

"You'd shoot me?" asked Frank. His legs were shaking.

Joker let the vest fall back in place and picked up a knife from the counter that had been lying next to a roll of salami. He cut a slice, speared it with the knife and stuck it in his mouth.

"Nah," he said, as he casually chewed the meat. "I ain't gonna shoot you. Guns are too noisy."

CHAPTER THIRTEEN

"I like your shoes," said Myrtle, as she took George's arm. "They look real snazzy."

"They're Capezio black jazz oxfords," he said. "I'm told they're good for dancing. They have extra smooth soles."

"Then we must dance every dance, mustn't we?"

The walk across the street to the Hoatson Mansion took less than three minutes.

Myrtle paused for a moment, gazing up at the enormous house that loomed in front of her. Four massive pillars extending all the way to the roof graced the front of the home.

She'd gotten a glimpse of it earlier when she and George arrived at the MacDonald home down the street.

Neither George nor Margaret had exaggerated: the Hoatson Mansion was, indeed, far grander than the MacDonald home.

Myrtle watched as carriages, sleighs, and automobiles inched their way up the drive on the far side of the house to unload their passengers under the portico.

They were met at the front door by Persis, one of the Hoatsons' maids, a middle-aged woman who had immigrated in 1893 from the Greek town of Laurium, renowned for its silver mining. At first, Persis had served as a housekeeper for the Reverend Matthew Gipp and his wife, Isabella, and their eight children, but she'd been hired away by the Hoatsons when they built their new home.

In 1895, when the Post Office Department notified the residents of Calumet they could have their own branch, but that it couldn't be called the Calumet branch because there was already one by that name across the road in Calumet Township, the people had decided to change the name of the town.

It was Persis who suggested Laurium, after her hometown.

Taking everyone's outerwear, Persis disappeared down the fifty-foot long hallway and around the bottom of the stairway that led to the second floor. On the other side was a ten-foot wide mirror that extended from one side of the hallway to the other. Eight feet high, it still failed to reach the ceiling.

"I'm sure Cornelia wouldn't mind if I took you on a little tour," said Margaret. "If you'd like to, that is."

"Oh, my, yes, I would," gushed Myrtle. Never before had she been in a house quite like this, not even the mansions her parents frequently took her to in New Orleans when she was a child.

"I'll head on upstairs with Norman," said George. "I've been in this house so many times it almost feels like home."

Minnie led Myrtle into the library where Hoatson's books and mineral collection occupied an oak cabinet, fronted by leaded glass doors. A fireplace flanked by two enormous bookcases took up one wall. Above the bookcases, beautiful stained glass windows looked out onto the side porch.

Across the hallway from the library was the parlor, its vaulted dome ceiling covered with hand-painted canvas. A box grand piano occupied one corner.

In the den, a hand-carved oak fireplace with glass tiles kept the men warm on cold winter nights when they would adjourn there after dinner to discuss business while the women retired to the parlor.

The dining room held a fireplace similar to that found in the den, except it contained a Celtic knot pattern that matched the design on the ceiling, the walls, and the stained glass in the door and hutch. A table with twelve chairs filled the middle of the room.

Myrtle ran her hand over the wall covering.

"Minnie, what is this?" she asked.

"Elephant hide," replied Margaret.

Myrtle stepped back. "Elephant hide?"

"Yes. Check out the chairs. They're also covered with elephant hide."

"Is Mr. Hoatson a big game hunter?"

Margaret cocked her head as if trying to remember. "I don't know," she said.

As they passed through the second floor on the way to the third floor and the ballroom, Myrtle wished she and George could have stayed in this grand mansion, or at least had been able to peek into one of the bedrooms. George had told her there were four more on the same floor as the ballroom, where the maids slept. But she knew far more important personages than the two of them were guests of the Hoatsons that evening, including a United States Senator, a Cardinal who had made the trip up from Detroit, a duke from some country in Europe, and the heads—presidents and chief executive officers—of various companies with whom Mr. Hoatson did business.

Myrtle gasped when she and Margaret stepped through the portieres into the ballroom. At thirteen hundred square feet, its vastness was almost overwhelming.

A Christmas tree, decorated with ornaments of blown glass, spun glass and spun cotton, all imported from Germany and the Czech Republic, occupied one corner of the room. Though not as tall as the one at the boarding house, it still reached almost to the top of the nine-foot-high ceiling. No popcorn strand for this tree: a garland of blown glass, also from the Czech Republic, and strings of electric lights brought from Japan provided a festive glow, while dozens of candy canes hung from the branches.

In another corner, a five-piece band played dance music.

Between the band and the tree, the doors were opened and put back to reveal a large cedar closet that normally held a profusion of clothes, mostly summer wear. For this occasion, however, everything had been moved to other closets along either side of the room, which allowed three separate bars to be set up, where three different bartenders tended to the needs of the guests.

If one didn't know better, one would have thought there was no such thing as Prohibition.

Myrtle glanced up at the ceiling, at a blue sky filled with stars.

"Is the roof open?" she asked Margaret.

Margaret giggled. "No, it's painted like that. But it certainly does look real, doesn't it?"

Two rows of chairs along one wall afforded seating, while on the opposite side, tables running the length of the room, over thirty feet, beckoned. They were loaded with food: pastries such as torchetti, pizelle, safransbullar, pepparkakor and mini Christmas tree cakes; meats such as bacala, kielbasa, maakana, gravlax, and Swedish meatballs; sandwiches of all varieties; apples, bananas, oranges, and clementines brought in from more temperate climes; a variety of crackers to go with juustoa and Wisconsin cheeses; vegetables—cauliflower, radishes, olives, broccoli, peppers—for dipping into onion and spinach dips; and, finally, kroppkakor and hard-boiled eggs.

That was where Myrtle found George, his plate loaded down.

"You didn't get enough to eat at the MacDonald's?" she asked.

"I'm not about to pass up this smorgasbord," George replied as he popped an olive into his mouth.

"I guess I better get some, too," said Myrtle. She headed for the end of the tables where the plates were stacked up.

"Would you like something to drink?" asked George as he and Myrtle settled into their seats.

"Do you know what is available?"

"In addition to alcohol, they have tea and lemonade and . . . oh, and grog, Norman said."

"Grog?"

"It's an alcoholic drink, hot, made with rum and cider. Tastes pretty good."

"Fine. I'll have that," said Myrtle.

"George, do you know the name of the band?" Myrtle asked when George returned with their drinks.

"Some fellows from the Calumet and Hecla Band. They're quite popular. At one point the whole band had about thirty members."

"They are very good," said Myrtle. "We are going to dance, aren't we?"

George smiled. "I certainly hope so."

Over the next several hours, George and Myrtle danced almost every dance: the Foxtrot, the Kangaroo Hop, the Castle Walk, the Tango. Myrtle appreciated that occasionally there was a chance to relax with something less strenuous, waltzes such as *I Met You Dear In Dreamland, A Perfect Day* and *On the Beautiful Blue Danube.* George's favorite was *Waltzing With the Girl You Love.*

At five minutes 'til midnight, the band stopped, and Thomas Hoatson strode to the middle of the dance floor.

"My friends," his words rang out in a sonorous tone. "It has been a good year. May 1921 be a better one. And a wetter one, eh?"

The room filled with laughter. It was obvious no temperance advocates had been invited to this party.

"Please lift your glasses," Hoatson continued, "to a glorious and profitable New Year."

"To a New Year," everyone replied as they lifted their glasses and drank.

"And now," said Hoatson, "according to my watch . . ." he studied the watch he had pulled from his watch pocket. ". . . it is five, four, three, two, one . . . Happy New Year!"

As the band broke into a rendition of *Auld Lang Syne*, George took Myrtle in his arms and kissed her.

Not as passionate as Henri's kisses thought Myrtle. *But every bit as satisfying.*

CHAPTER FOURTEEN

George pulled the Briscoe to a stop in front of the library and hurried around to help Myrtle from the car.

"I really had a good time," she said, as she stepped down.

"Me, too," George replied.

"Mr. and Mrs. MacDonald are lovely people, and their home—it was beautiful."

"But not as elegant as the Hoatson Mansion," said George.

"No, not nearly as elegant."

Myrtle glanced around, a puzzled look on her face. "I don't see Mr. Mitchell's carriage. I thought sure he'd be here by now. What time is it, George?"

George pulled a watch from his vest pocket. "Twenty after one."

"He said he'd be here by noon. Come, let's see if he's inside."

A quick walk through the library showed Frank nowhere to be found.

"Can we call him?" asked George.

Myrtle nodded. "I have the key to his office. There's a phone there."

After several rings, Maribel, the telephone operator said, "Doesn't sound like he's there, honey."

Myrtle returned the mouthpiece to its hook and turned to George. "Can we go to his house? Make sure he's okay?"

Twenty minutes later, George parked his car in front of Frank's home. A knock on the door brought no response.

"George, I'm worried," said Myrtle. "With what happened last week, you know, Mr. Mitchell getting stabbed on the street."

"Let's check his studio," said George.

Together, they walked around to the back of the house, where George had a small studio attached to the carriage house. The door was partly open.

Myrtle made as if to enter, but George put his hand on her arm.

"No, wait here. Let me check it out."

Minutes later, George returned, a distressed look on his face.

"You'd better come in," he said.

Myrtle wasn't prepared for what she saw: Frank lay on the sawdust-covered floor, his unseeing eyes staring at the ceiling. Blood covered what appeared to be a deep wound on the right side of his neck. Splotches of blue and green paint and what appeared to be blood also could be seen on his face and the frock he wore.

Myrtle's hands flew to her mouth. "Oh, no!" she exclaimed. "Is he . . . ?"

"Yah, he's dead, all right. I'll get into the house and call Henri and Doc Sherman. You okay to stay here?"

Myrtle nodded.

While George made the calls, Myrtle looked around the room. It appeared Frank had been painting; a half-finished canvas, a rendering of his favorite subject, the Booker Falls, rested on an easel some six or seven feet away from where the body lay. To one side, a small table held two open bottles, one with Southern Comfort, the other Old Grandad whiskey. A glass with a small amount of slush in the bottom sat next to one bottle, while another glass lay smashed to pieces on the floor under the table.

"They'll be here in a few minutes," said George when he returned. "What do you think happened?"

"He was murdered, there's no doubt about it. It looks to me as if he were stabbed."

"I think you're right. Both Henri and Doc Sherman said don't touch anything, so let's wait for them."

Ten minutes later, Henri and Ambrose Sherman arrived.

"Oh, my," said Ambrose.

Henri turned to Myrtle. "Are you all right?"

"I'm fine. A little shaken, that's all."

Myrtle pointed out to the three men what she had observed about the half-finished painting and the bottles and glasses.

"I think he was here painting, but someone else was here, too, and they were drinking, celebrating New Year's Eve, I would venture to say. The Southern Comfort is Mr. Mitchell's. I don't think he ever drank Old Grandad. And the glass on the floor—could there have been a struggle, and it was knocked off the table?"

"That's all possible," said Ambrose.

With his gloved hand, Henri picked up the glass from the table and smelled it.

"Southern Comfort," he said.

He bent down, picked up a large piece of glass from the floor and smelled it. "That's whiskey for sure. I'll take the good glass and the broken pieces and have Captain Wysocki check for fingerprints."

"You know, Henri," said George, "if these kinds of things keep happening here in town, you better get your own fingerprint kit."

"I hope these kinds of *things,* as you put it, definitely do *not* keep happening," said Henri. "We've had enough murders to last a lifetime."

"Well, okay, then," said Ambrose, who'd knelt down to examine Frank's body. "I'd say it's definitely a homicide, but I can't make it official 'til I get him in my office and do an autopsy. Here, Henri," he added, holding his hand out to Henri.

"What is it?" asked Henri. He took the object from Ambrose.

"'Pears to be a button of some sort. Must have ripped it off the coat or shirt of whoever killed him."

"Can I see it?" asked Myrtle.

Henri handed the button to Myrtle, who studied it and turned it over in her hand.

"It has an eagle with its wings spread out," she said.. "And a shield on its breast with the letter 'C.'"

"An initial?" said George.

Myrtle handed the button back to Henri. "Possibly."

"This is strange," said Ambrose. 'Pears he was stabbed. That's funny, though."

"What is?" asked Henri.

"He was stabbed in the neck. Where's all the blood? A wound like this, he would have bled a lot more than what I'm seeing here on his face and neck and his . . . what is this he's wearing?"

"A smock," said Myrtle. "I'm sure to keep paint off his clothes. But I think there's something else that's strange."

"What?" asked the doctor.

"First of all, you see what looks to be an indentation in the sawdust? Like a large square?" Myrtle indicated an area to the left of where Frank lay.

The three men looked to where she indicated.

"I believe you're right," said Ambrose. "Wonder what caused that?"

"I think it was a canvas like the other one there." She pointed back toward the canvas with the partially painted scene of the falls.

"Looks as if that could be what it was," George agreed.

"And see here," said Myrtle, indicating an area at the bottom of the indentation. "There's a trail of blood that leads right to the square, then stops. But that's not where Mr. Mitchell is. He's over here, next to the square. And the blood is farther down, not where you'd expect it to be if it were from his face or neck."

"What do you make of it?" asked Ambrose.

"I think there *was* a canvas here," said Myrtle, "probably on an easel—I wouldn't think it was just lying on the floor, though it might have been. After Mr. Mitchell was stabbed, he staggered toward it, while his blood dripped on the floor. He ran into the canvas, knocked it down and fell on it. That's why the blood trail ends there. And it could be why there's not much blood: it got on the canvas."

"And whoever killed him rolled him over off the canvas, picked it up and left," said Henri.

"That is my theory," said Myrtle.

"But why? Why would they have taken the canvas?" asked George.

"That's a good question," said Myrtle.

"Ambrose, how long you figure he's been dead?" asked Henri.

"It's freezing cold in here, so that has to be taken into consideration, but I'd say no longer than twenty-four hours. Okay, now here's one more strange thing to add to the list."

Ambrose looked up at them. "He's missing that gold tooth of his."

"What do you mean, 'he's missing his gold tooth?" asked Henri.

"Just what I said. It's not in his mouth, and I don't see it anywhere here on the floor."

"You think he might have swallowed it?" asked Myrtle.

"That's possible," said Ambrose. "It probably came loose when he fell and hit his head."

"There is one other possibility," said George.

"What's that?" asked Ambrose.

"Whoever killed Frank took it."

*****

The main topic of conversation at the dinner table that evening was the murder of Frank Mitchell.

"So you stumbled across another dead body," said Daisy, directing her comment to Myrtle.

"What do you mean 'another' dead body? This is the first one."

"I guess technically that's correct," said Daisy. "But you were right there when Mr. Folger's body was found."

"But *I* didn't find it," said Myrtle. "Penelope did."

"All I'm saying is, death—murders—seem to track you down."

"That's what I said," added Henri, wiping his mouth with his napkin.

"I can't help it if I happen to be around when people get murdered," said Myrtle.

"But from what I've heard," said Pierre, "you've been a great help in finding out who the culprit was."

"Thank you," said Myrtle, beaming.

Henri looked disgusted.

"Has any headway been made in finding out who this malefactor is?" asked Pierre.

"Not yet," said Henri. "But Doc Sherman asked me to come to his office tomorrow morning. Said he could tell me more then. Oh," he said, turning to Myrtle, "and he insisted you accompany me."

"He did?" said Myrtle, caught by surprise.

"Yah, it seems he has as high a regard for you as a crime fighter as does Pierre."

"An opinion shared by all of us," said Daisy.

"Miss Tully, what's going to happen now at the library?" asked Pierre.

Myrtle looked at him. "What do you mean?"

"With Mr. Mitchell's demise, does that mean you will now be the head librarian?"

Myrtle sat back in her chair. "Oh, my goodness! I hadn't even given that any thought."

"I bet you will," said Daisy. "What else could they do?"

Myrtle shrugged. "I don't know. I . . . I just don't know."

CHAPTER FIFTEEN

"I hope you don't mind my coming with you," said Myrtle, as Henri gave her a hand up into the car.

"It wasn't my idea," said Henri, coolly.

Doctor Sherman had been impressed with Myrtle's deductive skill and her ability to process pertinent information when she'd been instrumental in helping solve not one, but two, murder cases in the past year.

He had suggested to Henri—quite strongly—that her talent could be useful in the current case, and she should accompany him when the two met following the autopsy.

"You could have told Doctor Sherman you preferred I not come," said Myrtle.

"I didn't feel like he gave me a choice."

Myrtle turned and looked away so Henri couldn't see the grin spread across her face.

"Well, okay then," she said.

*****

The sight of Frank Mitchell's dead body on the table in Ambrose Sherman's office was something for which Myrtle was not prepared, in spite of her assurances to Henri that she would be fine. Tears sprang immediately to her eyes.

He had been her boss ever since she'd arrived in Booker Falls over a year ago. And although they had never been what she considered friends—indeed, at times, what could best be described as an uneasy truce existed between them—she knew he appreciated the job she did.

She took a handkerchief from her pocket and dabbed her eyes.

"Are you all right?" asked Ambrose.

Myrtle nodded. "Yes, I'm fine."

"Ambrose, what do we know?" asked Henri.

"Okay, then," said Ambrose. "He definitely died from the wound in his neck. In fact, other than the fact his tooth was missing, and his lip was split, I found no other wounds. There should have been a great amount of blood which, as I stated last night, there was little of at the scene."

"But he was definitely killed there?" asked Myrtle.

"Oh, yah," said Ambrose. He removed his glasses and wiped them on his apron, carefully avoiding the blood that had accumulated there. "There's no doubt about that."

"Do you know when it happened?" asked Henri.

"Because of the cold temperature in the room due to the door being left open, I can't say with great certainty, though my best guess is between ten and two."

"That can help," said Henri. "Once we can narrow down any suspects we'll know what time to look for on their alibis."

"Can you speculate on *how* he was murdered?" asked Myrtle. "I mean, you say he was stabbed—but how?"

"I can. Frank was about five foot nine. I believe the killer was at least that tall and perhaps a little taller."

"What makes you say that?" asked Henri.

"Let me demonstrate. Turn around."

Henri did as Ambrose ordered. Ambrose came up behind him and placed his left arm around Henri's chest. With his right hand, he made an upward thrust, as though stabbing Henri in the throat.

"I believe this is how the act occurred," said Ambrose. "The wound is at an upward angle. Then the killer released his hold on Frank, who stumbled forward and fell face down. The killer then, for whatever reason—maybe to get the canvas as Miss Tully here suggested—rolled Frank over onto his back, which is how he was when he was found."

"So the killer was right-handed," said Henri.

"And Mr. Mitchell was stabbed with a knife?" asked Myrtle.

Ambrose cocked his head. "That's a little strange. If it was a knife, it wasn't your common, ordinary kind of knife."

"What do you mean?" asked Henri.

"The point of the weapon was not nearly as wide as the rest of the blade. I'd say it was shaped more like a spade or . . . well, something you'd serve cake or pie with."

"A cake server?" said Myrtle.

Ambrose nodded.

"Or a *spade*?" said Henri. "You mean like a garden spade?"

"Yes, like one that would be used in a garden."

"Either of those would be a most unusual murder weapon," said Henri.

"Yes," said Ambrose. "That's what I thought."

"Is there anything else?" asked Myrtle.

"There is," said Ambrose. "In addition to all the blood on his face and his neck, as you might have noticed when you saw him, he was smeared with paint."

"I think that proves my theory," said Myrtle.

"What's that?" asked Henri.

"There was another canvas there. That's where the paint on Mr. Mitchell came from."

"She's right," said Ambrose. "That could mean that Frank was killed so the killer could steal the painting."

Myrtle laughed. Both men turned to look at her.

"I'm sorry," she said, "but I have to ask—who in the world would want to steal any of Mr. Mitchell's paintings? I mean, they weren't that good."

"She has a point," said Ambrose. "Frank was a terrible artist."

"For some reason, the killer wanted it," said Henri.

"*Somebody* wanted it," said Myrtle.

"What do you mean?" asked Ambrose.

"Someone could have come in after the murder happened and taken it. We don't know for sure that the killer took it."

"You're right," said Ambrose. "We *don't* know for sure the killer took it." He looked at Henri. "Looks as if you've got your work cut out for you, son. Good thing you got Miss Tully here to help you."

Henri looked at Ambrose and scowled.

*****

"Where to now?"

Myrtle and Henri had left Dr. Sherman's office and were back in Henri's car.

Henri turned and looked at Myrtle. "What do you mean, 'where to now?'"

"Suspects. Do we have any suspects?" asked Myrtle.

"You got anybody in mind?"

"Yes, several, as a matter of fact," replied Myrtle. "First of all is the man who stabbed Mr. Mitchell last week. He might have come back to finish the job. Then there's Eloise's father: he threatened to kill Mr. Mitchell if he didn't stop seeing his daughter, and I'm pretty sure he hasn't—he hadn't."

"You may be right," said Henri, "but we don't know who the man is who stabbed Frank and . . . ."

"Except we think he's a member of the Ku Klux Klan," said Myrtle, "and he's probably from Marquette."

"As I said," Henri continued, visibly irritated at the interruption, "we don't know who that is. And as for Mr. Blanchard, he lives in Iron Mountain, which is over a hundred miles from here."

"Hmm," said Myrtle, as she settled back into her seat. "You're right."

"What I'm going to do is take you back to the boarding house, and then I'm going to my office."

"What are you going to do there?"

"I don't know;" said Henri, "but whatever it is, it will be without you."

CHAPTER SIXTEEN

Daisy was waiting for Myrtle when she came through the front door. "What did the doctor have to say?" she asked.

Myrtle told her everything Dr. Sherman had shared with Henri and her, including his theory of the murder weapon.

"A cake server? A spade? Seriously?" said Daisy.

Myrtle shrugged. "That's what he said. I'm going to take Penrod for a walk downtown to visit Mr. Abramovitz."

*****

One of Myrtle's favorite things to do on a Sunday afternoon was to walk Penrod into town and stop by the pawnshop owned by Mr. Abramowitz.

During nicer periods—the four to six months when snow didn't cover the ground—they often cut across the fields, making the trip a little shorter than the two miles by taking the road.

Today was not one of those days.

Over forty inches of snow had fallen in December, and most of it was still around. So Myrtle donned her snowshoes, and she and Penrod took off down the road.

Forty-five minutes later, they straggled through the door of the shop, setting off the little bell overhead that alerted Mr. Abramovitz of the appearance of a customer.

He hurried out from a back room. A smile spread across his face when he saw who it was.

"Miss Tully!" he exclaimed. "Und Penrod, my little friend."

Mr. Abramovitz put his hand into his coat pocket. "Penrod, you know vat I haff for you?"

Penrod's ears perked up. He strained forward. It was all Myrtle could do to hold the leash steady.

Mr. Abramovitz pulled a Milk-Bone from his pocket and held it out. This time Myrtle couldn't restrain Penrod as he bolted to the old man.

"Ah," said Mr. Abramovitz, "but first let's zee if we can get you to zit."

Mr. Abramovitz held the treat up out of the reach of Penrod, who obediently sat back on his haunches and raised his two front legs.

"So good," said the old man, as Penrod gently took the bone from his fingers.

"So, Miss Tully. Vat brings you out on a day like today?"

"I wanted to see what wonderful new and exotic things you've gotten in," Myrtle responded, smiling while snuggling up closer to the pot-bellied stove that kept both the store and the room behind it where Mr. Abramovitz lived, comfortably warm.

Myrtle always found the pawn shop to be a veritable cornucopia of treasures.

In a room no larger than four hundred square feet, seven display cases held the various objects people had, over the years, decided they either no longer required or needed less than they did the cash brought by pawning the items: cameras; ladies' combs and hairbrushes; pipes of various sizes and designs; jewelry; ambrotypes, daguerreotypes and union cases; music boxes; silverware; coins and old paper money; a harmonica; fine place settings; handguns, knives and a set of brass knuckles; assorted toys; belt buckles; pocket watches, wristwatches, five ladies' watches on chains; tools;

medals; a 1908 campaign button for William Jennings Bryan and John W. Kern; a set of dental tools in a leather embossed box; and countless other articles.

"I tink I might have someting dat vould maybe interest you," said Mr. Abramovitz.

He walked to one of the cases, removed two books and walked back to where Myrtle waited.

"Dis is a Bible in two volumes, printed in 1764. It is a Purver Quaker Bible, over a hundred und fifty years old, but still in wery good shape."

"I've never heard of a Purver Bible," said Myrtle.

"Yah, it vas never wery popular."

Myrtle took the book and thumbed through it. "It looks interesting . . . but I don't think it's exactly what I'm looking for."

"Vell den . . . ."

The ringing of the bell over the door interrupted Mr. Abramovitz. He and Myrtle both looked to see who had entered the store.

Myrtle's eyes got big.

It was the woman she'd seen coming around the corner of the courthouse, the one who rode a motorcycle, the one Henri had referred to as "Kitty," a journalist, he'd said.

She wore the same outfit she'd had on that day, and Myrtle felt sure her original estimate that the woman was close to six feet tall was accurate.

"Good afternoon," said Mr. Abramovitz. "How may I help you?"

"I was told you sharpen knives," said the woman.

Myrtle thought she denoted a western accent.

"Yah, I do," said Mr. Abramovitz. "Vat kind of knife do you haff?"

The woman pulled back the coat from her side and removed a knife from the leather sheath attached to a belt.

Myrtle's eyes got big again: the knife had to be over a foot in length!

"Dat is vun big knife," said Mr. Abramovitz. "Is dat a Bowie knife?"

"Similar," the woman replied. "It's called an Arkansas Toothpick."

I couldn't imagine picking my teeth with that, thought Myrtle.

"Oh, yah," said Mr. Abramovitz. "I haff heard of such a knife. Yah, I can sharpen dat up for you real good."

"Would I have to leave it?" asked the woman.

"No, no, I can do it vile you vait. But I do have a customer right now I'm taking care of."

"Oh, no," said Myrtle. "Go ahead and help the lady. I'm just hanging around here anyway."

Mr. Abramovitz nodded, picked up the knife, and disappeared into his room at the back.

"That sure is a cute dog," said the woman, kneeling down to pet Penrod.

"His name is Penrod," said Myrtle.

"That's a strange name," said the woman.

"It's from a character in books by Booth Tarkington."

"I don't think I'm familiar with him. I don't read much."

Strange thing for a journalist to say, thought Myrtle.

"I'm Kitty, Kitty Vanderliet," said the woman, extending her hand.

As she did, the sleeve of her coat slid back, and Myrtle noticed a tattoo circling her wrist: a chain of red roses entwined with thorns.

Myrtle took the woman's hand. "Myrtle Tully. Nice to meet you. You're new to town?"

"Temporarily," said Kitty. "I'm a writer, working on a story."

"A story?"

"The triple murder you had here a few months back? I'm writing an article for the *Argosy All-Story Weekly.*"

"Never heard of it," said Myrtle.

"It's not a very big publication," said Kitty. "You don't sound like you're from around here."

"I was born in Louisiana," said Myrtle. "I've been in Booker Falls for a little over a year. Where are you from? Sounded like a western accent."

"Yeah, I can't shake it. Phoenix—Phoenix, Arizona."

"I've heard of Phoenix—never been west of the Mississippi River, though. Okay, that's not exactly true: a part of New Orleans where I'm from is on the west bank of the river. Is Phoenix a big town?"

"I imagine . . . twenty, twenty-five thousand."

"Wow," said Myrtle. "That is big. We're maybe a couple thousand here."

Mr. Abramovitz returned with Kitty's knife. It gleamed in the sunlight coming in through the store windows.

"All done," he said. "Good as new."

"One other thing," said Kitty. "You carry ammunition too, don't you?"

"Yah, I do. Vat kind of gun do you haff?"

Kitty pulled back her coat on the other side and from her holster removed a Smith and Wesson revolver. As she handed it to Mr. Abramovitz, Myrtle noticed the piece had an engraved pearl handle.

"That's very pretty," said Myrtle.

"Thanks," said Kitty. "But I don't carry it for show."

"How much you vant?" asked Mr. Abramovitz.

Kitty looked at him. "I'm sorry—how much what?"

"Ammunition," said Mr. Abramovitz. "How much you vant?"

"Oh," said Kitty, replacing the gun in her holster and the knife in its sheath. "One box should do it."

"I own a gun," said Myrtle. "In fact, I bought it here at the shop. It's a double barrel derringer. But it works for me."

"Altogether, dat vill be a dollar und sixty-five cents," said Mr. Abramovitz, placing the box of ammunition on the counter. "Dat includes da sharpening."

Kitty counted out the money from her purse, laid it on the counter and picked up the box of ammunition.

"Thank you," she said, turning to leave.

"Have you ever fired your gun?" asked Myrtle.

"On occasion. You?"

Myrtle nodded. "A couple of times. You ever shot someone?"

Kitty smiled. "A couple of times."

"Ever killed anyone?" asked Myrtle. A thought had begun to creep into her head.

By this time Kitty had reached the front of the store. "Killed someone? Of course not—except when I absolutely had to," she added, as the door shut behind her.

Myrtle's mouth fell open.

*****

"A gun? And a knife? What kind of journalist is she?"

Myrtle had shared with Daisy what had transpired at the pawn shop.

"That's my question, too," said Myrtle. "And what journalist would never have heard of Booth Tarkington?"

"Yes, even *I*'ve heard of Booth Tarkington," said Daisy. "And you know I'm not much of a reader. And she had a tattoo?"

"There's something about her," said Myrtle, "that I can't place my finger on. Why does she carry a gun and a knife?"

"What are you thinking?"

"She showed up in town about the same time Mr. Mitchell was killed."

Daisy drew in her breath. "You don't think . . . ?"

"I don't know what to think right now. But I'm going to have a talk with Henri."

CHAPTER SEVENTEEN

Henri had not been in Joker's establishment since the day nearly three months earlier when he'd arrested Mickey McInerney for robbing the Booker Falls Bank and Trust.

He knew that even on Sunday, Joker would be serving up drinks as he did every other day.

The country was finishing the first year of Prohibition, which had gone into effect the seventeenth day of the previous January. Everyone in Booker Falls knew about the illegal bar Joker ran in the back room of Alton Woodruff's barbershop.

But no one cared. Not even Henri, who was charged with enforcing the law.

Even Mrs. Livermore, president of the Women's Bible Study Group at St. James, the Finnish Lutheran Church in town, had never lodged a complaint. It was generally understood that people, especially men, who called Michigan's Upper Peninsula home, required a sufficient amount of spirits to deal with the hard-scrabble life they lived, particularly in the dead of winter when the ground was often not visible under the snow for more than half the year.

Joker was understandably surprised when Henri walked through the door.

"Constable?" said Joker, a hint of caution in his voice. *Was this the time the law was going to shut him down?*

"Morning, Joker," said Henri. "I'm here on official business, but not your business."

Joker let out a sigh of relief. "Well, okay, then. How about a drink, eh? On the house."

"A little early for me," said Henri.

"What can I do for you then?"

"Andy Erickson stopped by my office this morning. I assume you heard about Frank Mitchell?"

"Yah," said Joker. "Terrible thing." Joker wiped an imaginary spot off the bar. "You got any leads, any suspects?"

"Not yet," said Henri. "But Andy said he saw Frank coming in here the night he was killed—New Year's Eve? Was he here that evening?"

"Oh, yah, he was here. Came in with that friend of his."

"Friend?"

"Yah. Some short feller. Only had one hand."

"Did he mention the friend's name?" asked Henri.

Joker thought for a minute. "Howard, I think. No, wait—Herman. It was Herman."

"Last name?"

Joker screwed up his mouth. "He said it, but I don't remember. But I'm pretty sure the first name was Herman."

"What time were they in here?"

"Came in 'bout a quarter of nine. Stayed long enough for one drink. Then they left—right at nine, it was."

"You say they were friends?"

Joker nodded. "That's what Frank said. Oh, he said they was business partners, too."

"Business partners? What kind of business?"

"Don't know. He never said."

*****

Henri left the barbershop and walked across the street to George's office. He knew George sometimes stopped by there after church.

While Henri's office could best be described as 'shabbily utilitarian,' George's was impressively appointed, as befitted his position as mayor.

The main feature of the room was an imposing roll top desk that George's father had purchased in 1899 from an Amish community in Luce County, in the eastern part of the Upper Peninsula.

Constructed of solid oak, it boasted three bottom drawers on each side of the kneehole, and a drawer in between, with two pull-out work surfaces, one on either side. The upper portion of the desk contained a total of twenty-two smaller drawers plus six open slots.

An English leather office chair of matching oak with casters allowed George to glide smoothly across the beautifully patterned Persian Tabriz rug, colored in muted shades of brown, rust, and orange, to access the four-drawer filing cabinet on the opposite side of the room.

Two photographs hung on the wall: one of Woodrow Wilson, the outgoing President of the United States; and the other of Albert E. Sleeper, the former governor who had just left office.

"You know you're going to have to replace both of those photographs," said Henri, as he settled into the chair across from George.

"George looked up at the photographs. "I know," he said. "We're waiting for Groesbeck's. I don't know if we'll get Harding's before he's sworn in or not."

"You still have over a month. Who'd you vote for?"

George chuckled. "It was a choice between two Buckeyes, so I wasn't too keen on either of them, eh? But I voted for Cox."

"Me, too," said Henri. "I wasn't too thrilled with him, either, but I liked the fellow running with him."

"Roosevelt?"

"Yah. I think we'll see more of him in the future. Anyway, I need some information."

"Like what?"

"I just left Joker's," said Henri. "He told me Frank was there the night he was killed with some friend of his. I wonder if you might know who."

"A friend?" said George. "I didn't know he had any friends except those of us in the poker group."

"Joker said the man's name was Herman."

"Oh, sure, I remember now: Herman Hutchinson."

"Who?"

"Herman Hutchinson. Remember, Miss Wasserman mentioned him the day we put up the sign at her boarding house? He's a tenant there now."

Henri nodded. "Right. I remember now. I think I'll walk over there and see what he can tell me."

*****

The Wasserman Boarding House, a two and a half story Victorian that boasted eight bedrooms, took up a full third of the first block of Thimbleberry Road.

Until recently, it had been the home of Isaiah Steinmyer and his twenty-eight-year-old unmarried daughter, Rachel. After both of them were murdered by Nate, Isaiah's son and Rachel's older brother, the property passed to the housekeeper, Mildred Wasserman, who had transformed it into a boarding house.

Her first boarder was Herman Hutchinson, who rented not only a room but the space above the carriage house as well. Like his friend, Frank Mitchell, Herman was an artist.

Miss Wasserman was delighted when Henri rang her bell.

"Constable de la Cruz," she exclaimed. "How good to see you. Come on in. Would you care for some hot tea?"

"No, thanks, Miss Wasserman. I'm here to see one of your boarders, Mr. Hutchinson?"

"Oh, yah. Well, I tink he's in. He was here for breakfast, and I never heard him leave. Let me go upstairs and knock on his door."

"Would it be all right if I went?"

"Oh, yah, sure. It's da fourth one down da hall on da left."

"The one that used to be yours?"

"Yah, I'm in da big one now," said Miss Wasserman, a broad grin on her face

*****

A knock on the door brought a quick response.

"Can I help you?" asked Herman, eyeing Henri's uniform.

"I'm Constable de la Cruz. I'm investigating the death of Frank Mitchell."

"Oh, yah, I heard about that," said Herman.

"You and he were friends?"

"Old friends. We graduated together from Adelaide."

"But you haven't been in town long?"

"Yah, that's true," said Herman. "I left about twenty years ago. Floated around here and there. Did some time in the army. Couple of months ago I up and decided to come back and put down some roots."

"Joker said Frank mentioned the two of you were business partners."

"That's what Frank hoped would happen," said Herman. "But it didn't. I've worked in the import, export business, and Frank hoped we could do that together, you know, artwork. But even though he was my friend, I knew he was no businessman, so I never pushed real hard for it."

"Where did you go after you left Joker's?" asked Henri. "He said it was about nine?"

Herman nodded. "Yah, that's right. We went back to Frank's studio and had a few drinks to welcome in the New Year. He wanted me to see what he was working on."

"What *was* he working on?"

"He had another one of those damn paintings of the falls he likes—liked—so much. He was still working on it."

"And was there another painting besides that one?"

Herman furrowed his brows.

"Uh, yah, yah, I guess there was another one."

"What was it?"

"I'm not really sure. I didn't pay any attention."

"What happened to it?"

"The painting?"

"Yah, the painting. It wasn't there when we discovered Frank's body."

Herman looked confused. "Then how'd you know it had been there?"

"The impression in the sawdust, and the paint on Frank's face and smock. We think he fell on it. Then the killer rolled him over and took the painting."

"Huh."

"So you don't know anything about it?" asked Henri.

Herman shook his head. "Nope. Sure don't."

"Was Frank alive when you left him?"

"What! You think I killed him! Yah, he was sure enough alive when I left him."

"And what time was that?"

"Around ten."

"Around ten? You're having drinks to celebrate New Year's Eve, and you left before midnight?"

"To tell you the truth," said Herman, "we'd both been drinking pretty heavy even 'fore we stopped over at Joker's. After we had a couple of drinks at Frank's place, I was plain pooped, so I took off. But he was still alive when I left. If you want to accuse somebody, accuse Joker."

"Joker? Why would I accuse Joker?"

"Because he threatened to kill Frank if he didn't pay him back the money he owed." Herman proceeded to tell Henri about the conversation at the bar.

"Joker never mentioned that," said Henri.

"No, I don't reckon he would have. And I tell you who else you should talk to: Lars Jørgensen."

"Lars? And why should I want to talk with him?"

"Because when I left Frank's place that night, I saw Lars down the street, under one of the street lamps. He must have been drinking pretty heavy, too, 'cause he wasn't too steady on his feet."

"And what would make you think Lars killed Frank?"

"Lars worked for him. Frank had him doing some gardening in the summer and handyman jobs other times. Frank sure liked the flowers in his yard, but he didn't fancy getting his hands dirty."

"And you're sure it was Lars you saw?" asked Henri.

"Oh, yah, I'm sure. I know Lars, 'cause I've had him do some work for me, too."

"You said you left Frank's place about ten. Where did you go?"

"Here. I came straight here and fell into bed. Didn't wake up 'til after seven the next morning."

"Can anyone verify when you got back here, and that you were here the rest of the night?"

"Well, now, since I ain't married and I didn't pick up no woman that night, no—I was here all by myself."

"Miss Wasserman didn't see you come in?"

"I doubt it. The old lady's usually in bed right after she feeds us supper."

"Us?"

"Me and a couple of the guys who work in the mines and that Miss—what's her name?—oh, yeah, Vanderliet; Miss Vanderliet. She moved in right after Christmas. She's a looker, that one is. If I was thirty years younger . . . anyway, anything else, Constable?"

"No, that's all I guess."

"I'll walk you out."

As they reached the front door, Miss Wasserman came out of the parlor. "Constable, how did Mr. Mitchell die?" she asked.

"He was stabbed to death. Doc Sherman said it was a strange kind of knife, shaped like a gardening spade or a cake server."

"A spade, huh?" said Herman.

"A cake server?" said Miss Wasserman.

*****

After dinner that evening, Myrtle caught Henri before he headed upstairs to his room.

"Henri, do you have a minute?" She nodded toward the parlor.

"What is it," he asked when they were in the room. Myrtle had closed the pocket doors from the hallway.

"It's about this new woman in town," said Myrtle. "This Kitty Vanderliet. How much do you know about her?"

"Why do you want to know?"

Myrtle told him what had happened at the pawn shop that afternoon. "Henri, is it possible she had something to do with Mr. Mitchell's death?"

"Now, why would you think that?" asked Henri.

"She shows up, Mr. Mitchell is killed. She carries a gun and a whopping big knife. And I'm pretty sure she's no journalist."

Henri headed for the door. "I can assure you Miss Vanderliet had nothing to do with Frank's death."

"Shouldn't you check out her whereabouts for that night?"

Henri slid open the doors.

"As I said, I can assure you that Ki . . . Miss Vanderliet had nothing to do with Frank's death."

Myrtle stiffened. "Were you with her that evening?" she asked.

"That is none of your business," said Henri, as he disappeared into the hall.

CHAPTER EIGHTEEN

Henri took his watch from his pocket and checked it: ten a.m. He knew Lars should be at work at the train depot. If he even came in, that was. Lars Jørgensen wasn't the most dependable of employees.

Today was one of those days Lars *did* show up for work. Henri found him unloading freight from one of the rail cars.

"Morning, Lars."

Lars looked up from the crate which he'd just set down and grinned when he saw who it was.

Lars had initially been a suspect in the death of Rachel Steinmyer. The two had been secretly seeing each other.

Henri understood what Rachel saw in the man, physically at least. He was a good six feet in height, with a body sculpted from moving crates and other items weighing as much as a hundred pounds or more. A set of almost perfect white teeth blazed out of a face tanned by being outside almost all the time. A mop of blond hair fell down to his shoulders.

"Morning, Henri," said Lars. He took off his glove and stuck his hand out to Henri, who took it. "Whatcha up to?"

"You heard about Frank Mitchell?"

"Yah, I sure did. Sorry to hear it, too. He was a good guy. Let me do some odd jobs for him, so's I could make a few bucks."

"So I heard. You did some gardening?"

"Dat and a lot more, sure."

"Lars, I gotta ask you, you know anything about his death?"

Lars's brows knitted and a confused look crossed his face. "Me? No, why should I know anyting 'bout dat?"

"You were seen near his house the night he was killed."

Lars looked even more confused. "I was? You sure?"

"Were you?" asked Henri. "Were you near his house?"

"Man, Henri," said Lars, "I couldn't tell you if I was or if I wasn't. I got so soused dat night, I don't hardly 'member nutting 'bout it. Maybe I was—I sure don't know."

"You did gardening for him. You knew where his tools were kept?"

"Yah, sure. I used dem."

"You ever use a spade?"

"Yah, I used dat to dig da holes when I would be plantin' da flowers."

"Frank was killed with a spade—or something similar."

Lars held his hands out in front of him in a defensive position.

"Now, Constable, if you a'tinking I done did old Frank in, you got another tink coming. I admit I get drunk as a skunk and can't 'member nutting, but I sure as Hell would 'member if I went and killed a man!"

"I have somebody over at Frank's house now looking for the spade," said Henri.

In truth, Henri planned to go later himself to look. "If we find it and it's got blood on it, I'll be back to see you. Don't go anywhere."

"I din't do it," said Lars. "I can tell you dat. And I sure ain't going nowhere."

Henri got back into his car, drove around the corner, parked and got out. He walked back to where he had a clear view of Lars, who had resumed unloading crates, making sure Lars couldn't spot him.

If a spade really was the murder weapon, thought Henri, *and Lars was the culprit, he might make a bee-line to Frank's house to find it.*

Fifteen minutes later, after Lars gave no indication of going anywhere, Henri got back into his car and drove to Frank Mitchell's house in search of a bloody spade.

*****

Henri parked his Packard in front of his office and got out. An hour of searching Frank's property had produced no evidence of a spade or anything remotely resembling one.

With only three cars in town and many of the carriages put away for the winter, finding a parking space was no problem. In truth, parking was never much of a problem in Booker Falls, other than the Fourth of July, when Main Street was closed off for the five blocks it stretched through downtown in order to make room for the annual parade, which always drew hundreds of people from all over the county.

He was about to enter his office when he heard someone shout his name. He knew immediately who had called out, not so much from the familiar voice, but from the unpleasant odor that preceded its owner.

He turned to find Andy Erickson hurrying toward him.

Andy was the man responsible for keeping the streets clear of horse droppings. From sunup to sundown he made his rounds throughout the town, scooping up what the animals left behind, dumping it into the wheeled-barrel he pulled behind him.

Inevitably, the stench of the barrels' contents seemed to find their way onto Andy's clothes.

Henri remembered that when Andy had testified at the trial of Paul Momet the past summer, Judge Hurstbourne had given him clear instructions to ensure that Andy had a bath before entering the courtroom.

"Hey, Andy," said Henri.

"Hey, Henri. Say, I was wonderin' if you knew if anybody was a'hirin'."

"Hiring? Why—you looking for a second job?"

"Nope," said Andy. "I'm a'lookin' for a first job."

Henri looked puzzled. "You've already got a job," he said.

"Yeah, well, I don't know how much longer. We got tree cars in town now, includin' yours, and I seed two more tother evening. I can see da handwriting on da door, eh? Pretty soon all we're going to have 'round here is autymobiles. Ain't gonna be no horses pulling carriages no more. Which means no work for old Andy no more."

Henri chuckled. "On the wall."

"Huh?"

"You see the handwriting on the wall, not on the door."

"Wherever it's written, I can see it."

"I didn't know you could read, Andy."

"I can't. But I know what it says: Andy, you better be a'lookin' for another job."

Henri thought for a moment. "I can't think of anyone who's hiring right now. But I'll keep it in mind. You say you saw two other cars in town?"

"That's right. Tother night."

"What night?"

"New Year's Eve. I seed them parked over at da Walther."

"Did you see them the next day?"

Andy shook his head. "Nope. Just that night. 'Course, I was a bit late makin' my rounds da next day—kinda hungover, ya know?"

"Okay," said Henri. "Thanks. And I'll keep it in mind about a job for you."

Andy turned and headed back toward Main Street. Henri hesitated, then took off in the same direction.

*****

Marvin Halderman had been a fixture at the Walther Building for over forty years.

In his mid-fifties and never married, he served as the desk clerk for the hotel part of the building, where rooms could be rented by the day or week. He'd begun working at the Walther at the age of fifteen, sweeping the halls and carrying out the trash. When Augie McAllister, the original night clerk, dropped dead of a heart attack thirty-five years ago, Marvin took over the position. When Jim Lemon, the day clerk, followed Augie to the cemetery five years later, Marvin took his job too. He'd set up a bed in a small room off the office so that he could attend the desk day and night.

His personal needs were served by the bathroom down the hall and his meals delivered to him from Miss Madeline's Eatery, a few blocks away, so he had little reason to venture into the outside world.

Though friendly and outgoing, Marvin Halderman was not the most intellectually gifted person in town.

Henri found him nodding in his rocker behind the desk.

"Marvin," said Henri.

Marvin jerked upright. "Huh?" he said, shaking his head and looking around, still groggy.

"Marvin, it's Henri. I need some information."

Marvin stared at Henri, his mind clearing somewhat. "Oh, Henri. Sure, what can I do for you?" he asked, getting up from the rocker and coming to the window.

"There were two cars parked out in front New Year's Eve. Did you have some out of town people staying here that night?"

Marvin thought for a minute, then said, "New Year's Eve. Yup. Sure did. Two fellers. They wasn't together, though."

"Can you give me their names?"

"Yah, sure. Let's see," said Marvin. He opened the ledger in front of him. "One feller, da black one—his name was Otis Blanchard."

Eloise's father! thought Henri.

"Now, he's from—"

"From Iron Mountain—I know," Henri interrupted.

"Yup, you're right. And da other feller, he gave his name as Nick Clearmont."

"Nick Clearmont? Did he say where he was from?" asked Henri.

"Yup—from Marquette."

"What did this second fellow look like?"

Marvin stroked his chin. "Young, in his late twenties or thirties, I'd venture. Tall: maybe six feet. Built pretty good—might could be a athlete of some sort."

"You have a street address for him?" asked Henri.

Marvin shook his head. "Nope. All it says is Marquette."

The first thing Henri did when he returned to his office was telephone Captain Leonard Wysocki of the State Police, at his office in Marquette.

"Hey, Leonard, I wonder if you could check on someone for me. You know, we had another murder here in town this past Friday . . . ."

"New Year's Eve?"

"Yah, New Year's Eve. Anyway, there were two strangers—okay, one was a stranger, I know the other one—anyway, this fellow was in town, and he's from Marquette. Name's Nick Clearmont."

"Yah, I know Nick Clearmont."

"You do?"

"He's one of those Klan members we been keeping an eye on."

"Aha! I'm wondering if he might have been one of the men who attacked Frank last year, and maybe the fellow who stabbed him last week."

"Frank Mitchell? He was stabbed?"

"Yah, right out on the street. In broad daylight. Then the fellow got in his car and took off."

"When did this happen?" asked Leonard.

"Three days before Christmas; the twenty-second."

"We'll pick him up and find out where he was those two days. I'll let you know what we find out."

*****

The grandfather clock had struck five when Henri hurried into the room and took his place at the dinner table.

"Cutting it pretty close there, Henri," said Daisy.

"It's been a busy day," he responded.

"You catch the killer yet?" asked Pierre.

Henri shook his head. "Not even close. Although . . . ."

No one spoke for a moment. Then Mrs. Darling, who had just entered the room said, "Although what?"

"Oh, nothing," said Henri. "I shouldn't be talking about the case."

Mrs. Darling set down the bowl she'd been carrying and turned to Henri. "We got sugar cream pie for dessert tonight. But you ain't getting none if we don't get some information."

"You tell him, Mrs. Darling," cried Daisy.

"Okay, then. But I don't want any of this to go any further than this room."

He proceeded to tell them about his day, everyone he'd interviewed.

When he finished, Myrtle said, "I told you Mr. Blanchard might be a suspect."

"Sounds as though he's not the only one," said Pierre. "So, what's next?"

"Tomorrow I'm driving down to Iron Mountain to talk to Mr. Blanchard. I want to find out why he was in town. Could be he came to see his daughter, of course."

"I don't think so," said Myrtle. "Eloise came into the library today, quite upset. We talked for a long time. I assured her you'd find Mr. Mitchell's killer. I asked her about her father. She said she hadn't seen him since she came back to school."

"What about this Kitty Vanderliet?" asked Daisy.

Henri scowled. "What about her?"

"Myrtle told me about meeting her yesterday at Mr. Abramovitz's pawn shop. I'm wondering what a journalist—if that's what she really is—needs to carry a gun and a knife for. I'm a journalist. I don't carry a gun or a knife."

"I reckon that's her business," said Henri, picking up a forkful of beans.

"Sounds suspicious to me," said Daisy.

"Well, you're not the police, are you?" said Henri.

"I have some news," said Myrtle. "I'm the new head librarian."

"That's great!" exclaimed Pierre.

"Congratulations," said Daisy. "With an increase in pay, I assume."

"Mr. Forrester said there would be something. I don't know what, yet. But he did say I could hire an assistant to take my place. I hired someone today—one of the students at the college, a junior girl. That way . . ." she turned to Henri, ". . . I'll have a lot more free time to help you with your investigation."

Henri looked at her, laid down his fork, pushed back his chair, got up and strode out of the room.

"I'm not sure he was overjoyed by that bit of news," said Pierre.

*****

Henri hadn't looked forward to the drive down to Iron Mountain; not in the dead of winter when the roads were covered with snow.

He'd thought about having the constable there talk with Otis, but decided he should do it in person.

He'd left early in the morning before anyone else was up, particularly Myrtle. He knew she'd want to tag along. This time, it wasn't that he didn't want her to go—he didn't know how dangerous the trip might be with the weather.

After a jaw-clenching journey of four hours, including nearly skidding off the road, not once, but twice, he arrived in Iron Mountain. He stopped and asked directions to the bakery Otis owned, then drove there and parked his car in front of the store.

"Mr. Blanchard," said Henri, entering the shop, "do you remember me?"

Otis looked up from the cake he'd been decorating.

"Yah, you da constable from up Booker Falls way. Whatchoo doin' down here?"

"I came to talk to you about Frank Mitchell's murder," said Henri.

Otis's face lit up. He laid down the cone-shaped pastry bag he'd been using.

"Da son-of-a-bitch is dead?" he said.

"He is," said Henri. "What do you know about it?"

A look of surprise flashed across Otis's face.

"Me? Why would I know anyting 'bout it?"

"You threated him—in his office that day. And you were in town the night he was killed."

"New Year's Eve? He was killed New Year's Eve?"

"That's right. Mr. Halderman at the Walther confirmed you spent the night there."

"Yah, I did—but I didn't kill dat s.o.b. Tought about it. But I didn't do it."

Henri picked up a cake server from the counter in front of him.

"He was stabbed with something that looked like this."

"A cake server?" said Otis. "If I was gonna kill him, I'da used sometin' better'n dat."

"How many of these do you own?" asked Henri.

Otis shrugged. "Six or seven I s'pose. Why?"

"I'm going to have to take all of them with me."

"What! What for? I need dose!"

"I have to have them tested, to see if any contain remnants of blood."

"Blood? You kidding? You tink I use cake servers wit blood on dem?"

"Mr. Blanchard, you have a choice. Either give me all of these you have, or I'll have to take you back to Booker Falls with me and hold you as a suspect."

Henri was pretty sure he didn't have any authority to either make Otis give him the servers *or* transport him back to Booker Falls, but he was betting Otis wouldn't know that.

Otis shook his head. "Well, I sure ain't goin' back to Booker Falls wit you, so I guess you can take da servers. But you ain't gonna find no blood on dem, dat I can tell you."

CHAPTER NINETEEN

Myrtle stared at the body of the man who had been her boss for the past year.

Though she had never felt close to Frank Mitchell, she couldn't help but feel a sense of loss at his passing. Outside of the other residents of the boarding house and George, he was the first person she'd met after arriving in town.

He had spent hours instructing her on how to perform her duties as his assistant. More than thirty years his junior, she had almost begun to look at him as a father figure.

In spite of his taste—overconsumption, to be honest—for Southern Comfort, his leaving her to lock up most evenings, and his sudden attraction to a student young enough to be his granddaughter, there existed a sense of connectedness between the two of them, a mutual appreciation of their roles: they were fellow librarians, caretakers of books, those vessels of knowledge, of enlightenment and illumination, of just plain enjoyment.

Yes, thought Myrtle, *I will miss you, Mr. Mitchell.*

"He looks nice, doesn't he?"

Myrtle turned to see who had spoken. It was George.

"He does," replied Myrtle, slipping a handkerchief from her sleeve and wiping her eyes.

"Gonna miss him at our Friday night poker games," said George.

"I imagine so," said Myrtle.

"Yah," said George, "he was the one player in the game I could always count on beating."

Myrtle laughed. "You're terrible," she said.

"All kidding aside," said George, "we will miss him. I haven't talked with Henri; anything new on the case?"

"He drove down to Iron Mountain yesterday to interview Mr. Blanchard."

"Oh? How did that go?"

"He brought some cake servers back with him. You know, Doctor Sherman said the murder weapon could have been something shaped like a cake server. Turns out Mr. Blanchard is a baker."

"A baker?"

"Yes. This morning Henri sent them over to Captain Wysocki to have them tested for blood stains."

"Speaking of Mr. Blanchard," said George, "do you think his daughter will be here for the funeral?"

Myrtle shook her head. "I'd be surprised if she were. She might want to pay her respects, but I'm not sure she'd want to show up in the midst of so many people who might have mixed feelings about her and Mr. Mitchell."

"I'd say you're mistaken," said George, looking over Myrtle's shoulder. "I see her coming in right now."

Myrtle turned to see Eloise heading toward her. As the young girl moved through the crowd that was milling about, people stepped aside. Some began to whisper among themselves.

"George, excuse me," said Myrtle.

Myrtle met Eloise halfway down the aisle. She took her hand, then embraced her. The young girl was shaking.

"My dear," said Myrtle, "are you all right?"

Eloise nodded, unable to speak.

"It was brave of you to come here today," said Myrtle. "Come, let's go up and pay our respects to Mr. Mitchell."

*****

The number of mourners present for Frank's service surprised Myrtle, especially those from the college. She knew he had lived in Booker Falls for the last forty years of his life but didn't realize how many friends and acquaintances he had acquired over that time. She always considered him to be somewhat reclusive and, indeed, he had been for the last ten years of his life. Before that, he' been very much involved in the life of the community.

She had secured a place in the front row for herself and Eloise. Henri, George, Judge Hurstbourne and Malcolm Middleton, the remaining members of the Friday night poker club, joined them there.

"Where will he be buried?" Eloise whispered to Myrtle.

"At the Catholic cemetery. But not right away."

Eloise turned to look at her. "Why not?"

Myrtle explained to her what George had said—that the ground was too frozen; the actual burial would have to wait until spring when the earth thawed enough to dig it up.

"What happens to his body until then?" Eloise asked.

"Mr. Reynolds has a refrigerated room where it will be kept."

"Mr. Reynolds?"

"The funeral director," said Myrtle. "We need to be quiet now; Father Fabian is ready to start the service."

*****

Everyone agreed it was a nice service—as funerals go.

"Eloise," said Myrtle, "can Henri give you a lift back to your dorm?"

"No, thank you," said Eloise. "I want to walk. I have a lot of thinking to do."

*****

Myrtle looked through the window of Miss Madeline's Eatery at the snow falling at a rapid pace outside, gigantic flakes piling up on what was already on the ground. Henri sat across the table from her.

When she'd found out at dinner the previous evening that he'd gone to Iron Mountain without telling her, she'd gotten upset.

"Why didn't you take me with you?" she'd asked.

"It was too dangerous."

"Pshaw. That's no excuse. You just didn't want me along."

Henri had decided to try to make it up to Myrtle by taking her to lunch following Frank's funeral. While they ate, he filled her in on his conversation with Otis Blanchard.

They had finished their meal—Miss Madeline's famous corn chowder—and were enjoying their coffee.

"Don't you ever get tired of it?" she asked.

Henri stopped a cup of coffee on the way to his lips.

"Tired of what?" he asked.

"The snow. Don't you ever get tired of the snow?"

"I would think after one winter here you'd be used to it. You told me all about how terrible the winters were in France when you were stationed there."

"It was *cold*," said Myrtle. "But it didn't snow all the time. It was just *cold*."

"I have to admit," said Henri, dabbing his mouth with his napkin, "sometimes I *do* get tired of it."

"Well, halleluiah!" exclaimed Myrtle. "So it's not just me."

Henri shook his head. "No. I think only the crazy people never get tired of it."

"Like . . . . ?"

"George, for one. He goes on and on about how great it is here. And Mrs. Darling—okay, I'm not saying she's crazy—like George, she's lived here all her life. But she thinks this is all merely a beautiful Christmas card."

"You haven't lived here all your life," said Myrtle, sipping her coffee.

"No, I was born in French Guiana. I didn't come here until my mother took the position at the college. I was seventeen."

"What's the weather like there?"

"It's a paradise. The temperature hardly ever gets below seventy and hardly ever over ninety. There's no snow, but lots of rain, especially during the rainy season."

When is that?" asked Myrtle.

"From December to June," said Henri. "Except for March."

"Wow. That's like half the year."

"April and May are the worst; December and January not so bad. What's really bad is the humidity. My mother and I lived on the coast, in Kourou, so at least there was some breeze. Inland was hardly tolerable."

"Which do you prefer? Here or there?"

Henri thought for a minute. "Here," he said.

Myrtle was surprised. "I was sure you would have said there. Why here?"

"For one thing," said Henri, "you're not there."

Before Myrtle could respond, the front door opened and a blast of cold air blew into the room. Everyone turned to look, including Myrtle and Henri.

It was Kitty Vanderliet.

She came straight to the table where Myrtle and Henri were sitting.

"Henri, I heard the news about Mr. Mitchell."

"Yah, he's dead. Murdered," said Henri.

"Do you have anyone in custody?" Kitty asked.

"Nah. Have some suspects, though."

"Is the Englishman one of them?" asked Kitty.

Myrtle looked at Kitty. "What Englishman?"

"The one who was staying at Miss Wasserman's the night Mr. Mitchell was killed. I heard him and Mr. Mitchell engaged in a heated argument."

"I wasn't aware of his presence in town," said Henri. "Was your Mr. Wickersham here?" he asked, turning to Myrtle.

"Wickersham! That's the name," said Kitty. "Thomas Wickersham. I thought the two of them might come to blows. Something about a painting."

Myrtle was stunned. *Thomas had been in town?*

"I didn't know he was here," she said. "I'm sure he would have contacted me."

"You say he was staying at Miss Wasserman's?" asked Henri.

"Yes. He was in the parlor when Mr. Mitchell came to see Mr. Hutchinson that evening."

"Was Mr. Hutchinson there, too—during the argument?"

"He came in just before it got serious and hurried Mr. Mitchell from the room."

"Is Mr. Wickersham still at Miss Wasserman's?" asked Henri.

"No," said Kitty. "He was gone the next morning."

Henri looked at Myrtle. "And you knew nothing about this?"

Myrtle shook her head. "I had no idea Thomas was in town."

"Do you know how I can contact him?" asked Henri.

Myrtle nodded. "I have his address."

CHAPTER TWENTY

Friday night dinners at Mrs. Darling's Boarding House always followed the same menu: fish—baked cod, fried perch, or any other type of fish Mrs. Darling had around—boiled potatoes, peas or green beans, canned beets, biscuits, a salad of some sort, and thimbleberry pie for dessert.

When Mr. Pfrommer was in residence, the meal was always served promptly at five o'clock. Even after he went away to prison, that time was pretty much adhered to, though with a little more flexibility.

Until now, it was a meal at which Myrtle was seldom present since, as Frank's assistant, she'd been responsible for closing the library those days on which she worked—Friday being one. Mrs. Darling always saved a plate for her to warm up when she arrived home, but she missed eating with her fellow boarders.

However, since she had recently been made head librarian, she decided her new assistant, Lydia Westerman, could be entrusted with the job of locking up, allowing her to enjoy the evening meals at the regular time with everyone else.

She was doubly delighted to learn that Mrs. Darling had invited George to join them for this night's meal.

"I thought you had your poker club on Friday nights," said Myrtle, addressing George as she popped a small potato into her mouth.

"We don't have enough players anymore," said George. "With Rudy and Frank and Mr. Steinmyer all gone, the only ones left are myself, Judge Hurstbourne and Clarence."

"Maybe it's time you let me in," said Myrtle.

George wiped his lips with his napkin. "As I said before, I fear it may be a little too expensive for you."

"Are you kidding?" asked Daisy. "Myrtle's got a new job now and a pay raise. She's rolling in dough."

"I wouldn't go that far," said Myrtle. "But I suppose you're right—it would probably be too rich for my blood."

"Might you consider a newcomer?" asked Pierre.

Everyone turned to look at him.

"You play?" said George.

"I've been known to bluff my way through a hand now and then."

"We do play for pretty high stakes," said George, hoping not to embarrass his dinner companion.

"I have a bit of money coming in from a trust fund," said Pierre. "Let me sit in one evening, and I'll know if I'm in your league or not."

"Done," said George. "Next week—my house. Seven o'clock."

"Speaking of Mr. Mitchell," said Daisy. "How's the investigation coming, Henri?"

Henri hesitated for a moment, not sure how much he should share. Then he realized whatever he had wasn't all that confidential.

"We have a number of suspects, but none that stand out. They all have motives, and none of them have alibis—at least not provable alibis. Frank owed money to Joker, and according to Herman Hutchinson Joker threatened to kill him if he didn't pay up. Both Mr. Blanchard and that Klansman from Marquette, that Nick fellow, had the same motive: that Frank was involved with that young black woman from the college. I'm not sure what Lars's motive might have been: he could have been drunk and stumbled in on Frank at his studio and one thing led to another. Then there's Mr. Wickersham . . ." Henri turned to Myrtle, ". . . whom I would still like to talk to, to find out what he and Frank were arguing about. Any idea if, or when, he'll be coming back here?"

"He said he'd be back sometime this month," said Myrtle. "But I can't believe Thomas would have had anything to do with Mr. Mitchell's death. And what about Miss Vanderliet? What about her?"

"I've already told you I know she didn't do it," said Henri.

"So you say," Myrtle replied, a disgusted tone in her voice.

"Yes, so I say," said Henri. "So, right now, unless something turns up, I'm at a dead end in this investigation. My best bet is on Mr. Clearmont."

"The Klansman from Marquette," said George.

"Yah," said Henri. "Leonard is interrogating him tomorrow. We'll see what he comes up with."

CHAPTER TWENTY-ONE

Other than Frank's service, it had been several months since Myrtle had been to church. She hadn't even attended the midnight Mass on Christmas Eve, or the regular service the next day, opting instead to remain at the boarding house, playing games with Daisy and Mrs. Darling until three o'clock in the morning, board games such as *Round The World With Nellie Bly, Parcheesi* and *The Landlord's Game,* and card games like *Pit, Rook, and Flinch.*

The women had tried to persuade both Henri and Pierre to join them, but they were informed their souls would best be saved by being in church, and that they— the women—should be there too.

This Sunday, as Myrtle washed her face in the bathroom she shared with Daisy at the end of the hallway, she glanced up and saw in the mirror the crucifix on the wall behind her. It had the same effect as it had the previous fall, shortly after the murders took place. As far as she could recall, that was the last time she had been to a service.

She sighed. *Okay*, she thought, *today's the day.*

*****

"Nice to see you today, Miss Tully," said Father Fabian, shaking Myrtle's hand as she prepared to leave following the service.

"Bet you thought you'd never see me here again," said Myrtle. "Except for funerals, that is."

Father Fabian smiled. "Never crossed my mind."

"That was a very nice service you did for Mr. Mitchell," said Myrtle. "I didn't have a chance to tell you afterwards."

Myrtle turned to go, but Father Fabian didn't let go of her hand. "Don't wait so long until the next time," he said, smiling.

Then he released his grip and turned to the next person in line.

*****

Breakfast that morning had been more than plenteous: fried ham, fried potatoes, buttermilk biscuits, prunes, and scrambled eggs—not to mention an excess of coffee.

Myrtle decided she didn't need another meal quite yet.

Maybe I'll go see what Mr. Abramovitz has new today, she thought.

A few minutes later, she entered the old man's shop, setting off the little bell over the door that jingled, signaling the appearance of a customer.

Mr. Abramovitz hurried out from the back room.

"Miss Tully," he said, obviously pleased by her presence. "But vere is da little dog? Vere is Penrod?"

Myrtle explained she had come from church and had not yet been home.

"You must be hungry, den, eh?" said Mr. Abramovitz.

"No, not at all. That's why I came here instead of going back to the boarding house: so I wouldn't hurt Mrs. Darling's feelings by passing on lunch."

"But how 'bout a cup of tea? Vould you like dat?"

"Yes, I would," said Myrtle. A cup of tea sounded perfect.

While Mr. Abramovitz returned to the back room to fix the tea, Myrtle strolled around the store, peeking into the various cabinets that held a profusion of odd and curious items.

But she didn't see anything new that piqued her interest.

"Anyting you vant to look at?" asked Mr. Abramovitz, returning to the room with two steaming cups.

"Not really," said Myrtle. She was disappointed: she'd always found something before that grabbed her attention.

"How 'bout a gold nugget?" asked Mr. Abramovitz.

Myrtle's ears perked up. A gold nugget *did* sound interesting!

Mr. Abramovitz walked back to his room. When he returned, he held a small object in his hand.

"Here it is," he said, handing the item to Myrtle.

Myrtle looked at what he gave her. Her brow furrowed.

"My goodness!" she exclaimed. "Mr. Abramovitz, do you know what this is?"

"A piece of gold; a small piece, but still gold," Mr. Abramovitz replied.

"This is a gold tooth. Mr. Abramovitz, where did you get this, if I might ask?"

"Vy, dat young Mr. Jørgensen—he brung it in 'bout a week ago. I bought it from him."

Myrtle shook her head. "I think I know who this tooth belonged to."

The old man looked shocked. "You do? How can you know dat?"

"Because the man to whom this used to belong was my boss—I'd bet on it."

"Dat Mr. Mitchell?" said Mr. Abramotiz. "Da librarian who got killed?"

"That's right. Mr. Abramovitz, do you have a phone I can use?"

"No, I'm sorry; never had da need for one."

"All right," said Myrtle. "Now, do me a favor: do not get rid of this tooth—I think it's going to be valuable evidence in solving Mr. Mitchell's murder. I'm going to go get Henri—Constable de la Cruz—and bring him back so he can see this."

*****

Myrtle rushed from the shop and headed around the block to Henri's office at the courthouse, hoping he was there.

He wasn't.

Maybe George was in his office.

Myrtle hurried around to the other side of the building. George wasn't in his office either.

She stopped for a moment to consider her next move. Should she go to George's home? It wasn't far away, closer than the boarding house. From there she could call Henri and, if he wasn't home, perhaps track him down.

Moments later, she knocked on George's front door. It was opened almost immediately by Mrs. Delahanty, George's housekeeper.

"Miss Tully," said Mrs. Delahanty, "what a pleasant surprise. Mr. Salmon didn't tell me you'd be stopping by."

"No, he didn't know I was coming," said Myrtle. "But is he here?"

"Aye, lass, he is. Come in, come in."

While Myrtle waited for George to appear, her thoughts went back to the one other time she'd been in this house: last March, when he'd invited her for a St. Patrick's Day dinner. She wondered if she'd get another invitation this year. She hoped so. Besides Mrs. Delahanty's fabulous cooking, she had enjoyed playing—and beating—George at his billiard table in the basement.

"Myrtle," said George, smiling as he entered the parlor. "This is a pleasant surprise. To what do I owe the honor?"

Myrtle quickly explained what she had discovered at Mr. Abramovitz's pawn shop. "We need to call Henri and get him down there," she said.

"The phone is in the study," said George. "Come with me."

*****

"You found what?" asked Henri, after Myrtle filled him in on finding what she was sure was Frank Mitchell's gold tooth.

"You heard me," said Myrtle. "Come quickly. George is going to drive me back over there."

"George? Where are you?"

"I'm at George's home. I had to call you, and Mr. Abramovitz doesn't have a telephone."

"I'll meet you at his shop," said Henri.

*****

"What do you think?" asked Myrtle, as she, George, and Mr. Abramovitz watched Henri study the piece of gold.

"I think it's a gold tooth, for sure," said Henri. "But was it Frank's? George, you knew him as well as anyone. You played poker with him every Friday. What do you think?"

George took the object from Henri and turned it over in his hand. "My guess is, it was Frank's. It looks like what I remember it looked like."

"Mr. Abramovitz, I'm going to have to confiscate this," said Henri. "I'm not sure if the county can compensate you for it or not, but I need to get Doc Sherman's opinion. If it turns out not to be Frank's tooth, it will be returned to you."

*****

Even though it was Sunday, Henri found Ambrose Sherman in his office. As he, George, and Myrtle gathered around, the doctor carefully studied the tooth.

Finally, he looked up. "Yah, that's Frank's all right. I treated him once for an abscess on his gum right next to this tooth. I noticed it had a funny little ridge on one side like this one does. It's definitely Frank's."

George looked at Henri. "Time to make an arrest."

Henri nodded. "First, though, I'm going to find Judge Hurstbourne."

"What for?" asked Myrtle.

"To get a warrant to search Lars's place."

"I'll go with you," said Myrtle.

Henri looked at her and shook his head. "No, you won't. You'll go back to the boarding house. In fact, George will drive you there while I find the judge."

"But . . ." Myrtle started to protest.

Henri shook his head again and glared at Myrtle. "No way," he said, emphatically.

Myrtle shrugged. "You know, you wouldn't even be making this arrest if I hadn't spotted that tooth."

"And I thank you," said Henri. "The town thanks you. The county thanks you. And now I'll thank you to go with George. Then, George, if you'll come back here, we'll go out and arrest Mr. Jørgensen."

*****

Henri found Judge Hurstbourne in his chambers, located on the courthouse's second floor, right above his own office. He'd had no problem getting the search warrant after explaining about the tooth and the fact that Lars had been seen in the vicinity of Frank's home the night he was murdered.

When he reached the street, George was already waiting for him.

"That didn't take long," said Henri.

"She wasn't too happy about not being able to tag along."

"She's tagged along too many times," said Henri, hopping into George's car. "Let's go see if we can find Mr. Jørgensen."

CHAPTER TWENTY-TWO

The shack Lars Jørgensen called home made the modest homes in Greytown, where most of the miners lived, look like mansions.

Located a quarter of a mile down the road from where Lars worked at the train depot, the house was in grave danger of complete collapse. In fact, a part of the roof above the front porch had fallen down, almost blocking the door.

Traces of white paint, applied when the house was built, were still evident here and there, but the overall grayness of the wood gave testimony to the ravages of over sixty Northern Michigan winters.

Two of the six windows still had glass in them; the remaining four were covered with wood.

From the time Henri had discovered while investigating Rachel Steinmyer's murder that Lars was her boyfriend, he'd wondered what it was the woman saw in the man, other than his good looks. He was not in her league socially, intellectually and certainly not financially. After all, her father, before he, too, was murdered the same night as Rachel, owned the town bank.

Henri had to admit that, in his contacts with Lars over the years, he'd never found the fellow to be offensive in terms of physical hygiene, other than when they talked at the depot where Lars worked. But then, the man was engaged in physical labor, lifting and moving crates, bags, and boxes, and performing other menial tasks; a little body odor was to be expected.

What will his house look like inside? Henri wondered. Neat and clean like Lars—or in sad shape like the outside?

Henri knocked on the door.

No answer.

He knocked again.

Still no response.

He turned the doorknob, and the door inched open. Henri slid his pistol from his revolver and looked at George, who nodded.

Henri pushed the door open the rest of the way and entered the house, George close behind him.

They looked around in amazement. The room was spotless, everything in its place except for an empty whiskey bottle lying on the floor by the couch. The walls were bare save for one thing: a photograph of Rachel Steinmyer.

"Not what I expected," whispered Henri.

"I know what you mean," George whispered back.

Moving silently through the darkened house, they came to a closed door. Henri opened it a crack and peeked in. Lars lay fast asleep on the bed, still dressed in his jeans and sweater.

Henri placed his gun back in his holster. He walked over to where Lars lay and shook him.

"Lars!" said Henri.

Lars didn't budge.

"Lars!" said Henri, louder.

Still no response.

"I think he's passed out—probably drunk," said George.

"Go to the kitchen, will you? See if you can find a glass, fill it with water and bring it back here."

Minutes later, George returned with the glass. "It's nice and cold," he said.

Henri took the glass from George's hand and dumped its contents on Lars's unsuspecting head.

"Holy Whaa!" exclaimed Lars, sitting bolt upright. He looked at Henri.

"Constable? What's going on? What are you doing here? And how'd I get so wet?" He ran his hand over his dripping hair.

"You're under arrest," said Henri.

Lars's eyes opened wide. "Arrest? What'd I do now?"

"For the murder of Frank Mitchell," said Henri.

Lars's eyes opened even further. "Murder? Old Frank? What makes you tink I killed him? Me and him was friends. I already told you I din't do it."

"You sold his gold tooth to Mr. Abramovitz at the pawn shop. The same gold tooth you took out of his mouth after you stabbed him to death."

Lars shook his head vigorously. "No, no! That ain't right. I'm a lot of tings, but I ain't no killer!"

"Then how did you get his tooth?" asked George.

Lars looked at George. He hadn't realized he was there. "His tooth?"

"That's right—his tooth, his gold tooth," said George. "How'd you get it if you didn't yank it out of his mouth? Or perhaps when he fell, it came out and you thought, 'Why don't I take that—I can sell it.'"

"Now," said Henri, "get up and put your hands behind your back."

Lars got out of bed and did as Henri had instructed him.

"I found that tooth," said Lars.

"You found it?" said George. "Where? On the ground?"

"On my dresser," said Lars. "Dat dresser right dere."

He nodded toward the dresser sitting across the room. "Dat's where I found it—swear to God."

"It magically appeared there?" said Henri.

"I don't know how it got dere. But dat's where I found it—I ain't lying!"

"Lars, I have a warrant to search your property."

Henri handed his pistol to George.

"George is going to keep an eye on you here while I look around. Is there anything you think I shouldn't find?"

"Like what?"

"We've never found the murder weapon. That's one thing I'll be looking for. And whoever killed Frank might have stolen a painting."

Lars shook his head. "You ain't going to find no murder weapon, 'cause I din't do it. And you sure ain't going to find no painting here, neither."

"Well, okay, then," said Henri. "George, you okay here?"

George nodded. "Lars, why don't you have a seat on the bed there?"

*****

Fifteen minutes later, Henri returned to the bedroom. In one hand he held what appeared to be a bloody coat; in the other, a garden spade that also appeared to have blood on it. He held both items up in front of Lars, who stared at them, uncomprehendingly.

"I found both of these out back in the shed," said Henri. "Care to explain?"

Lars shook his head. "I don't know nothing 'bout neither one of dose tings. Dey ain't mine."

"I'm sure the spade is probably Frank's," said Henri. "But if the coat's not yours, why is it in your shed?"

"Constable, I ain't been in dat old shed since last Thanksgiving. I don't know half of what's out dere. But I can tell you dis—dat ain't my coat."

"Let's go," said Henri, pulling Lars up off the bed by his arm.

"Where to?" asked Lars.

"Why, jail. As I said before, Lars Jørgensen, you're under arrest."

*****

News of Lars's arrest quickly spread through town.

"Didja hear Lars got arrested?" "I always did think that feller was up to no good." "Thank God, they got the killer."

Twenty minutes after Myrtle heard the news she was in Henri's office.

"You arrested Lars," she said.

"Yah, I did. Should have expected you'd be here in record time. 'Spose you want to interrogate him."

"Well, I could . . . ."

"Forget it. He doesn't need interrogating. We got him dead to rights."

"He confessed?"

"Well, no, he didn't confess."

"So, all you have on him is the gold tooth. What did he say about that?"

"He said he found it on his dresser."

"On his dresser?" said Myrtle, a look of doubt on her face. "Golly, I could understand if he said he found it on the ground or at the depot—but on his dresser?"

"I know. You would think he'd have come up with a better explanation."

Myrtle thought for a minute. "Hmm. Unless it's true."

"What do you mean, 'unless it's true?'"

"If somebody framed him."

"Somebody framed him? Like, who?"

"The real killer."

"The *real* killer? We've got the real killer—he's sitting back there in a jail cell. And, besides, the tooth's not all we have."

"What do you mean?"

Henri reached into the burlap sack he'd carried the coat and spade in from Lars's home, pulled out the spade and laid it on his desk.

"We've got this," he said.

"The murder weapon?" said Myrtle

"And this." Henri pulled out the coat and held it up. "And I'm pretty sure we're going to find out the blood on both of them is the same type as Frank's."

"Which doesn't mean it's Mr. Mitchell's blood," said Myrtle, eyeing the coat. "Just that it's the same type. There's no way to know for sure it's his. And I don't think that's even Mr. Jørgensen's coat."

"What?"

"The coat—hold it up by the shoulders, so it's spread out."

"Why . . . ?"

"Humor me, okay?" said Myrtle.

Henri did what Myrtle asked him.

"That's not his coat," said Myrtle.

"Why don't you think so?" asked Henri, turning the coat around and studying it.

"It's too small. It might fit me—but it sure wouldn't fit Mr. Jørgensen."

"We found it in his shed. Who else's would it be?"

Myrtle shook her head. "I don't think so. Did he say it was his?"

"No, but . . . ."

"That could have been planted, too," said Myrtle.

"By the *real* killer," said Henri, sarcastically, replacing both the coat and the spade into the bag.

"Exactly."

"I like my chances with what I've got," said Henri. "And I have a feeling Jake will, too."

*****

Jake McIntyre had been the county prosecuting attorney for nine years. In his mid-thirties, he was a graduate of the University of Michigan Law School.

The previous year he had successfully prosecuted Paul Momet for the murder of a young woman some twenty-eight years earlier, although that verdict was later overturned when the real killer was found out. Later in the year, when the investigation was underway to uncover the murderer of three more people, Jake had invited Myrtle to join in the discussion about potential suspects and motives, an occasion at which she came to appreciate both his taste in scotch whiskey—Johnny Walker Black Label—and cigars. The aroma of *Little Beauties*, which Jake had shipped in from Kalamazoo, reminded her of her father, also a cigar aficionado.

Though not overpowering in stature—he stood barely seven inches over five feet and weighed close to three hundred pounds—Jake was a formidable foe in the courtroom, the number of his convictions far outnumbering his losses. And he was happiest and most enthusiastic when faced with a difficult case.

This wasn't one of those cases; at least not in Jake's opinion.

"This shouldn't take any time at all," he said when Henri presented him the next morning with the evidence he'd found: the bloody coat, the bloody spade, and the gold tooth.

"Not only that," said Henri, "but I also have a witness who saw him in the vicinity of Frank's house the night Frank was killed."

"Okay, then, let's take it to Hurstbourne and see what he says, eh?" said Jake, chewing on his cigar.

"Let's put it on the docket for tomorrow," said Judge Hurstbourne when Jake approached him. "It's been pretty slow around here. We could do with some excitement."

CHAPTER TWENTY-THREE

It may have been the fact that the town had been through two murder trials in the past four months—this being the fourth murder during that time; or that the fate of Lars Jørgensen was of little importance to the majority of the residents of Booker Falls; or that the minds of the town folk were on the upcoming hockey game at Dee Stadium in Houghton between the Booker Falls volunteer firemen and Hancock Central High School, but whatever the reason, of the fifty available seats the courtroom at the Booker Falls Courthouse held, scarcely a dozen were filled for the beginning of Lars's trial.

Unlike at the trials of Paul Momet and Nathan Steinmyer, Myrtle and Daisy had no trouble finding seats.

"All rise." The sonorous voice of Teddy Wilkerson, the bailiff, resounded through the room.

Judge Clarence Hurstbourne entered and waved his hand. "Sit down," he said, dismissively.

Like Jake McIntyre, Hurstbourne had also graduated from the University of Michigan Law School. Other than that, the two men shared little in common.

An imposing man some four inches over six feet and who now weighed two hundred and seventy pounds, in 1879 Hurstbourne had been a starting guard for the first football team ever to represent the University of Michigan. A face as hard as rock, adorned by a bushy beard, black, sprinkled with gray, further gave the appearance that Clarence Hurstbourne was a man not to be trifled with.

Though Jake never tired of trying.

"Your honor," said Jake, after the judge took his seat. "Permission to smoke my cigar?"

Judge Hurstbourne glared at Jake with steely eyes. "Mr. McIntyre, we have been through this before, have we not?"

Jake grinned. "Thought I'd give it another shot."

Hurstbourne glanced down at a sheet of paper lying on his desk. Jake thought he saw the hint of a grin on the man's face.

"The case before us today," said Hurstbourne, "is the state of Michigan versus Lars Jørgensen." He looked up. "Is Mr. Jørgensen in court?"

Jake rose. Henri, sitting next to Lars, took him by his arm and the two of them did likewise.

"Mr. Jørgensen," said the judge, looking at Lars, "who is representing you, sir?"

A blank look covered Lars's face. "Huh?" he said.

"Who is your attorney?" asked Hurstbourne. "Who is defending you?"

"I guess I ain't got no attorney, your honor," said Lars. "I can't afford one."

"Very well," said Hurstbourne. "We shall have one appointed for you. Teddy, can you bring me that list of lawyers?"

The bailiff opened a drawer in a cabinet next to the wall, removed a piece of paper and walked it over to the bench.

"Okay, let's see," said the judge. "I think Michael Gladstone will do."

"Uh, your honor," said Jake, "Mike is out of town right now—won't be back 'til the fall."

Hurstbourne screwed his mouth up in disgust.

"All right," he said, again studying the sheet in front of him. "London Flaxon."

This time it was the bailiff who spoke. "Your honor, Mr. Flaxon has moved to Wisconsin."

Hurstbourne's eyes narrowed. "How come nobody ever tells me what the hell's going on?" he asked, his irritation evident in his voice. "Okay, who *do* we have who can handle this case?"

"There's Mr. Brown," said Wilkerson.

Judge Hurstbourne looked at the bailiff. It was obvious the judge had no idea who Mr. Brown was.

"Who?"

"Brown—Baron Brown," said Wilkerson. "He just passed the bar and arrived here in town last week."

"Where from?" the judge asked, his brow furrowed.

"I'm not sure, sir," said Wilkerson.

Hurstbourne sighed. "Okay, then. Teddy, you tell Mr. Brown to get his butt over to the jail right away and confer with his client. And tell him I'm setting the start of this trial for next Tuesday."

*****

"Who is Baron Brown?" asked Daisy.

She and Myrtle had left the courthouse and gone across the street to Miss Madeline's Eatery for a cup of coffee. After returning Lars to his jail cell, Henri had joined them.

"Beats me," said Henri. "But I don't think it's going to matter much who represents Lars—we've got him dead to rights on this murder."

"You keep saying that," said Myrtle, "but I'm not so sure."

"You're hung up on that coat, aren't you?" asked Daisy.

"That's one thing," said Myrtle.

"What else?" asked Henri.

"How about the painting?"

"What painting?" said Henri.

"The painting Mr. Mitchell fell on when he was killed. What happened to it? You didn't find it in Mr. Jørgensen's home, did you?"

Henri shrugged. "He could have already sold it, maybe threw it away."

Myrtle shook her head. "I think if he had it, he would have taken it to Mr. Abramovitz's pawn shop like he did the tooth."

"Then there's your proof," said Henri. "There's no disputing the fact he had the tooth."

"Which he found on his dresser," said Myrtle. "Come on; he's not that dumb. He could surely have come up with a better story."

"Which he didn't," Henri reminded her.

"Which makes me think he's telling the truth," said Myrtle. "Someone put it there—the real killer. And Mr. Jørgensen is being framed."

"What do you think, Daisy?" asked Henri. "You've been pretty quiet."

"I think I may have to start writing another book," said Daisy, taking a sip of her coffee.

CHAPTER TWENTY-FOUR

Tuesday morning found Myrtle and Daisy back in the courtroom in time to see Henri enter with Lars in tow.

Sitting at the defense table was a young, pimply faced man, no more than twenty-three, dressed in a blue serge suit that did not quite fit him. When Henri led Lars over, Brown stood and shook his client's hand.

The usual routine of standing for the judge's arrival proceeded, and the trial was ready to begin.

"Mr. McIntyre," said Judge Hurstbourne, "you ready to make your opening statement?"

"I am, your honor."

Jake rose and walked over to the jury of ten men and two women who had been empaneled the day before.

"Ladies and gentlemen," he began, "I know being here is an inconvenience for most of you. Thankfully, this trial will not take long. The evidence the state will present will make it clear beyond a doubt that on the evening of December thirty-first last year, the defendant, Lars Jørgensen, did stab and kill one of the leading citizens of this community, Mr. Frank Mitchell. Thank you."

"Wow," Daisy whispered to Myrtle, "that was short and sweet."

"He thinks this is an open and shut case," Myrtle whispered back.

"You don't."

"We'll see what the defense has to offer," said Myrtle.

"Mr. Brown," said Judge Hurstbourne, as Jake returned to his table. "Your turn."

"Ahem," said Baron Brown as he rose to his feet.

He approached the jury box and stopped. For a few seconds, he didn't say anything.

"He's building up suspense," whispered Daisy.

Myrtle shook her head. "He doesn't know what to say," she whispered back.

"Um, ladies and gentlemen," said Baron. "Mr. Janiston is not guilty of this crime."

Myrtle shook her head again. "He doesn't even know Mr. Jørgensen's name."

"Jørgensen," said Judge Hurstbourne.

Baron turned to look at the judge. "Sorry?"

"Jørgensen. Your client's name is Jørgensen, not Janiston."

"Oh, uh, yes, sir, your honor." Baron turned back to the jury. "Mr. *Jørgensen* is not guilty of this crime," he said, emphasizing Lars name, "and we will prove that. I will prove that. Thank you."

"I think poor old Lars is in deep trouble," said Daisy.

Myrtle nodded. *Indeed he was.*

"Mr. McIntyre," said the judge. "You may call your first witness."

"We call Constable Henri de la Cruz," said Jake.

Henri took his place in the witness box and was sworn in.

Jake picked up the coat and the spade Henri had found in Lars's shed. He approached Henri, holding one of the objects in each of his hands.

"Constable," said Jake, "can you tell me where you found these items?"

"In the defendant's shed, out behind his house."

"The defendant, Lars Jørgensen."

"That's correct."

"These both appear to have blood on them. Was that blood tested?"

"Yah;" said Henri. "by the state police."

"And what was the result?"

"The blood type of both articles was the same as Frank Mitchell's."

"And were any fingerprints discovered on the spade?"

"There was a partial print—it belonged to the defendant."

Jake walked back to his desk, laid down the coat and spade and picked up the tooth. He returned to Henri and held the tooth out for him to take.

"Can you tell me what this is?" asked Jake.

"That is—was—is, I guess, a gold tooth that belonged to the deceased."

"And where was this discovered?"

"At Mr. Abramovitz's pawn shop. Lars—Mr. Jørgensen—had sold it to Mr. Abramovitz."

"Constable de la Cruz, did Mr. Jørgensen say how he came into possession of this tooth?"

"Said he found it on his dresser."

A titter ran through the room.

Judge Hurstbourne pounded his gavel. "Order!" he cried out. "I want order!"

"On his dresser?" said Jake, when the laughter subsided.

"That's right—on his dresser."

"Did he say how it got there?"

"Nah," Henri replied. "Just said that was where he found it."

"Did you believe him?"

"Object," muttered Myrtle.

But Baron said nothing.

"Heck, no," said Henri. "Would you?"

"No, I would not," said Jake. He turned to Baron. "Your witness."

Jake returned to his desk as Baron approached Henri.

"Constable," said Baron, "the fingerprint on the spade—you say it was a partial print?"

"Yah."

"If it's only partial, maybe it's not Mr. Jørgensen's."

"Objection," said Jake. "Calls for speculation."

"Sustained," said Judge Hurstbourne.

"Constable, was the blood on the coat found to be Mr. Mitchell's blood?"

"Wait—what about the spade?" muttered Myrtle. "He worked for Mr. Mitchell. He used that spade. Of course, his fingerprints would be on it!"

"Shush," said Daisy. "People are looking at us."

Judge Hurstbourne was one of them. And he didn't look happy.

"Nah," said Henri. "Leonard . . . ."

"Leonard?" Baron interrupted.

"Leonard Wysocki, a captain with the state police."

"And Captain Wysocki said?"

"Said they could match the blood type: A, in this case. But there was no way to tell if it came from Frank or not."

"Is blood type A pretty standard? Is that what most people have?"

"I have no idea," said Henri.

"No more questions," said Baron.

"Mr. McIntyre, you may call your next witness," said the judge.

"Wait a minute," Myrtle cried out, jumping to her feet. "Ask him about the size of the coat. Ask him why it's too small for Mr. Jørgensen. And what about the button? Ask him about that!"

Daisy took Myrtle's arm and tried to pull her back into her seat.

Mouths open wide in shock, everyone turned to see who had spoken.

Judge Hurstbourne's eyes were open as wide as Daisy's; but it was anger, not concern, that poured from them.

"Miss Tully!" he shouted. "You are out of order. Please sit down and be quiet or I will have you removed!"

But Myrtle wasn't done. "And the spade" she continued, "—Mr. Jørgensen worked for Mr. Mitchell in his yard; naturally, his prints would be on it."

Judge Hurstbourne rose to his full height and shook his gavel at Myrtle. "That is enough, young lady! Bailiff, please remove Miss Tully from the courtroom."

Suddenly, Myrtle realized what she had done.

"I . . . I'm sorry, your honor," she said.

"Out!" shouted the judge. "Out of my courtroom—now!"

Feeling thoroughly humiliated, Myrtle turned and started for the door. Daisy stood to follow her.

"No," said Myrtle, waving her back down into her seat. "You stay here." Then, whispering, "That way you can let me know what happens."

She fled through the door at the back of the room that led to the hallway. Daisy looked around and sat down.

"Mr. McIntyre, your next witness," said the judge, taking his seat.

For a moment, Jake just stood, frozen. Then, recovering, he said, "Uh, I call Simon Abramovitz to the stand."

"Mr. Abramovitz," said Jake, after the old man was sworn in, "you are the owner of the local pawn shop?"

"Yah, I am," said Mr. Abramovitz.

Jake showed him the tooth. "Do you recognize this?"

"Yah, I do."

"How did it come into your possession, sir?"

Mr. Abramovitz looked at Lars. "Young mister Lars, dere, he brought it in, and I bought it from him."

"Thank you, sir."

Judge Hurstbourne looked at Baron. "Mr. Brown?" he said when the man made no motion to get up.

"Oh, no questions your honor," said Baron.

"Your next witness, Mr. McIntyre," said the judge.

Doctor Sherman entered the witness box and was sworn in.

"Doctor Sherman," said Jake, "you were the coroner who handled this case?"

"I was," said Ambrose.

"Please tell us your conclusion."

"Mr. Mitchell was stabbed in the neck," said Ambrose, "which caused him to bleed to death."

"Did you determine what type of weapon was used?"

"Because of the nature of the wound, I determined it was not a standard blade, but perhaps something similar to a spade."

"Like a garden spade? Like this spade?" asked Jake, holding up the spade.

"Yah, that could do it, I think."

"And you offered a scenario on how the crime was committed. Can you show us?"

Ambrose stood and demonstrated what he had previously shown Henri and Myrtle, how the killer had been behind the victim and, using his right hand, stabbed from the front at an upward angle into Frank's neck.

"So the killer was right-handed," said Jake.

"That was my conclusion," said Ambrose.

"And how tall would you say he would have been?"

"At least five-foot-nine or taller."

"And what makes you say that."

"That's how tall Frank was," said Ambrose. "With the angle of the wound, the killer would have to be at least as tall."

"You've seen plenty of bodies. How tall would you say Mr. Jørgensen is?"

"Objection," said Baron.

"Overruled," said Judge Hurstbourne. "Mr. Jørgensen, please stand up."

Lars did as the judge had ordered.

"Doc?" said the judge.

"Why, I would say Mr. Jørgensen must be close to six feet."

"Thank you," said Jake. "Now..." He picked up Frank's gold tooth, "...you're the one who identified this tooth as belonging to the deceased, is that correct?"

"Yah, it is. I know that tooth, 'cause I did some work in Frank's mouth once. I recognize the ridge along one side."

"No more questions, your honor."

Judge Hurstbourne looked at Baron. "Mr. Brown?"

Baron stood and walked to the witness box.

"Doctor Sherman, you said the murder weapon was a spade?"

"I said it *could* have been a spade."

"You also mentioned it might be something like a cake server?"

"Yah, I did."

"Since we don't know if the blood on the spade Mr. McIntyre produced is Mr. Mitchell's, and since the murder weapon might have been something else—a cake server, for instance—then we can't be sure this spade—or any spade for that matter—is the murder weapon, can we?"

"Objection," said Jake. "Calls for speculation."

"I'll allow it," said the judge. "Since the answer seems pretty obvious to me."

"No, we cannot," said Ambrose.

"Thank you," said Baron. "No more questions, your honor."

"Mr. McIntyre," said Hurstbourne, "you have one more witness?"

"I do, your honor."

"I think we shall break for lunch," said the judge. "Reconvene at one o'clock."

CHAPTER TWENTY-FIVE

"What happened after I left?" asked Myrtle, as she and Daisy ate their lunch at Miss Madeline's.

Daisy told her about Mr. Abramovitz and the tooth, and how Doctor Sherman described the attack.

"But I thought Mr. Brown made a good point about the spade," said Daisy, recounting the testimony he'd elicited from Doctor Sherman.

"Good for him," said Myrtle, dipping her spoon into her white chicken chili. "It's about time he started putting up a defense. I don't think he's anywhere near as good as Mr. Lawrence was."

"The lawyer who defended Mr. Momet?"

"Yes."

"You do remember Mr. Momet was found guilty?"

"But Mr. Lawrence put up a great defense," countered Myrtle. "Besides, Mr. Momet was later exonerated."

"So what you're saying is that Mr. Lawrence was such a great lawyer he couldn't get his client off, even though he was innocent?"

"Well . . . regardless, I don't think I would want Mr. Brown to defend me even if it was for spitting on the sidewalk."

"Is spitting on the sidewalk against the law?"

"I don't know, but it should be. I swear, I could do a better job than he's doing."

"I think you already did," said Daisy.

"Yeah, and it got me kicked out of the courtroom."

*****

By the time Daisy returned to the courtroom, the proceedings were underway. Myrtle had made her promise to take notes, to share later, and then headed back to the library to make sure everything was going all right there.

As Daisy settled into her seat, she saw Herman Hutchinson sitting in the witness box.

"Now, Mr. Hutchinson," said Jake, "you told Constable de la Cruz the night Mr. Mitchell was murdered, you saw Mr. Jørgensen in the vicinity of his house."

"Yah, that's true, I did."

"And you were coming from Mr. Mitchell's house?"

"Yah. We'd had a few drinks to celebrate the New Year coming in."

"And Mr. Mitchell was alive when you left him."

Herman nodded. "As alive as you or I."

"What time was this?" asked Jake.

"Around ten o'clock."

"Where was Mr. Jørgensen when you saw him, exactly?"

"Down the street, under one of the street lamps. Like I told the Constable, he must have been drinking pretty heavy, too, eh, 'cause he was stumbling all around."

"Thank you. No more questions."

"Mr. Hutchinson," said Baron, approaching Herman, "what was your relationship with the deceased?"

"With Frank? We was friends. Ever since college. We graduated together."

"And you say Mr. Mitchell was alive when you left his house. How do we know that to be true? How do we know you didn't kill him yourself?"

"Why would I?" asked Herman. "Like I said: we was friends."

Baron thought for a moment.

What would have been the motive?

"No more questions," said Baron, returning to his desk.

Judge Hurstbourne shook his head. "Very well. Mr. McIntyre, any more witnesses?"

"No, your honor," said Jake, rising to his feet.

"Mr. Brown, do you have any witnesses to call?" asked the judge.

"Your honor, I call my client, Lars Jørgensen."

"Mr. Jørgensen," said Baron, after Lars was sworn in, "do you know why you're here in this courtroom?"

"'Cause they tink I done killed Mr. Mitchell," replied Lars.

"And did you?"

"No, sir, I would never do nothing like dat. Mr. Mitchell was my friend."

"You told Constable de la Cruz you found Mr. Mitchell's tooth on your dresser. Was that true—is that where you found it?"

"Yes, sir, it is—dat's where I found it."

"Do you know how it got there?"

Lars scratched his cheek. "No, sir, I ain't got no idea."

"What about the spade and the coat? Do you know how they got in your shed?"

"No, sir, like I told the constable, I ain't been in dat shed since last Thanksgiving. Only went dere den to get my hatchet."

"Your hatchet?"

"To kill da turkey wit. See, I'd caught dis wild turkey a couple days before. I killed it and dressed it and sold it to da Juicy Pig."

"I see. So, *were* you in the vicinity of Mr. Mitchell's home the night he was murdered, as Mr. Hutchinson testified?"

Lars hesitated. "Uh . . . maybe. I got pretty drunk dat night. I ain't right sure where all I went after I left Joker's."

"What time did you leave Joker's?" asked Baron.

Lars shrugged. "I ain't rightly sure 'bout dat, neither."

For a few minutes, Baron didn't speak. Then he walked back to his desk and turned to face the judge.

"I guess that's all the questions I have, your honor," he said, and sat down.

"Mr. McIntyre, your witness," said Judge Hurstbourne.

Jake stood and strode to the witness box.

"Lars, you're in a lot of trouble, you know that?"

Lars hung his head. "I reckon so."

Jake nodded and turned to the judge. "No questions, your honor."

"Mr. Brown," said Hurstbourne, "do you have any other witnesses to call?"

"No, your honor," Baron replied.

"Anything else?" said Hurstbourne, directing his question to Jake.

Jake shook his head.

"Well, okay, then," said the judge. "We're adjourned for today. Ten o'clock sharp tomorrow—we'll hear closing arguments."

*****

"That's it? That was all he asked him?"

Following the adjournment, Daisy had headed straight for the library. She knew Myrtle would want to know what had happened at the trial.

They were sitting in Myrtle's office; the office that once belonged to the man whose murder trial they were now discussing. Daisy had filled Myrtle in about Herman Hutchinson's testimony as well as Brown's questioning of Lars.

"He didn't ask him to try on the coat?" asked Myrtle. She was furious.

"Nope."

"What did Mr. McIntyre ask Lars?"

"If he knew why he was there."

Myrtle stared blankly at Daisy when she didn't continue. "That's it?"

"That's it. I think Mr. McIntyre felt sorry for him. There's no way the jury's going to find him innocent."

"He is, you know," said Myrtle. "He didn't do it."

"How can you be so sure?"

"First of all, what's the motive?"

"The tooth? The missing painting? Money?"

"Oh, the tooth was an accident; it just came out when Mr. Mitchell fell into the other painting. And about the painting . . . where is it? There's no proof Mr. Jørgensen ever had it. If he did, I'm convinced he would have tried to sell it to Mr. Abramovitz, just as he did the tooth."

"What about the coat—and the spade?" asked Daisy.

"They're not evidence at all!" exclaimed Myrtle. "It's not *his* coat—anybody who took a minute to look at it would know that. It's much too small. And his fingerprints were sure to be on the spade: he used it when he worked for Mr. Mitchell. Besides, we don't know for sure if that's the murder weapon."

"But they were both found in his shed. And as far as finding the tooth just sitting there on his dresser—who would believe that?"

Myrtle looked hard at Daisy. "I would," she said. "Someone is trying to frame Mr. Jørgensen."

"If that's true," said Daisy, "they're doing a bang-up job of it."

CHAPTER TWENTY-SIX

Myrtle was determined to be present for the closing arguments. But in order to pull it off, she needed to make sure the judge couldn't recognize her. She knew she could find one at de Première Qualité Women's Wear Shop.

"Isabell, I'd like to see your wigs."

Isabell Dougherty stared at Myrtle. "Why would you need a wig? You have beautiful hair?"

Myrtle leaned over and whispered in Isabell's ear. "I want to be in that courtroom today."

"I heard what happened yesterday," said Isabell.

"I couldn't sit there and not say anything. Mr. Jørgensen's lawyer, I'm sorry to say, is incompetent."

"You think someone is trying to frame Lars?"

"Yes, I do."

"Okay," said Isabell, "let's see what we can find."

A few minutes later Myrtle found herself in front of a mirror, sporting a dark, shoulder-length wig and green-tinted glasses.

"What are these?" Myrtle had asked when Isabell brought the glasses out from the back room.

"They used to be my mother's," said Isabell. "They were supposed to help her vision."

"Did they?"

Isabell chuckled. "Not a bit. But they did help her attract men after my father passed away."

Myrtle laughed. "Let's hope they have the opposite effect for me; I don't want to stand out."

"Don't sit with Daisy," said Isabell. "Find someone else, and sit with them."

*****

"Daisy."

Daisy looked around to see who had spoken to her. At first, she didn't recognize Myrtle.

"Myrtle? Is that you?"

"Shh," said Myrtle. "Yes. I'm going to sit in on the trial today."

"What will the judge say?"

"Nothing, if he doesn't spot me. You take your normal place. I'm not going to sit next to you—I'm going to sit somewhere else, somewhere in the back. I'll see you outside afterward."

Daisy nodded, then entered the courtroom.

A few minutes later, Myrtle followed her. She stopped, looked around, and spotted a large man in the second row from the back.

If I sit behind him, she thought, *the judge won't be able to see me.*

She had just slid into her seat, adjusting herself so the tall man was directly between her and where the judge would sit when the bailiff ordered, "All rise."

"Be seated," said Judge Hurstbourne, taking his seat. "Mr. McIntyre, are you ready?"

"I am, your honor," said Jake, getting up out of his chair. He walked over to the jury.

"Ladies and gentlemen," he said, "this is a pretty simple case, really open and shut. The defendant is charged with killing Mr. Frank Mitchell by stabbing him in the neck with this spade . . ." Jake walked over to the table, picked up the spade and returned to the jury. He held the spade up so they could see it. ". . . which contained the defendant's fingerprints and traces of blood, and was found in the defendant's shed along with . . ." He walked back to the table, laid down the spade, picked up the coat and walked back to the jury box. ". . . this coat, which also contains traces of blood."

Jake returned to the table, laid down the coat, picked up the tooth and again walked back to the jury.

"Finally, there is this tooth, which Doctor Sherman has identified as having belonged to the deceased, and which the defendant admits having sold to Mr. Abramovitz. Now, Mr. Jørgensen claims he found the tooth on his dresser at his home, but he doesn't know how it got there. It 'mysteriously' appeared.

"In addition to the physical evidence I have presented, we also have a witness, Mr. Herman Hutchinson, who saw the defendant in the vicinity of the victim's home the night of the crime. Mr. Jørgensen does not deny being there, claiming he was so drunk he doesn't know where he was.

"Ladies and gentlemen, based on the evidence presented and the testimony given, you can do nothing less than find the defendant, Lars Jørgensen, guilty of the murder of Frank Mitchell. Thank you."

Jake returned to his table and sat down.

"Mr. Brown?" said Judge Hurstbourne.

"Ladies and gentlemen," said Baron, standing and walking over to the jury box. "What you see before you here is an innocent man. Mr. Jørgensen has testified he has no idea how the spade and coat the prosecution has produced got into his shed and that he had not been in that shed since last Thanksgiving, long before Mr. Mitchell was murdered.

"If the spade came from Mr. Mitchell's home, it is understandable how my client's fingerprints would be on it since he did gardening work for the deceased. As far as the blood on it and the coat are concerned, while it has been identified as human, and as the same type as the deceased, there is no way to prove it *is* the deceased's."

Tell them about the coat, mumbled Myrtle. *It doesn't fit.*

The man sitting in front of her turned around. "What?" he asked.

Myrtle waved her hand at the man. "Nothing," she said quietly. "Nothing."

"As far as the tooth is concerned," Baron continued, "by Mr. Jørgensen's own admission, he is prone to overindulge on occasions. It is perfectly plausible that on one such occasion he might have found the tooth on the street, picked it up, taken it home and placed it on his dresser. The next morning when he arose, he discovered it but did not remember how it got there."

Good point thought Myrtle. *Wish I'd thought of that.*

"While my client does not dispute—indeed, does not remember—being in the vicinity of the deceased's home the night of the murder," Baron went on, "there is no evidence to show he was actually there—in the studio, that is. In fact, Mr. Hutchinson testified *he* was in the studio that evening, having drinks with Mr. Mitchell and when he left, Mr. Mitchell was still alive. But was he? Still alive, that is. How do we know Mr. Hutchinson is telling the truth?

"Ladies and gentlemen, the decision is up to you. Is this flimsy evidence sufficient to sentence a man to prison for the rest of his life for a crime he did not commit? I do not think so. And I hope you will not think so, either. Thank you."

"Mr. McIntyre," said Judge Hurstbourne after Baron returned to his table, "anything more?"

"No, your honor," said Jake.

"Very well, then," said the judge.

For the next few minutes, Judge Hurstbourne gave the jurors their instructions, then directed them to retire to the jury room.

"You will let the bailiff know when you have reached a decision," he said. "Court is adjourned."

The jurors all stood but, instead of leaving, began whispering amongst themselves.

"What's the meaning of this?" asked the judge.

"Your honor," said the foreman, "we don't need to go to the jury room. We got a decision."

Everyone who had gotten up, ready to leave, stopped where they were.

"You do?" asked Judge Hurstbourne. He had never had a jury that didn't adjourn to the jury room to determine their verdict.

"Yes, your honor," said the foreman, "and it's a unanimous one."

Judge Hurstbourne threw his hands up. "Well, okay, then, sit back down so we can have it read. Court is back in session. Everybody who's not leaving, sit down."

Everyone sat down.

"And your verdict is a unanimous one, you say?" asked Judge Hurstbourne.

"Yes, your honor."

"Let's hear it," said the judge.

The foreman stood up. "We find the defendant guilty, your honor."

A ripple of conversation went through the room.

"Quiet," said the judge. But he didn't bang his gavel this time. Instead, he asked, "So say you all?"

He wasn't ready to accept that every juror had voted guilty without reviewing the evidence and the testimony.

"Yes, your honor," they all answered in unison.

"Okay," said the judge, "I guess we have a verdict. Would the defendant please rise?"

Lars and Baron stood up. Lars was visibly shaken.

"Having been found guilty by a jury of your peers," said Judge Hurstbourne, "I now sentence you to life in prison, such sentence to be served at Marquette Branch Prison. *Now*, court is adjourned."

He banged his gavel, got up and strode from the courtroom.

For a moment, no one moved, stunned by what had happened. Then, one by one, they got up and straggled out of the room. Daisy stopped at the row where Myrtle sat. Myrtle didn't look at her, so she continued on and left with the others.

Henri walked over to the defendant's table, took Lars by the elbow and led him out a side door.

Jake and Baron gathered up their papers, shook hands, and exited through the big double doors at the rear of the room.

Myrtle found herself alone.

I can't believe that just happened, she thought.

*****

The mood at the supper table at the boarding house that evening was somber. No one spoke.

Myrtle started to cut her ham, then paused. She laid her fork and knife on the table and folded her hands in her lap.

"That was a travesty of justice," she said.

Everyone stopped eating and looked at her.

"You mean the trial?" asked Daisy.

"Yes," said Myrtle, "the trial. I'm convinced Mr. Jørgensen is innocent. That jury had its mind made up before he ever even entered the courtroom."

"I think I have to agree with you about him being innocent," said Daisy.

"Well, I don't," said Henri. "All the evidence pointed to him."

Pierre decided to stay out of this conversation. He remained silent.

"There's something else," said Myrtle.

"What's that?" asked Daisy.

"Doctor Sherman said Mr. Mitchell's assailant was behind him when he was stabbed, and that the killer thrust the knife—or whatever it was—upward into his throat."

"What's wrong with that?" asked Henri.

"Humor me for a moment. Would each of you pick up your knife and hold it as though you were about to stab someone?"

Henri sighed. "What's the poi—"

"Oh, come on, Henri," said Daisy, picking up her knife. "Humor her, will you?"

Grudgingly, Henri complied, as did Pierre.

"Now," said Myrtle, "look at how each of you is holding your knife, with the blade pointed down."

"So?" said Henri.

"Mr. Mitchell was about five-foot-nine, Doctor Sherman said. You're about that tall, aren't you Henri?"

"Yes."

"Doctor Sherman said Mr. Mitchell's killer was probably as tall as he was, maybe a bit taller," said Myrtle. "Mr. Longet, how tall are you?"

"Five-eleven."

"Could both of you get up, please?" asked Myrtle.

Pierre stood immediately. Reluctantly, Henri followed.

"Now," said Myrtle, "Mr. Longet, would you stand behind Henri and put your left arm around his chest?"

Pierre did as Myrtle asked.

"Thank you," said Myrtle. "Now, with your right hand, pretend to stab Henri—in the throat."

Pierre started to comply, then stopped.

"That would be difficult to do holding the knife like this," he said.

"So turn the knife around," said Henri.

"Yes," said Myrtle. "Turn it around so the blade is pointed upwards."

Pierre switched the knife.

"Now, you can stab him, can't you?" asked Myrtle.

"Yes," said Pierre.

He pretended to stab Henri, then released him.

"What's your point?" asked Henri, turning to Myrtle.

"If you were going to stab someone, how would you hold your knife—blade up or blade down?" said Myrtle.

Together, Daisy and Pierre answered, "Blade down."

"That's what I think, too," said Myrtle.

"But," said Henri, "let's say you hadn't planned on stabbing the other person and at the last minute picked up the weapon from the table. Then you'd be holding it blade up."

"I thought so too," said Myrtle. "But Doctor Sherman said the murder weapon wasn't an ordinary knife; more like a cake server or a spade. The murder took place in Mr. Mitchell's art studio. What would either of those be doing there?

"Here's another theory. What if Mr. Mitchell wasn't attacked from the back, but from the front, by someone shorter than him, not taller? That could explain the upward thrust of the weapon."

"But again," said Pierre, "that would mean the killer was holding the weapon pointing upward, not downward."

Everyone retook their seats at the table.

"Hmm," said Myrtle. "You're right about that."

"In any case," Henri continued, "it's over now; nothing more to be done about it."

"We shall see," said Myrtle. She picked up her knife and resumed cutting her ham. "We shall see."

CHAPTER TWENTY-SEVEN

The hockey game between the Booker Falls Volunteer Firemen's Association and the Hancock Central High School team had been scheduled back in December before the town became embroiled in the whole affair of Frank's murder.

Reverend Albrecht, one of the volunteer firemen, had made the arrangements with Frank Williams, an old friend of his from his days at Suomi, now the coach of the high school team.

Eddie O'Halloran, the fire chief, was not too enamored by the arrangement.

"Preacher, what if dere's a fire; we'd all be twenty miles away—in our skates. Okay, not me, because at my age I ain't about to get out on da ice again. But all da rest of our men would be. Who'd be left to answer da bells?"

"I have it all arranged with the fellows over in Chassell," said Reverend Albrecht. "They'd come down and spend the day here. They all want an excuse to come here anyway and eat at the Juicy Pig. Besides, we haven't had a fire here in six years. And as cold as it is, I think the chance of having one this winter is pretty slim."

O'Halloran had finally given his reluctant okay. "But I ain't going. As I said, I couldn't play anyway. I'll stay here and keep dose Chassell fellows in line."

*****

The seven volunteer firemen piled into Chuck Zeering's hay wagon for the hour and a half ride to

Houghton, located across Portage Lake from Hancock. Trailing along behind them came a procession of carriages and wagons carrying other town residents making the trip as spectators and cheerleaders.

An hour after this caravan departed, Henri's car followed, with Myrtle, Daisy, and George as passengers. Despite their entreaties, neither Pierre nor Mrs. Darling had exhibited any interest in going. They caught up with the earlier crowd just as they reached the arena, where the game was to be played.

The Amphidrome, constructed in 1902, had been built specifically for hockey. A vast, barrel-roofed building that could hold over five thousand spectators, it appeared deserted with the small crowd of less than a hundred people who turned out for the game, most of them from Hancock, rooting for the home team.

Some of the Booker Falls players had been in the building before as spectators. But for Alex Coldtrain and Jacques Lemieux, it was a first time experience.

Alex, in fact, had never played hockey on any surface other than an ice-covered pond. "Holy Whaa!" he exclaimed as he looked around. "Dis be one big place!"

"Come on guys," said Reverend Albrecht, "let's go to the locker room and get dressed."

Fifteen minutes later, they returned to the rink and skated out to the middle, where the Hancock team waited with the referee.

"Gentlemen," said the referee, "I'm . . . ."

"You're Willard Hyppio?" said Alex, his mouth wide open.

"Yah, I am," said Willard. "Okay, gentlemen, here are da rules we're playing wit tonight."

"Who is Willard Hyppio?" Jacques whispered to Alex.

"He plays right wing for da Red Jackets team."

"Hockey?" asked Jacques.

"Well, yah," said Alex. "What else? And he's really good."

"And that's it, gentlemen," Willard finished. "Let's have a good clean game."

Reverend Albrecht controlled the opening face-off and sent the puck rocketing over to Pete, who swished it swiftly across the ice to Gus Palmer, who fired it over to Alex who put it in the goal.

Booker Falls Volunteer Firemen: one; Hancock Central High School: zero.

"Man, this gonna be easy," Gus said to Pete, as the teams took their places for the next face-off.

Twenty-eight minutes later, at the end of the first period, the score was Booker Falls Volunteer Firemen: one; Hancock Central High School: four.

Pete ladled a glass of beer from one of the buckets his cousin, Morris, had been kind enough to run over to the Douglas House Saloon and return with. He turned to Gus. "I don't tink it's gonna be as easy as you tought," he said.

Both men were breathing hard. In fact, all seven of the Booker Falls skaters were having trouble catching their breaths, even Reverend Albrecht, who was easily in the best shape of any of them.

"Preacher," said Alex, "I'm tinking maybe we're a little bit out a shape to stay up wit dese young sprigs for tree periods."

"Alex, I think you're right," said Albrecht. "But let's see what happens this next period."

After a much-appreciated intermission of seventeen minutes, the second period got underway.

Thirty-one minutes later it ended. Score: Booker Falls Volunteer Firemen: one; Hancock Central High School: seven.

"Man, dey're killing us," said Lawrence, another of the Booker Falls players as he collapsed onto the bench. "Where's da beer?"

"All gone," said Alex. "We finished it after da first period."

"Fellows, gather around," said Reverend Albrecht. "Let's take a vote: who wants to play a third period?"

No one moved.

"Who wants to call it and go home?" asked the reverend.

All six hands shot up.

"I'll go tell the other team," said Reverend Albrecht.

"What?" said George, when Reverend Albrecht came back and announced to the spectators the game was being called. "You're giving up?"

"Mayor," said Lawrence, "you strap on a pair of skates if you want and get out dere and play. We done had enough."

"I think we should give our men a hand for a game well played," said Myrtle, standing and applauding. The rest of the Booker Falls fans stood and joined her.

"It was a fun experience," said Myrtle. "Thanks to all of you for a great game."

"Okay," said Henri, as the firemen skated away to change their clothes. "I guess that's that."

"Oh, I don't know," said George.

"What do you mean?" asked Daisy.

"It's about a half hour drive up to Red Jacket. I say we go up there and make a stop at Shute's."

"What's Shute's?" asked Myrtle.

"You'll see," said George. "What say, Henri, make a day of it? It's only four o'clock."

Henri shrugged. "Sure, why not? If the ladies are up for it."

George looked at Myrtle and Daisy. "What say? A side trip to Red Jacket?"

Myrtle looked at Daisy, who shrugged.

"Why not?" said Myrtle. "Let's go see what Shute's is."

*****

Shute's Bar had been meeting the drinking needs of Red Jacket's citizens—primarily male—for a quarter of a century, first as Curto's Saloon, later under its current name.

And though Prohibition had been the law of the land for over a year, Mike Shute, who owned the place, was not about to let that minor inconvenience stop him from continuing to provide what his customers desired.

While the drink list reflected nothing more than near beer and soda as being available, the room in the basement provided spirits of a more enjoyable nature. A communications tube that ran from the bar down to the lower level provided a means of warning the patrons of the imminent presence of any law enforcement officer—which was seldom.

The upper room on the second floor was a social hall, hosting meetings of the Cigar Makers Union Local Number 413 in addition to several Italian groups such as the Guiseppi Garibaldi Celebri Society—which consisted of young Italian bachelors—and Club Alpino Pont and Locono.

It was the bar that most impressed Myrtle when the four of them came through the front door: forty feet long, it made even the grandiose bar at the Michigan House pale by comparison.

"Oh, wow, would you look at that!" she exclaimed. "Isn't it gorgeous?"

A stained glass canopy hung over a crystal clear mirror. The long counter behind the bar was conspicuously noticeable by its absence of any alcohol.

"I have to use the ladies room," said Daisy.

"It's up those stairs, through that opening and clear back on the right," said George, pointing.

"Evening folks, evening George," said Ethan, the bartender. "What can I get you?"

"Doesn't look as though you have much of an assortment," said Myrtle. "We were hoping for something a little more, uh, *substantial*, if you know what I mean."

Ethan smiled. "Miss, I don't know you. But you're lucky because I do know George. George, you know how to get to our *other* serving area, don't you?"

"I do," replied George.

"Why don't you take your friends there," said Ethan. "And I shall escort the other young lady when she returns."

George nodded. "Okay, this way."

He took off, and Myrtle and Henri followed.

*****

Minutes later Daisy joined them. They were seated at a small table, drinking homebrewed beer and listening to the accordion music of Giuseppe Bianchi. Several dozen other patrons sat at similar tables, some drinking beer, others moonshine, all brewed and distilled by the owner.

"Wow, he's good, isn't he?" said Daisy, taking her seat.

"Yah," said George. "You should have heard his rendition of *There'll Be a Hot Time in the Old Town Tonight.*"

For the next half hour, the four of them sat entranced, as Giuseppe belted out such favorites as *Whispering* and *Swanee*.

"Myrtle, let's dance," said George, getting to his feet.

As they twirled to the strains of *Santa Lucia*, Myrtle said, "George, I'm always amazed how nimble you are on a dance floor when you have to use a cane to get around."

"It depends on who I'm dancing with," said George, smiling.

"Well, I'm glad it's me."

"Me, too," said George.

"Ain't this fun?" asked Daisy as she and Henri glided by.

"We should do it more often," cried Myrtle, as George took off with her across the floor.

*****

By the time eight o'clock rolled around they all decided they had drunk enough, danced enough and gorged themselves sufficiently on hard-boiled eggs, fish and chips, and fried pickles to last until the next time.

"Time we should be getting back," said Henri.

"Yah," said George. "Church tomorrow."

Myrtle groaned and laid her head down on the table.

*****

When Myrtle, Henri, and Daisy arrived back at the boarding house, Mrs. Darling was waiting for them in the parlor.

"Mrs. Darling, you're up late," said Daisy.

"I been waiting up for Miss Tully," said Mrs. Darling.

"Oh?" said Myrtle. "Why? Is something wrong?"

"Oh, no, dearie, it's dat young man, dat Mr. Wickersham—he called for you."

"He was here?" asked Myrtle, a surprised look on her face.

"Oh, no, he wasn't here; he called on da telephone. Said he's staying over at Miss Wasserman's. Just got into town."

"Did he want me to call him?" asked Myrtle.

"Nah, said he'd stop by tomorrow afternoon if dat was okay wit you."

"Hmm," said Daisy. "So the Englishman's back in town."

Henri said nothing but turned and headed up the stairs.

"I wonder what he wants," said Daisy, a mischievous grin covering her face. "Oh, that's right—he wants you, Myrtle."

"Oh be quiet," said Myrtle, a blush coming to her face. "What he better have is a good explanation as to why he didn't tell me he was in town on New Year's Eve and didn't contact me."

CHAPTER TWENTY-EIGHT

The next morning at breakfast, Daisy regaled Pierre with a running account of the previous day's excursion to Houghton for the hockey game.

"We had so much fun," she enthused. "You should have gone with us." She turned to Myrtle, who had been silent throughout the whole meal, hardly touching her food. "Shouldn't he have gone, Myrtle?"

Myrtle sat up and looked at Daisy.

"Huh?" she said. "Gone? Gone where?"

"Not wherever you just went to," said Daisy. "What's wrong with you?"

"Nothing," said Myrtle. "Nothing's wrong with me."

"She's thinking about seeing Wickersham again," said Henri, in a not too friendly voice.

Myrtle's face turned red. "What if I am?" she asked. "What's it to you?"

"Nothing now that we've got Lars for Frank's murder," said Henri. "But if that weren't the case, I would definitely want to talk with the fellow. He *was* a suspect, you know."

"Half the town were suspects," said Myrtle, getting up. "And I'm telling you, you still don't have Mr. Mitchell's killer. But it's not Thomas," she added, walking away from the table with a polite, "Please excuse me."

Myrtle had barely reached her room when she heard the telephone ring downstairs. Then came the sound of Mrs. Darling's voice.

"Miss Tully, it's for you, dearie. It's dat nice Mr. Wickersham."

For a moment Myrtle hesitated. *Did she even want to talk with him?* She sighed, turned and started back down the stairs.

Of course, she did.

When she reached the hallway, she took the receiver from Mrs. Darling's hand.

"Yes," she said, speaking into it, a definite tone of iciness in her voice.

"Myrtle?" came back the voice on the other end.

"Yes."

"Myrtle, is that you?"

"Yes, it's me. Who did you think—the Queen of Sheba? What do you want?"

Thomas didn't speak for a few seconds. Then: "You sound upset. Are you upset?"

"What is it you want, Mr. Wickersham?" asked Myrtle.

"I take it you are upset, but I don't know what about."

"You were in town on New Year's Eve," said Myrtle.

"Yes, yes I was. I tried to contact you, but Mrs. Darling said you were out of town; at a party over in Laurium."

Now Myrtle was confused. "Mrs. Darling? When did you talk to her?"

"That night; New Year's Eve. I had a sudden change of plans and was able to stop by Booker Falls just for one night. I'd hoped if you weren't busy we could bring in the New Year together. But then I found out you weren't home. And I had to leave early the next day."

"Mrs. Darling didn't tell me you stopped by."

"No, I didn't stop by; I telephoned."

"I see." Myrtle's voice was softer now. "And now you're back in town."

"Have lunch with me today? At Miss Madeline's?"

Myrtle took a deep breath. "All right. What time?"

"Noon works for me. What do you say?"

"Okay," said Myrtle. "Noon it is."

*****

Myrtle's eyes lit up when she saw Thomas enter the restaurant. While she had occasionally thought of him over the past year, ever since the night they'd spent together in his apartment in Paris before she returned to America, the idea she would ever see him again never crossed her mind until he'd shown up three months ago.

An inch shy of six feet and weighing one hundred and eighty-five pounds, Thomas wasn't as tall as George, who stood about three inches taller.

As if having a face handsome enough to seduce any number of women, both before and after Myrtle wasn't enough, he also possessed style and charm, qualities sometimes lacking in many of the male inhabitants of Copper Country, populated in large part as it were by uneducated and uncultured men who made their living as miners.

Though, Myrtle admitted, both George and Henri possessed those qualities, though to a somewhat lesser degree than Thomas.

What first captured her interest that night in Paris at Le Chat Noir cabaret where they'd met was the jet-black hair he had tied back in a ponytail. The second thing was his eyes, dark and deep-set, like a matching pair of black pearls.

Today, when he entered the restaurant, the eyes were still there, but the hair was cut short and neat, more befitting of the position he now held. Myrtle noticed he wore the same outfit he'd had on when he'd surprised her last fall: a black, Chesterfield overcoat over a beige colored tweed suit with a matching vest and a patterned silk tie. A black herringbone Cashmere wool scarf lay loosely around his neck.

Must be his favorite outfit, she thought.

Unlike that day, today Thomas was not uncovered— a black top hat rested perkily atop his head.

Myrtle felt her heart jump a little. *Did he really still have that effect on her?*

He strode quickly over to where she sat, bent down and kissed her on the cheek.

"Thank you for coming," he said. He removed his hat and coat and hung them on the hook on the wall, then sat down.

"You sounded a little peeved on the phone when we first spoke," he said. "I was afraid you wouldn't meet me."

"I was peeved," said Myrtle, "until I found out you'd tried to contact me. I thought you were in town and didn't bother to come by."

"Well, now you know. While you were out gallivanting with the mayor, I spent the night alone in my room at Miss Wasserman's."

"Yes, I'm afraid there isn't a great deal to do in Booker Falls, even on New Year's Eve, though I hear Mr. Mulhearn's establishment was quite busy. Are you here for a week, now?" asked Myrtle.

Thomas frowned. "'Fraid not. I've been called back to London. I don't think I'll get back to the states before May. But I wanted to see you before I went."

"May!" exclaimed Myrtle. "But that's three months from now!"

"It will go by before you know it," said Thomas. "I'll write you."

CHAPTER TWENTY-NINE

During Myrtle's first year at the boarding house, the grandfather clock in the corner of the dining room was the bane of her existence.

Every hour on the hour between six o'clock in the morning and eleven o'clock in the evening, the chimes would strike, loud, obtrusive bongs, announcing the time. And on each of those occasions, Myrtle, startled, would jerk involuntarily. It had only been over the last several months she had finally been able to ignore the strident sound.

The fifty-year-old clock came with the farmhouse when Mrs. Darling bought the property in 1885 and turned it into a boarding house.

Eight feet high, it was constructed of solid mahogany, and mahogany veneer. The numbers were Roman numerals and the upper half of the face displayed a beautiful painted wooded scene: two deer drinking placidly from a pond surrounded by trees and a soaring, snow-capped, mountain in the background. A montage of carved animals—bears, elk, deer, moose, and wolves—marched in a parade around the top, crowned by an imposing eagle that reigned over the whole assemblage. Spiraled, wooden columns descended elegantly down all four sides, ending at four huge claw feet which supported the whole structure.

The bottom part of the case consisted of a glass front and glass sides, and a solid wooden back. Inside, hung a magnificent brass pendulum and three weight-driven chimes.

A silent mode was set that prevented the chimes from ringing at night when everyone was asleep.

Today, as Myrtle bounded down the stairs, she counted the strikes as the chimes announced seven o'clock: breakfast time.

Bong, Bong, Bong, Bong, Bong . . . .

Myrtle stopped, frozen, two steps from the bottom.

Where was bong number six? And seven?

She turned the corner of the hallway into the dining room and found everyone staring up at the now silent clock. Henri had gotten up from his chair and opened the lower front panel to see inside the case.

"What happened?" asked Myrtle.

Daisy turned to look at her. "The clock stopped."

"The clock stopped?" said Myrtle. "Why did the clock stop?"

"I think it's broken," said Henri, still peering into the case. "The weights aren't moving at all."

"Perhaps it needs to be wound," said Pierre.

"No, I wound it last Sunday," said Henri.

"But that was five days ago," said Myrtle.

"It's an eight-day clock," said Henri. "It only needs to be wound every eight days. I've been winding it every seven days, every Sunday, after breakfast, like Mr. Pfrommer did when he was here."

"How do you wind it?" asked Daisy.

Henri reached into the case and withdrew an object.

"This is the crank," he said, holding it up for them to see.

He opened the upper panel covering the face.

"You put the crank in the arbor and turn it. That makes the weights come up. You raise them almost all the way, but don't let them touch the top of the lower case. That's all there is to it. They'll slowly lower over the next eight days—seven on the schedule I kept."

Henri inserted the crank into the arbor and turned it. Nothing happened.

"Yep," he said. "Something's broken, for sure."

"I'll call over to da watchmaker's shop in Houghton and see if dey can send someone to look at it," said Mrs. Darling, heading for the hallway and the phone.

"How will we know when it's meal time?" asked Daisy.

"You'll just have to rough it," said Myrtle, trying not to laugh.

"I bet Mr. Pfrommer could fix it if he was still here," said Daisy.

*****

Myrtle lay down the book she'd been reading, *The Moon and Sixpence*, and stared up at the ceiling.

What is it I want? she thought.

Pickles. She had a craving for pickles. *Daisy would say it's because I'm expecting,* thought Myrtle. But she knew otherwise. It had been more than two years since she had been intimate with a man—that one night in Paris at Thomas's apartment.

She remembered Mrs. Darling saying she had canned some pickles a few weeks ago. Maybe that's what made her think of them.

Myrtle swung her legs off the bed and slipped on the moccasins she had purchased for fifty cents from Mr. Kinnamon, a traveling salesman, the last time he'd come through town. They were leather and crafted, Mr. Kinnamon said, by an old Indian who lived out in the woods up by Copper Harbor. She didn't know whether or not to believe him about their origin, but they were comfortable and well-constructed and served her well.

Even after over a year of living in Michigan's Upper Peninsula, she had still not acclimated to the bitter cold that winter brought. And though Mrs. Darling was not parsimonious about heating the house, the floorboards in her room always seemed to be at least twenty degrees colder than the room itself.

At the bottom of the stairs, she paused: what was that sound coming from the parlor?

Opening one of the pocket doors that separated the room from the hallway, she discovered Mrs. Darling sitting by the fire. She was dabbing her eyes with a handkerchief to wipe away the tears accumulating there.

"Mrs. Darling? What's wrong?"

The old lady looked up at Myrtle.

"Oh, I'm sorry, dearie, I didn't mean to disturb you."

"No, no," said Myrtle. "You didn't disturb me. I was on my way to the kitchen to get a pickle, and I thought I heard something in here. You're crying—what happened?"

Mrs. Darling picked up a slip of paper from her lap and handed it to Myrtle.

"It's Mr. Pfrommer. He's . . . he's dead."

Myrtle took the paper from her landlady's hand and read it. It was a telegram.

ADOLPH PFROMMER DECEASED. STOP. YOU WERE TO BE NOTIFIED. STOP. BODY WILL BE INTERRED IN PARK CEMETERY ON FRIDAY, JAN 28. STOP. CONDOLENCES. STOP.

"Oh, my," said Myrtle, her hand going to her mouth. "Mr. Pfrommer is dead."

"Yah," said Mrs. Darling, "and dey'r going to bury his body in da cemetery up dere."

For a moment, Myrtle was silent. Then she said, "No, they're not. We're not going to allow him to be buried there where nobody cares."

"But what can we do?" asked Mrs. Darling.

"We shall have the body brought back here to Booker Falls and give him a proper funeral. And he'll

be buried in St. Barbara's cemetery, like Mr. Mitchell
was. Leave it to me."

CHAPTER THIRTY

"I'm sorry, Miss Tully, but it isn't possible."

Myrtle had approached Father Fabian and inquired about having Mr. Pfrommer's funeral at St. Barbara's, with the burial in the church cemetery.

"Not only was he not a member of this congregation," continued Father Fabian, "I'm not even sure he was Catholic. And, besides, he was a convicted murderer—a double murderer, at that. While I wish I could honor your request, I'm afraid the rules of this congregation forbid it."

"But I'm sure Mr. Pfrommer was repentant. He told me himself how sorry he was."

"He told you he was sorry for having killed that woman in Quebec and the young woman in the library?"

Myrtle thought for a moment. "Not exactly. He said he was sorry for trying to kill me."

"I'm sure he was. But that does not absolve him of his previous offenses."

"Doesn't the Church believe in forgiveness, though?" asked Myrtle. "I thought that was a tenet of the Christian faith."

"Yes, you're right, it is. Our God is a forgiving God. Unfortunately, many of our members are not so compassionate. May I make a suggestion?"

"Certainly," said Myrtle.

"Talk to Reverend Albrecht across the street. As much as I hate to admit it, those Finnish Lutherans are often much better at following our Lord's examples than our good Catholics are."

*****

"Of course, the funeral can be held here," said Reverend Albrecht, when Myrtle made her request. "And the burial can take place in the township cemetery. As I'm sure you know, the burial won't be able to take place for a few months."

"Because of the ground being too frozen," said Myrtle.

"Exactly. The funeral can be held right away—just not the burial."

"What will be the cost of your services, reverend?"

"My services? You mean, to conduct the funeral?"

Myrtle nodded.

"Oh, my dear, there will be no charge for my services. I would be honored to do so, eh? As far as the other costs are concerned, you would need to talk with Mr. Reynolds over at the funeral home."

*****

Although L. L. Reynolds was but fifty-eight-years-old, he had been the funeral director in Booker Falls for forty-two of those years.

He was sixteen, the oldest of five children, when his father, Roger, unexpectedly keeled over from a heart attack.

Roger was L. L.'s first client.

The other children had eventually grown and left Booker Falls so that only L. L. and his mother remained. Never married, he made it his lifelong responsibility to take care of her.

He was known as a fair man and someone who treated the families of those who had passed on with the utmost respect, so when Myrtle and Mrs. Darling entered his office and made known their needs, he did his best to put them at ease.

Myrtle had decided to take Mrs. Darling with her, so she could have some say in selecting Mr. Pfrommer's casket. Henri drove them there in his car.

"Call me at the office when you're finished," he'd said. "And I'll drive you back home."

"Ladies, would either of you care for some coffee or tea?" asked Mr. Reynolds after Myrtle and Mrs. Darling were seated.

"None for me," said Myrtle.

"Tea would be good," said Mrs. Darling.

"I have Thimbleberry," said Mr. Reynolds.

"Oh," said Myrtle, "in that case, I would love to have some, too."

Thimbleberry tea was Myrtle's favorite; she'd become hooked on it at the boarding house, where Mrs. Darling served either that or dandelion tea—the latter of which she didn't care for at all.

"I was sorry to hear of Mr. Pfrommer's passing," said Mr. Reynolds.

He pulled a watch from his pocket and held it up. "I took this in to Mr. Becker's shop . . . oh, I think it was twenty-five years ago now. I couldn't get it to keep the correct time. As you know, Mr. Pfrommer worked there. He kept it overnight, and the next day I went back to retrieve it. I have not had a moment's problem with it since.

"When would you want the service to be held?" he asked, returning the watch to its resting place.

"We were thinking this coming Saturday," said Myrtle, "if that's possible."

"Yes, quite possible," said Mr. Reynolds. "Now, I think the first thing we should decide on is the casket. I have a number of selections in stock. But if you should not find one that suits your needs, I have a catalog we can look at. We could definitely have it here by Saturday."

As they wandered among the caskets, Mrs. Darling would stop, check the price tag, and shake her head. Finally, Myrtle asked, "Don't you like *any* of them?"

"Oh, dearie, dere all beautiful. But so much! Da only one I could afford is dat cheap pine one, da one wit nothing on it. He deserves someting better dan dat, I tink, eh?"

Myrtle laid her hand on the old lady's arm. "Mrs. Darling, don't even think about the price. You're not going to be paying for any of this."

"I'm not? Den who is? Somebody has to."

"Mr. Pfrommer is paying for his own funeral," said Myrtle.

Mrs. Darling looked confused. Her eyes wrinkled up. "He is? How? He's dead."

"You remember his watch collection he gave me?"

Mrs. Darling nodded. "Yah. Dat was nice of him."

"I've been thinking what I wanted to do with it. When we decided to have the funeral and burial here in Booker Falls, I took it to Mr. Abramovitz, and he paid me a generous sum for it, more than enough to cover all the expenses."

Mrs. Darling's eye lit up. "Oh, my, dat is wonderful."

"Let's take another look around, shall we?" said Myrtle. "And this time let's not bother to look at the price tags."

"I tink dis one," Mrs. Darling said at last, pointing to a plain wooden casket priced at forty-nine dollars.

"That is nice," said Myrtle, still eyeing the most expensive model, one with a satin lining, handles and a plaque where Mr. Pfrommer's name could be etched.

"Den dat's it," said Mrs. Darling.

"Excellent choice," said Mr. Reynolds. "Why don't we return to my office and go over the other items and services that will be required?"

Myrtle and Mrs. Darling sat and listened as Mr. Reynolds ticked off a list of necessities: embalming—nineteen dollars; opening the gravesite—seven dollars; one hearse and one carriage to the cemetery—fifteen dollars each; the plot—twenty-five dollars; various other services, such as clothes and newspaper notice—thirteen dollars.

"The last two items," said Mr. Reynolds, "are the charge for my services and the marker."

"We won't need a marker," said Myrtle. "That has been taken care of."

"It has?" said Mrs. Darling, turning to Myrtle.

Myrtle placed her hand on Mrs. Darling's. "It has. Mr. Reynolds, your services—how much are they?"

"Thirty-five dollars," said Mr. Reynolds.

"Very well," said Myrtle. "And what is the total we owe you?"

"You will need someone to set the marker," said Mr. Reynolds. "My man can do that for eight dollars."

Myrtle nodded. "That is acceptable."

Mr. Reynolds bent over and added up the figures. When he was finished, he looked up.

"The total—without the marker—comes to one hundred and seventy-eight dollars."

"Oh, my," said Mrs. Darling.

Mr. Reynolds looked at Myrtle. "Is that too much?"

Myrtle smiled. "No, that is fine."

She turned to Mrs. Darling. "Mrs. Darling, you did like the casket with the plaque better than the one we chose, didn't you?"

"I really did," said Mrs. Darling, nodding. "But so expensive: ninety-two dollars!"

Myrtle turned back to Mr. Reynolds. "We will take the ninety-two dollar casket. And I'm assuming there is no additional charge for having Mr. Pfrommer's name engraved on the plaque?"

"No charge," said Mr. Reynolds, smiling. "So . . ." he said, turning back to his paper and making some quick adjustments, "the new price is now . . . two-twenty-one."

Myrtle opened her purse and took out a roll of bills. Counting off exactly two hundred and twenty-one dollars, she handed the money to Mr. Reynolds who put it into an envelope.

"I will call tomorrow and arrange for Mr. Pfrommer's body to be transported here," he said.

*****

"I still don't understand about da marker," said Mrs. Darling, as she settled into the car seat behind Henri and Myrtle.

"Pierre told me we can get a marker from Sears and Roebuck a lot less expensive than if we bought it through Mr. Reynolds. And since we won't need it for a while, we can order it through the catalog and have it shipped here."

"Very smart," said Mrs. Darling, nodding.

*****

"Now," said Myrtle when they arrived back at the boarding house, "shall we take a look at the catalog?"

"Yah," said Mrs. Darling. "First, though, let me make us some tea."

A half-hour later Myrtle said, "You think this is the one we want, then?"

"Yah," said Mrs. Darling, smiling. "Dat's da one."

The marker was almost two feet high, including the base, made of White Acme Rutland Italian Marble. For the inscription, they chose four lines: Adolph Pfrommer; 1840-1921; A good friend; Rest in peace.

"How much is dat?" asked Mrs. Darling.

"Don't worry," said Myrtle. "It's taken care of."

"I'd still like to know."

"Okay," said Myrtle. "The marker itself is eighteen dollars and forty cents. The cost for the letters is two dollars and seventy cents. And the shipping is . . . let's see . . . three dollars and seventy-eight cents. Altogether that comes to twenty-four dollars and eighty-eight cents. And it says it will be shipped in four to six weeks, so it should arrive in plenty of time."

"Dat's nice," said Mrs. Darling, her words a little strangled.

Myrtle looked at her landlady: she was crying.

Myrtle began crying, too.

CHAPTER THIRTY-ONE

Myrtle watched the people milling around in the sanctuary of St. James Lutheran Church. She estimated that at least several dozen town folk had come out for Mr. Pfrommer's funeral. She, Daisy and Pierre had walked into town from the boarding house. Henri said he'd bring Mrs. Darling in his car.

As she glanced around the room, she was struck again by its starkness, so different from the Catholic churches she was used to. The walls and ceiling were all painted white. A single stained glass window at the front of the chancel provided the only color, a depiction of a man draped in a gold cape, hands folded around a staff, looking heavenward.

Myrtle remembered Rev. Albrecht telling her that the cross suspended in front of the window was made of downy birch, which she later learned had been brought from Finland. She still couldn't get used to the fact it was empty, that there was no figure of Christ hanging on it.

The open casket containing Mr. Pfrommer's body sat at the front of the sanctuary. Several people had already passed by, paying their last respects. Myrtle overheard more than one of them remark on what a good man he had been, and their connection with him at the watch shop.

She was waiting until Mrs. Darling arrived so they could go up together.

"Miss Tully?"

Myrtle looked around and was surprised to find Mrs. Sinclair, the mother of the young woman Mr. Pfrommer had been found guilty of murdering twenty-eight years earlier, the crime for which he had been sentenced to spend the rest of his life at the Marquette Branch Prison.

"Mrs. Sinclair?" said Myrtle.

"You're surprised to see me here," said Mrs. Sinclair.

"Why . . . why, yes, I am."

I thought you were dead, thought Myrtle. The last time she'd seen Mrs. Sinclair was last year, just before Mr. Pfrommer was arrested. At that time the old lady looked so frail Myrtle didn't think she was long for this earth.

In truth, she didn't look much better now.

"I came to pay my respects," said Mrs. Sinclair. "I got to know Mr. Pfrommer quite well over dese past months."

"You have?" *Why?* Myrtle wondered. *How?*

"About a month after he went to prison, I went to see him," said Mrs. Sinclair. "He told me how sorry he was about what he did to my little girl, and I could see he was. I could also see he was very lonely. So I started visiting him once a week. We got to be good friends. Eventually, I was able to tell him dat I forgave him for what he done. I was so sorry to hear of his passing."

Myrtle's eyes were moist; *to think that this woman was able to forgive the man who'd murdered her daughter!*

Myrtle took Mrs. Sinclair's hand. "I'm waiting for Mrs. Darling to arrive. We'll be sitting together. Why don't you join us?"

"Yah, I'd like dat. Can I go up and see him?"

"You go ahead; Mrs. Darling and I will come up when she gets here."

*****

A few minutes later Mrs. Darling walked in, accompanied by Henri. Myrtle joined them, and they approached the casket.

"He looks very nice," said Henri.

"He does," said Myrtle.

"Too thin," said Mrs. Darling. "He's too thin."

Mrs. Darling began softly crying. Myrtle put her arm around her landlady's shoulder. Then she started crying, too.

*****

"That was a wonderful service," said Mrs. Darling, as she stood outside the church building. Myrtle, Henri, Daisy, Pierre, and Mrs. Sinclair were gathered around her.

"What happens next?" asked Mrs. Sinclair.

"The body will be taken back to Mr. Reynolds's funeral home," said Myrtle, "along with the casket. They will be kept there until spring when the ground will thaw enough to allow the grave to be dug. Mrs. Sinclair," Myrtle continued, "do you think you'll be able to come back for that?"

Mrs. Sinclair shook her head. "Nah, I don't tink so."

Myrtle had to agree. She didn't think she would be, either.

CHAPTER THIRTY-TWO

Myrtle stood behind her desk, staring out the window at the small garden at the side of the library. There were no flowers to be seen now to show how beautiful the place could be when blazing star, goldenrod, red baneberry, smooth aster, and tickseed carpeted the ground.

A snow-covered picnic table and three benches, all blanketed with a foot of the fluffy white stuff, gave the only hint that when spring eventually came, town folks and the students at the college would spend long, languorous hours there, reading, talking, eating, napping—courting.

A streak of gold, a gift from a sun that had deigned to appear after a week of gloomy days, ricocheted off the still ice-covered pond.

Myrtle watched as two raccoons chased each other across its surface, performing fancy turns and twirls while sliding on their posteriors.

Inside the library, several dozen students sat at long tables, immersed in their books and papers, reading and writing, and studying. The only sound was the footsteps of Else Booth on her way to the bathroom at the rear of the building, though she tried her best to be quiet.

From the far side of the room came an almost imperceptible cough, followed by an equally quiet, "Sorry."

The stillness was as pervasive indoors as one would expect it to be outside.

Suddenly the quiet was shattered by a cry.

"He's eating her! He's eating her! Somebody help!"

Myrtle turned to see a young female student standing at the front door, a terrified look on her face. She waved her arms around as if trying to swim through molasses.

"Hurry, somebody help—she'll die!"

Myrtle raced from her office and grabbed the now hysterical woman.

"Sit down!" she said and pushed her toward the waiting arms of another student.

Hurrying outside, Myrtle stopped, frozen at the sight before her.

A black bear, easily two hundred pounds, had pinned down another female student. The girl's screams punctuated the air as the animal scratched and bit her.

Myrtle gasped. What could she do?

Then she felt, rather than saw, a blur rush past her. The next thing she knew, Claude was clinging to the creature's back, stabbing him over and over with a knife at least as long as the one Kitty Vanderliet had brandished at the pawn shop.

Though no more than four foot four and one hundred and fifty pounds, Claude was exceptionally strong.

The bear released its hold on the young girl and swung around in an effort to rid itself of this intruder on its back.

But Claude refused to be unseated.

The bear continued to twist and turn, unsuccessful in his attempt to rid himself of this unwelcomed guest.

Reaching around behind with one paw the bear swiped it across Claude's legs, tearing through his pants and flesh.

Blood started running down Claude's leg.

By now other students had joined Myrtle. They watched, transfixed, as Claude continued to attack the beast, even as blood covered his jeans.

The bear, sensing whatever was on its back was not going to let go, tumbled backward, crushing Claude underneath its massive body. Fortunately, the heavy layer of snow on the ground cushioned the impact.

The bear stood and turned to confront his attacker.

As he did so, Claude, though groggy and struggling to catch his breath, struggled to his feet.

Now Myrtle saw it wasn't only Claude who was bleeding; massive wounds, inflicted by Claude's knife, were visible on the bear's back, along with large splotches of blood.

The bear lunged for Claude. But instead of avoiding the charge, Claude held the knife out in front of him, both hands wrapped around the shaft. The blade sank deep into the bear's chest, instantly killing the huge beast.

The animal's momentum knocked Claude backward onto the ground. Before the bear could fall on him, crushing him, Claude managed once again to roll to one side, the creature's body coming to rest against his arm.

"Quick!" cried Myrtle, as she rushed to aid the young woman who had been the victim of the animal's assault and who now lay moaning, half-conscious, on the blood-splattered snow. "Somebody help Claude! Be careful—we don't know for sure that thing's dead. Lydia, there's a first aid kit in the closet by the restroom! Oh, and there's a blanket and some towels there, too—bring everything!

"Phillip, go to my office—call Doctor Sherman and then call Constable de la Cruz! Hurry, all of you!"

Myrtle knelt down beside the young woman.

"Mary Margaret," she said, using the sleeve of her blouse to wipe blood away from the girl's face. "Can you hear me?"

Mary Margaret stirred but didn't respond.

Myrtle turned to see how Claude was doing. Three of the male students had helped him to his feet.

"Quick, get him inside!" said Myrtle. "You boys," she said to two of the other students still standing on the steps, "come help me get Mary Margaret inside."

Minutes later, the wounded girl lay on one of the study tables, covered by a blanket. Myrtle wiped away blood while one of the students applied gauze and bandages to the wounds that were visible.

Outside, the jingle of Henri's police car bell could be heard as it came closer and closer. Then it stopped. Doctor Sherman rushed through the door, followed closely by Henri.

"How is she?" Ambrose asked Myrtle.

"She hasn't opened her eyes or said anything," said Myrtle. "I don't know."

"Let me have a look," said the doctor.

While Doctor Sherman examined Mary Margaret, Henri checked on Claude. The boys had wrapped bandages around his wounds, and he was sitting up in one of the chairs.

"Claude, you okay?" asked Henri, looking into Claude's eyes.

"Is he dead?" asked Claude.

"The bear?" said Henri.

Claude nodded.

"I'm pretty sure he is," said Henri. "He was still laying out there in the snow when the doc and I got here."

"Good," said Claude, taking a deep breath. "Da little girl—she okay?"

"I don't know," said Henri. "Can you walk?"

"I tink so."

Claude struggled to get to his feet, aided by Henri and one of the boys.

"Let's get you in my car," said Henri. "We're taking you and the girl to Doc's office."

Moments later, the car sped off with Mary Margaret sprawled out in the back seat. Claude sat up front with Henri. Ambrose stood on the running board, hanging on for dear life.

All the students gathered around Myrtle, eyeing the bear.

"What's going to happen with it now?" asked one of them.

Myrtle shook her head. "I don't know."

"I do," said one of the male students. "My dad killed a bear once. He and I dressed it. I can dress this one, too. The meat could go to the lunchroom. We could be eating bear meat for some time."

The news elicited a chorus of agreement, mostly from the male students standing around.

"What about the skin?" asked another student.

Myrtle looked at the young man who had volunteered to dress the bear. "You can take the skin off in one piece, can't you?"

"You betcha," said the young man.

"Then that can be made into a coat for Claude," said Myrtle. "He deserves it."

"And the head?" asked another student.

"It would look good on a wall inside," said one of the students.

"I suppose so," said Myrtle, not all that sure she wanted a bear head in the library. "I'll talk to President Forrester and see what he says. What now?" she asked the student who said he could dress the bear.

"We'll get the big sled from the barn, and get the carcass on it. Then we can drag it back to the barn, and I'll dress it there."

"Very well," said Myrtle. "For now, let's get all those bloody towels together so I can take them home with me to have them laundered."

*****

The buzz around Booker Falls that evening was how Claude Amyx, the dwarf custodian at Adelaide College, single-handedly killed a bear that outweighed him by at least fifty pounds.

"He should get a medal," said Andy Erickson. "He saved that little girl's life."

Indeed, it did appear Mary Margaret would survive the attack. After Doctor Sherman did what he could to make her stable, he accompanied Henri who drove her to Houghton to St. Joseph's Hospital where she could receive better care.

The attack was also the topic of conversation at dinner at the boarding house.

"Wow!" exclaimed Daisy as Myrtle provided her and Pierre and Mrs. Darling a blow by blow account of what had happened. "Weren't you terrified? I know I would have been. What if Mr. Amyx hadn't been able to kill the bear? What would you have done then?"

"I would have gotten all the students back inside the building and had some of the boys put tables up against the door to block it. Then I would have called Henri and told him what was happening."

"And the young lady out in the yard?" said Pierre. "And Mr. Amyx?"

Large tears filled Myrtle's eyes as the full realization of how much of a tragedy the event could have been hit her.

"I don't know," she said between sobs. "We couldn't have done anything. No one had a gun. I couldn't send anyone out there to help poor Mary Margaret or Claude as long as the bear was there. I don't know what I would have done!"

"Everything turned out all right," said Henri, as he joined them at the table.

"You're back," said Myrtle, wiping her eyes with her napkin. "How is Mary Margaret? Will she be okay?"

"The doctor over at St. Joseph's looked her over and said she'll recover. She'll have scars, but at least she's alive. Claude's doing fine, too. I took him over to Miss Wasserman's. She's going to put him up for the night so she can keep an eye on him."

"I'm so relieved," said Myrtle.

Pierre raised his water glass. "Well, all's well that ends well."

The others all raised their glasses.

"Yes," said Myrtle, "all is well."

CHAPTER THIRTY-THREE

Daisy sat at her desk at the newspaper office, a scowl on her face.

Besides the fact it was Monday, not her favorite workday, she was also not at all happy that Mr. Donaldson, the editor, had told her she'd have to handle the classified ads while Mary Ellen was out with the grippe.

She was a reporter, she'd told him, not a secretary. He'd told her she'd be an out-of-work reporter if she didn't take the job.

So she took it.

But she wasn't happy.

Until Eddie O'Halloran came in to place an ad.

Eddie was the captain of the Booker Falls Volunteer Fire Department, composed of men who held regular jobs but responded at a moment's notice whenever a fire broke out anywhere in the county. Fortunately, the last time they'd had to do so was six years ago when Patrick Monahan's cow kicked over a lantern in his barn, causing the whole structure to burn to the ground.

The standing joke for months afterward was that Patrick must be related to Catherine O'Leary, whose cow—name lost to history—allegedly started the Great Chicago Fire of 1871, which burned down a good portion of the city.

While the other firemen were volunteers, Eddie was employed full time as the Fire Chief. At six feet four and two hundred and forty pounds, he cut an imposing figure, especially with the handlebar mustache he'd cultivated over the years.

When Daisy looked up and found Eddie towering over her, she felt her heart flutter.

"Can . . . can I help you?" she managed to get out.

"Aye, I hope you can," replied Eddie. "I'm looking to buy a good used double harness. Da one we got now is getting pretty frayed."

"I'm sorry, I'm not sure what that is," said Daisy.

"Oh," said Eddie, "I'm da Fire Chief. Da harness is for Lilly and Gordon."

"Lilly and Gordon?"

"Our horses—da ones what pull da engine."

"Oh," said Daisy, starting to understand. "And you want to place an ad."

"Aye, an ad," said Eddie.

When Daisy finished taking down Eddie's information, she asked, "How long have you been the Fire Chief, Mr. O'Halloran?"

"Been chief for ten years; been on da job near to forty. And not Mr. O'Halloran—my men call me Chief. My friends call me Eddie."

"And what should I call you?" asked Daisy.

Eddie grinned. "You can call me Eddie."

Daisy stuck out her hand. "Daisy," she said, "Daisy O'Hearn."

"You're Irish?"

"No, my late husband was. I'm German." Daisy wasn't about to tell Eddie that O'Hearn was just a name she'd taken when she was hiding from her husband's brother, whom she thought was looking for her.

"You look fla enough to be Irish," said Eddie.

Daisy brushed the hair back from her face. "I'm not sure what that means," she said.

"It's a compliment. Say, it's near lunch time. Care to grab a bite wit me?"

"Sure," said Daisy. *I'm not about to say no to that invitation.* "Miss Madeline's?"

Eddie hesitated for a minute, then said, "I usually eat at da Juicy Pig, but . . . ."

"No, no," said Daisy. "The Juicy Pig is fine. I've never eaten there. I'd like to see what it's like."

"It ain't much to look at, but da food's damn good . . . pardon my French."

Daisy laughed. She liked Eddie O'Halloran. She *really* liked Eddie O'Halloran.

*****

The Juicy Pig was not what Daisy expected.

She knew it was the only restaurant in town other than Miss Madeline's Eatery and was mostly frequented by the men and women who lived in Greytown. And while she had never been in any of those homes, it was apparent from the street that, though the places were kept up well, the people who lived in them definitely belonged to the lower income class.

Daisy had pictured the restaurant living up to its name; shabby, and less than a paragon of cleanliness. What she discovered instead was a large, brightly lit room with a spotlessly clean floor, filled with long tables where food was served family style. Five smaller tables that could seat up to four people each were lined up against one wall. Folded linen napkins lay at every place. Eddie chose one of the smaller tables for them.

A block from the train depot, the building itself had previously served as a storehouse for merchandise being shipped into or out of Booker Falls. Then, twenty years ago, when the Duluth, South Shore and Atlantic Railroad Company built a brand new storage facility next to the tracks, the structure was abandoned. It had sat empty for the next four years until Percy Armstrong bought the building and converted it into the Juicy Pig.

"What do they have to drink?" asked Daisy, looking over the menu.

"Deir specialty is what dey call Keweenaw Brown Tea," said Eddie.

"Keweenaw Brown Tea? What's that?"

Eddie pointed to a man at a nearby table drinking from a pint Mason jar containing an amber-colored liquid.

"Dat's it," he said.

"So it's tea in a Mason jar?" asked Daisy.

Eddie leaned over and whispered, "It's someting a bit stronger dan tea if ya know what I mean."

Daisy's eyes lit up, and she nodded. "I think I do."

After the waitress, a young woman whom Eddie introduced as Ann Marie, the owner's daughter, took their orders, Daisy leaned back and glanced around.

Unlike Miss Madeline's Eatery, which featured photographs on the walls of people and town buildings from over the past three decades, the walls of the Juicy Pig were filled with the head mounts of a bevy of animals: four elk; a dozen deer, including four with racks of eight points or more; two black bears; and three moose—two more than Miss Madeline's one mounted head.

Full body mounts—wolves, coyotes, red foxes, badgers, beavers, a bald eagle, one cougar, and numerous other small animals and birds—were displayed on platforms attached to the walls.

A blazing fireplace kept the occupants warm, though few were present at this time of day. The difference between this one and Miss Madeline's was that, where hers reached six feet across, the one here was half again that wide.

"It's not very full," said Daisy, glancing around at the nearly deserted room.

"Nah, not at lunchtime," said Eddie. "Da workers in da mines, dey take deir lunches with dem. What you see here are fellers who either ain't got a job or dey'r retired—or just too damn lazy to work. Dis evening is when da place fills up. Da single men, dey come to eat dinner and meet da lassies, and da married men will bring deir wives, let dem have a night off from cooking."

Daisy spotted one person she recognized.

"Is that . . . is that. . . ."

"Judge Hurstbourne? Aye, da judge, he likes to come here and eat. He's a real pork and ham man. Likes to mingle wit da fellers, too. He's a pretty regular guy when you come right down to it."

By the time Daisy finished her hot ham and cheese sandwich with a side of potato salad, and Eddie had wolfed down a generous portion of bangers and mash with fried onions and peas, she had learned he had immigrated with his mother from Ireland in 1868, when she came to work as a cook at one of the logging camps. He was three. His father had died the previous year, a casualty of the Fenian Rising.

"That's when we tried to kick da British out of Ireland," he'd explained.

"Were you successful?" asked Daisy.

"Nah, we weren't. Dat's when Mam decided to come to America and start a new life."

"I'm glad she did," said Daisy, smiling.

Eddie smiled back. "Aye, me, too."

Eddie had lived in the area his whole life, starting work when he was fourteen years old at the same logging camp where his mother worked. When he turned eighteen, she had given him permission to join the fire department as a volunteer. Twenty-nine years later, he became Chief and gave up logging.

Since he was the only paid member of the force, he lived in two rooms above the station, so he'd always be available if a fire broke out.

"You ever been in da station?" he asked Daisy.

Daisy shook her head. "No, never have."

"Want to see it?"

"Sure."

CHAPTER THIRTY-FOUR

Thirty minutes later, after a brief walk back to the fire station, they stood next to a horse-drawn, steam pumper.

Daisy stared up at the copper and brass tank that towered some five feet over her, polished to the point where her face gazed back at her from the bottom section.

"Dis is good old number One Eleven," said Eddie, the pride evident on his beaming face.

"One Eleven?" said Daisy.

"Yep, bought it new from da Ahrens Company down in Cincinnati back in ought six. You shoulda seen it crossing da straits on dat ferry. Dat was some ride, I tell you."

"Why One Eleven?" asked Daisy.

"Dat's da serial number. Tought it sounded like a good name for her, too."

"So it's a 'she'?" asked Daisy, amused.

"Sure is. And dis . . ." Eddie walked them around to the other side of One Eleven to a fire engine on sleds, ". . . dis is Whippoorwill."

"Wow! I've never seen a fire engine on sleds!"

"Yep. Back in ought eleven, right after I'd taken over as Chief, we had a fire at da Ranscott place outside town. Dere'd been a big snowfall da day before, and da roads was all snow-covered, impassable, even for One Eleven. We couldn't make it dere, and da whole house burned down. Dat's when I got da idea of having Whippoorwill here, built.

"I'd seen one like dis over in Negaunee, so I go over dere and found da guy what built it, Clancy Chevrette. I had him build one for me, too. It's an old Studebaker wagon dat he modified. We've used it a couple times over da years when da weather got too bad."

"Pretty ingenious," said Daisy. "What are these buckets for?" she asked, turning back to One Eleven, where four buckets hung on a line strung along the side of the pumper.

"We use da buckets in a bucket brigade. Sometimes we can get water out of farm ponds or lakes: makes da water in our pumper go farther."

"But they have rounded bottoms. How do they stand up?"

"Dey don't. But dat's what makes dem so good, eh? Wit da rounded bottoms, we can trow da water farther. Besides, dey're a real money saver."

"A money saver?"

"Aye. Since dey can't stand up straight, da only ting dey're good for is trowing water at fires: discourages our men from taking dem home to use and making me have to buy new ones. We got another engine out back, but we ain't used it in a while, 'cept in da parade."

"What's this big thing on the wall for?" asked Daisy, eyeing a board full of bells and a map of the county.

"Dat's where da alarm boxes is located. You ain't never seen any of our alarm boxes 'round town?"

"Oh, I have. But, thankfully, I've never needed to use one."

"Well, all da boxes are connected to dis board, ya see. When someone pulls one, it sets off a series of rings. The number tells me which box it is so's we can get to da right place real quick like. All seven of our men got a box in deir homes, too, so dey know where dey have to go. Oh, and da preacher, he's got one at da church. Sometimes he's across da street and on da pumper 'fore I ever get it out of da station.

"We also get blasts on da horn up in da tower. Dat's another way of letting everybody know where da fire is. It's helpful especially if I happen to be away from da station, 'cause I can hear it anywhere."

"Pretty neat," said Daisy. "Did you figure all that out?"

"Wish I could take da credit, but dey had a system like dis over in Red Jacket long 'fore we ever got ours. Dat's where I got da idea. Come on; I'll show you our horses."

"I remember these horses," said Daisy, as she and Eddie stood in front of the stalls's open doors. "They pulled a fire engine in the Fourth of July Parade. I'd forgotten all about that."

"Aye," said Eddie. "Every year I drive 'em down Main Street in da engine out back."

"They're huge. How much do they weigh?"

"Gordon, here, he tops out a little over fifteen hundred pounds. Lilly's a tad smaller, eh? 'Round fourteen and fifty. But she can pull almost as hard as old Gordon does.

"Say, Miss O'Hearn . . . ."

"Daisy—please call me Daisy."

"Well, all righty. So, Daisy, dis Tuesday is St. Patrick's Day. Da fellers and me, we always have a get together dat night, dey bring deir wives and girlfriends. We get a little band to come in and provide da music. Dere's always someting to whet your whistle if you know what I mean. I always come but I ain't got a wife or a girlfriend, so's I was a'wonderin' if you might like to be my guest dat evening."

"You mean, like a date?" asked Daisy.

Eddie blushed. "I guess you could call it a date, but if you didn't want to do dat, you could just consider it an invitation to attend."

"It's just your firemen—and their wives and girlfriends?"

"We always invite da mayor and da constable, but dey never come. I tink it's because of da drinks we serve, you know?"

"You mean like alcohol?"

"Well, no, I don't mean *like* alcohol—it *is* alcohol."

Daisy laughed and looked around. "Is there dancing?"

"Oh, yah, dere's dancing all right," said Eddie.

"It seems pretty crowded in here for dancing," said Daisy.

"Oh, we move da engines outside. Den dere's plenty of room. Also, we got da upstairs."

"Could Myrtle come if she got either George or Henri to come, too?"

"We would love to have her—and da mayor or da constable, either one—or both."

"I'll think about it," said Daisy. "Now, let me ask you . . . ."

Before Daisy had a chance to finish her question, one of the bells began to ring, while at the same time the big door at the front of the station started to open. The horn in the tower gave out four short blasts, loud enough to be heard for miles around.

"Is there a fire?" Daisy asked, staring in amazement as Gordon and Lilly walked out of their stalls and took their respective places at the front of the engine.

"Looks like," said Eddie, slipping into his firemen's boots.

"Where?"

"According to da board, right close to da restaurant."

"Miss Madeline's? Miss Madeline's is on fire?"

"Nah, da Juicy Pig; where we just ate. But dat don't necessarily mean it *is* da Juicy Pig—just in dat neighborhood, eh?"

Eddie quickly slipped the harness over the horses. As he turned to climb up on his seat, he found Daisy sitting next to him.

"What're you doing?" he asked.

"I'm going with you."

"What?"

"I'm going with you. It's a fire. I'm a reporter. It's a story."

Eddie didn't speak for a moment, then: "Okay, but stay out of da way, den. I don't want you getting hurt, eh?

"Hold on," he cried as Gordon and Lilly charged out of the station.

*****

Henri heard the blast from the horn in the fire station tower, then the bell of the fire engine as it rolled out of the firehouse.

He quickly ran the half block from his office to Main Street, where he was joined by everyone else who happened to be downtown at the time. Alton Woodruff, razor in hand, along with Roger Lampley, his face still half-covered with shaving cream and a barber cape wrapped around him, stood, both staring in the direction of the fire station.

Dozens of other people lined the sidewalks up and down the street, watching and waiting.

Seconds later they were rewarded with the sight of the pumper hurtling by them, Eddie driving, Daisy by his side.

She waved as they rushed by.

Henri couldn't believe his eyes.

What was Daisy doing riding on the fire engine?

CHAPTER THIRTY-FIVE

It *was* the Juicy Pig that was on fire.

By the time Eddie and Daisy arrived, four other firemen were there, doing their best to control the blaze by carrying buckets of water from a nearby watering trough. A large number of the people in town who had watched the engine pass by, including Henri, showed up minutes later. Right behind them came two more volunteer firemen.

Eddie quickly got the pumper working, and hundreds of gallons of water began pouring onto the blazing structure while volunteers continued the bucket brigade, first from one trough, then to another, after they exhausted the first.

By this time the fire had spread to the barn, from which a chorus of squeals emanated. In good weather, the hogs would have been outdoors. But with the temperature still below freezing, the passel of several dozen animals had been moved inside.

Eddie had positioned the fire engine so that one hose was trained on the restaurant, the other on the barn. It soon became evident, though, that both structures, being over seventy years old, were not going to be saved; the second hose was turned to join the first, aimed toward the barn.

Under the safety of the water from the hoses, two of the firemen made it to the barn door and unlatched it. As they swung the door open, a stampede of hogs nearly overran them, as a cheer went up from the onlookers.

For the next twenty minutes, the firemen continued to pour water onto the barn until the worst part was under control.

Eddie watched as his men finished dousing the last embers.

Daisy approached him.

"I'm glad I had a chance to eat here at least once," she said.

"Aye, we timed dat right, eh?"

"I'm taking off now," said Daisy.

"Oh? Where you off to, den?"

"Back to the office. We go to press tomorrow, and I want to get this story written—about the fire and about the fire station, too. Thanks for lunch. I had a good time."

She turned and started to walk away.

"How 'bout da party?" Eddie called out to her. "Did you tink about it?"

Daisy smiled and kept walking, but turned her head back to Eddie.

"Yes," she said, then turned back and continued on her way, still smiling. "I'll go."

"Well, okay, den," said Eddie, grinning.

*****

As Daisy approached the Y where the road she was traveling from town met the road from the library, she spotted Myrtle about a quarter of a mile away, heading towards her.

"Hey, kiddo," she shouted, waving her hand.

Myrtle waved back.

"You hear about the big fire today?" asked Daisy, when Myrtle reached her.

"Fire? What fire?"

"The Juicy Pig burned down."

"Oh, no!" exclaimed Myrtle. "Was anyone hurt?"

"No, they got the hogs out in time."

Myrtle looked at Daisy. "Were any *people* hurt?" she asked.

Daisy laughed. "No, I knew what you meant. I was kidding. Nobody was hurt. But the place is completely destroyed."

"Were you there?"

"Oh, yes, I rode in on the fire truck with Eddie."

Myrtle stopped and grabbed Daisy's arm, bringing her to a sudden halt.

"Wait a minute. Eddie? Who is Eddie and what fire truck were you riding on?"

"Eddie's the Fire Chief for the volunteer fire department, and the fire truck is the one they take to fires, and I have a date Thursday night."

Myrtle's jaw dropped. She didn't know what question to ask first.

Finally, she managed one word: "Date?"

Daisy beamed. "Yep—date. Eddie asked me to the St. Patrick's Day party at the fire station this Thursday. And you're coming, too."

Myrtle shook her head: *too much information too quick!*

"Okay, first of all, when did this all happen: you and this Eddie? Second, how'd you end up riding on the fire truck? And third, why am *I* going to this party?"

Daisy went on to explain how Eddie had come into the newspaper office to place an ad, how he took her to lunch—*before* the place burned down!—how they'd gone back to the fire station and when the bells went off she'd jumped onto the fire truck and ridden along to the fire.

"I filed the story a little bit ago," she finished. "It'll be in the paper tomorrow. I had my camera with me, so I took some pictures. I'm going to develop them tonight."

By now they had reached the boarding house.

"You want me to go to the party with you?" said Myrtle as they walked up the path to the house from the road.

"No, I don't want you to go with *me*. I want you to go with Henri or George."

"Why?"

"Why? Because you need to get out more. When was the last time you had a date?"

Myrtle shrugged. "I don't know. Why do I need to go out on a date?"

"Because you need to. So you don't wither away on the vine."

"Wither away on the vine, huh? You mean, like an old spinster?"

"Exactly."

"I'll think about it."

"Who would you ask?" asked Daisy. "If you decide to go."

"We'll see."

*****

When Myrtle and George arrived at the fire station, they saw the two fire engines sitting out in front. Loud music came from inside, and all the lights were turned on.

"Looks as though the party has begun," said George.

He was surprised when Myrtle had asked him to go with her. As mayor, he'd received invitations in the past. He would have felt out of place showing up by himself when most of the others had dates or wives. But an opportunity to be with Myrtle was not something he was about to pass up.

When they walked through the front door, Eddie met them with a glass of beer in each hand.

"Welcome, Mr. Mayor," he said, "and Miss Tully. It's an honor to have both of you join us. Come on in."

Once inside, Myrtle watched as four couples, including Daisy and one of the firemen, danced to the music of a five-piece band tucked away in a far corner.

"Do you know what that song is?" asked George.

"The dance is called the Camel Walk, so I assume that's the name of the song," replied Myrtle.

"How do you know that?"

"I haven't lived my whole life in Booker Falls, you know. Between New Orleans and France, I've been around a little bit."

"I bet you have," said George, smiling.

"Come on," said Myrtle. "Let's go over to that table and sit. I see Reverend Albrecht and Saija."

"Mr. Mayor," said Reverend Albrecht when George and Myrtle reached the table. "And Miss Tully. This is indeed a pleasant surprise."

For the next hour, while the band belted out dance songs, many of them by Scott Joplin—*Sunflower Slow Drag, The Easy Winners, Maple Leaf Rag*—Myrtle listened as Saija regaled her with the exploits of her three small sons, while George and Reverend Albrecht talked about the total destruction three days earlier of the Juicy Pig.

"Do you think it was arson?" asked George.

"I don't think so," said Reverend Albrecht. "I mean, who would want to burn it down? It was the prime eating place for a lot of the working men in town."

"Are they planning on rebuilding?"

"That's what I heard. I hope so. This town needs more than one restaurant."

Suddenly, a cry of "It's a bear!" came from the dance floor.

George and Myrtle both jumped to their feet.

The bear attack at the library barely a month earlier had left everyone jumpy.

"Where?" George called out. "Where's the bear?"

"Relax," said Saija. "There's no bear. It's the dance they're doing."

Myrtle and George stared as the dancers went through wild gyrations, imitating the lumbering movements of a bear.

"What's that all about?" asked Myrtle, settling back into her seat.

"It's a dance called the Grizzly Bear," said Saija.

"I've never seen anything like that," said George.

"Me, neither," said Myrtle.

"And like you said," said George, "you've been around."

Myrtle looked at him and stuck out her tongue.

"At one time it was banned in a lot of places in the country;" said Saija. "too risqué."

George and Myrtle watched, entranced as the dancers continued their weird movements, lurching first to one side, then to the other.

"Don't ever ask me to do that," said George.

"You can count on it," said Myrtle.

When the dance ended, Daisy came tripping over to their table.

"Wasn't that great?" she said.

"Where in the world did you learn that dance?" asked Myrtle.

"Remember, I'm from Chicago," said Daisy. "They're about ten years ahead of us here, in a lot of ways. Listen, Eddie says we can slide down the pole."

Myrtle stared at her, a look of confusion on her face.

"What?" she said.

"The pole—Eddie says we can slide down the pole if we want."

"What pole?"

Daisy pointed to a metal pole in one corner of the room, running down from the second floor.

"That pole."

Myrtle turned to look, then laughed out loud.

"You want to slide down that pole?"

"Sure, don't you?"

Myrtle started to answer, then stopped. She looked at the pole again. *It might be fun!*

"Okay," she said, getting up from her chair. "I'm game. Saija?"

"Thanks, but no," said Saija. "I've already had that experience. Remember—I'm married to a fireman."

"George, you better be at the bottom to catch me when I come down," said Myrtle.

"I wouldn't miss it for the world."

"And, George," said Daisy, "you be there for me, too, will you?"

"How about Eddie?" said George.

"I'm a'goin' up wit dem to make sure dey grab da pole right," said Eddie.

Two minutes later Myrtle found herself staring at a metal pole that extended from the ceiling through a hole in the floor down to the first level.

"I'm not so sure about this," she said.

"Oh, come on, scaredy-cat," said Daisy. "I'll go first."

Myrtle watched as Daisy leaned over the hole and Eddie positioned her hands around the pole.

"Now, jump on da pole, wrap your legs around and off you go," he commanded.

Daisy did as he said and immediately disappeared down through the hole, letting out a loud "Whooooop!" as she did.

"All right, lass, your turn," said Eddie, turning to Myrtle.

Hesitantly, Myrtle approached the pole, leaned over and allowed Eddie to position her hands.

"Okay, you seen what Daisy done. You do da same. See you at da bottom."

Myrtle took a deep breath, then jumped, wrapping her legs around the pole. It seemed like only seconds—which indeed it was—before she felt George's comforting arms around her as she hit the floor.

Everybody applauded.

Myrtle smiled.

"Let's do it again," she said.

After two more pole slides, Myrtle spent the rest of the evening dancing with George and a few dances with some of the firemen, including Reverend Albrecht, all the while drinking her fair share of beer.

At eleven o'clock, the band packed up their instruments.

George gave the two women a ride back to the boarding house, where Daisy scurried inside, leaving him and Myrtle alone on the porch.

"I had a good time tonight," said Myrtle.

"Me, too," said George. "I'm glad you asked me to go. I was wondering, though, why me and not Henri?"

Myrtle reached over and kissed George.

"I don't like to play favorites," she said, turning to the door.

"I don't . . ." George started to say.

But Myrtle was gone.

CHAPTER THIRTY-SIX

The only mourners present for Mr. Pfrommer's internment were the five residents of Mrs. Darling's Boarding House and Saija Albrecht, Reverend Albrecht's wife. Myrtle had learned a week earlier of the passing of Mrs. Sinclair.

"What a beautiful headstone," said Saija, admiring the marker that had been set the day before.

"Yah," said Mrs. Darling, "me and Miss Tully picked it out."

Reverend Albrecht's graveside service was a brief one. The weather might have warmed sufficiently to thaw the ground, but a brisk April wind still made it feel like winter.

Later, at the boarding house, Myrtle, Daisy, Henri, and Pierre gathered in the parlor. Mrs. Darling came in carrying a tray of glasses and the bottle of sherry she kept for guests and special occasions.

Myrtle looked at the tray: five glasses. She knew Mrs. Darling was a teetotaler.

"Henri," said Mrs. Darling, "will you pour, please?"

Henri filled the first four glasses, then hesitated. He looked at Mrs. Darling.

She nodded. "Dis is a special occasion," she said.

Henri poured the last glass.

CHAPTER THIRTY-SEVEN

Daisy bounced into Myrtle's room and threw herself onto the bed.

"Today's the big day, huh?" she asked.

Myrtle sat at her dressing table, applying her lipstick.

"Guess so," she said. She turned to Daisy. "Does this look okay?"

"You look ravishing;" said Daisy. "irresistible, enchanting . . . ."

"Oh, shut up," said Myrtle, turning back to the mirror.

"How you feeling?" asked Daisy, as she rolled over onto her stomach.

"Nervous." Myrtle picked up a brush and ran it through her hair.

"When does all this start?"

"I'm meeting him there in an hour."

"Can I come along and watch?" asked Daisy.

Myrtle turned back to her, a dumbstruck look on her face. "Are you kidding? I'm not about to let you see me half naked!"

"Kiddo, you seem to forget I've seen you *all* naked."

"Yes, but not in front of a man."

"You're embarrassed to have me see you naked in front of Thomas, who, as you have previously told me, though not in so many words, has already seen you naked before?"

"That was different."

"Right: you were in bed with him that time."

"Quit talking, will you? You're making me more nervous than I already am."

"Okay," said Daisy, moving off the bed and heading for the door. "But for sure, I want to see the finished product."

"Oh, get out!" said Myrtle.

But Daisy was already gone.

*****

Myrtle pulled the Model N to a stop in front of J. P. Finnegan's Fancy Groceries and Fresh Meats.

But she didn't turn the engine off.

Instead, she sat, staring through the windshield, watching people as they walked up and down Main Street, popping first into this store, then that one.

She wasn't sure how long she had been there when she heard a man's voice.

"Miss, there's no loitering allowed here."

She turned and saw Thomas, his hands leaning against the car, a smile on his face.

"You coming in?" he asked.

For a minute, Myrtle sat and stared at him. *Was she? That* was *the question.*

She sighed, nodded, and turned off the engine.

Thomas hurried around to her side and opened the door.

"I saw you sitting out here through the window," he said as he took her hand and helped her from the car. "I wondered if you might be having second thoughts."

Myrtle's eyebrows shot up. "Second thoughts? I'm on about the fifth or sixth thought."

Thomas laughed. "I promise it won't hurt. I'll be gentle. I've turned on the space heater," he said, as they climbed the stairs. "It should be nice and comfortable in there."

"That's considerate of you since I will apparently be scantily dressed," said Myrtle.

When they walked into the room that had been set up for the portrait, Myrtle looked around. In addition to the easel and the little table that had been there on her first visit, and the second table against one wall with a collection of books, there were a few new items.

Across the room from the easel was a Russian painted, water gilded daybed, with giltwood and a brown silk covering. At one end was a backrest, with a semi-curved back.

In another corner stood a Chinese folding screen. Myrtle walked over and studied it carefully.

"This is exquisite," she said.

The double-hinged screen contained three panels adorned with gold leaf. Across all three ran a painted scene of a gloriously colored pheasant perched on a gnarled pine tree. Bright flowers around the base provided a contrast to the stark grayness of the trunk. Small birds flew overhead.

Six feet high and four feet wide with all its panels, it was more than sufficient to provide a modicum of privacy for Myrtle while she changed clothes.

"Where did you find this?" asked Myrtle.

"Mr. Abramovitz," replied Thomas.

Myrtle turned to look at him in wonder. "Mr. Abramovitz? At the pawn shop? He had this there? I never saw it."

"He said the son of some woman who just died brought it in."

Myrtle nodded. "That would be Mrs. Hall. She passed away last week."

"I thought it might work well for you for changing."

"You mean, as opposed to standing out here in the middle of the room. Yes, you're right, and I appreciate it. Thank you."

She walked around the screen where a moose rack coat tree and a beautifully carved mahogany oval-shaped cheval mirror sat. A diaphanous, cherry and pink-colored gown hung on one rack of the tree, a plain, cotton house robe on another.

Myrtle breathed deeply. *So this is what she would be wearing!*

Gently, she pushed the glass on the mirror, which tilted slightly.

"This coat rack," she called out to Thomas. "Did this come from Mr. Abramovitz's shop also?"

"No. Mrs. Finnegan was kind enough to loan it to me, and the mirror as well."

Myrtle walked back around the screen into the room.

"Did she tell you where the coat rack came from?" she asked.

"No—why?"

"I'm pretty sure it belonged to her former lover, Mr. Folger."

Thomas gave her a wry look. "Oh?"

"I recognize it from when we found his body."

Thomas's eyebrows shot up. "*You* found his body? I never knew that."

"Not me," said Myrtle. "It was Penelope. I found Penelope standing over his body."

"Is this one of those murders that happened here last fall?"

"Yes," said Myrtle. "Mr. Folger and Mr. Steinmyer and his daughter, Rachel."

"Whose room I stayed in at Miss Wasserman's, as you pointed out."

"One and the same."

"Okay, so, are you ready to get started?" asked Thomas.

Myrtle took a deep breath. "I guess."

"You saw the gown back there?"

Myrtle nodded.

"Go try it on. Let's see what it looks like."

He watched as Myrtle disappeared behind the screen. Moments later, when she emerged, he had to catch his breath.

"Good Lord, you're beautiful."

Indeed, she was.

The red gossamer garment fell down over her body, concealing personal areas while still allowing a sufficient amount of flesh to be exposed, making her appear almost nude.

"I feel naked," she said.

Thomas smiled. "It's a good look on you. Now, if you will come over here to the daybed."

Myrtle followed him to the daybed.

"Here's how I would like you to pose," said Thomas, as he lay down, stretching out his legs. He posed one arm back over his head, the other laying on the daybed.

"Okay," he said, getting up. "You try it."

Myrtle lay down and positioned her body, attempting to imitate the pose Thomas had struck.

"Pretty good," said Thomas, moving the hand over Myrtle's head slightly.

"Is that comfortable for you?" he asked.

"Yes," replied Myrtle.

"Here, let me make one adjustment."

He reached over and took hold of a pleat and moved it, so it no longer hid one breast. As he did so, his hand brushed her skin.

Myrtle felt a tingle run through her.

She looked down at the now naked breast.

"Is that absolutely necessary?" she asked.

"Essential;" said Thomas, "absolutely essential. Now, a smile, please?"

Myrtle tried her best smile. It wasn't much.

"Not a grimace—a smile," said Thomas, frowning. "Think of something you like: your dog."

Myrtle smiled. She did love Penrod!

"That's it!" cried Thomas, hurrying back to his canvas. "Now, stay just like that. Don't move."

For the next hour, Myrtle watched as Thomas worked, occasionally glancing at her, then back to the canvas in front of him.

She allowed her eyes to wander over the apartment, though there was little to see.

She turned her eyes back to Thomas and watched as he worked.

CHAPTER THIRTY-EIGHT

"Time for a break," said Thomas, laying down his palette knife and emerging out from behind the easel.

"Oh, thank God," said Myrtle. She curled herself off the daybed.

"Do you have anything to drink?" she asked. "I'm thirsty."

"Go put the robe on," said Thomas, "and I'll fix us something."

When Myrtle returned from behind the screen, Thomas was waiting for her with two drinks. He handed one to Myrtle, who took a sip and licked her lips.

"Johnny Walker Black Label?" she said.

Thomas looked at her in amazement. "How in the world do you know that?" he asked.

"Did you get it from Mr. McIntyre?"

"Okay, now you're just showing off. Yes, Jake had a bottle he let me buy. But how would you know *that*? Are you and he . . . ?"

Myrtle laughed. "No. When Henri and George and I met in his office to sift through information on that triple murder, that's what he served. I never forget a good scotch."

"Miss Tully, you are a woman of many fine qualities," said Thomas, smiling.

"May I see the painting?" asked Myrtle, taking another sip.

"Absolutely not."

"No? Then when *can* I see it?"

"When it's finished."

"When it's finished?" exclaimed Myrtle. "Why do I have to wait until then?"

"Because you do," said Thomas.

Myrtle's shoulders slumped. "Well, how long will that be?"

"Maybe the end of this week. Depends on how long I can get you to pose at any one time."

"How am I doing so far?"

"Good. You're a good model."

"What are you going to do with it when it's finished?" asked Myrtle.

"Why, I thought I'd give it to you."

"Give it to me? What would *I* do with it?"

"I noticed there's an empty spot above the fireplace in the parlor at Mrs. Darling's. It would look perfect there."

"Oh, no!" said Myrtle, recoiling. "There is no way a naked picture of me is going up in the boarding house. You think I want Mr. Longet and Henri and . . . well, everybody who comes there to see it? What if Father Fabian was to walk in one day?"

"I bet Father Fabian is a fan of the female form," said Thomas, a grin spreading across his face.

"No way," said Myrtle.

"Eddie said he'd be happy to hang it at the fire station."

"What!" Myrtle was up in arms now. "The *fire station*? How did he even know you were painting it? Did you tell him?"

"Not me. I believe he told me Daisy mentioned it to him."

Myrtle jumped up off the floor. "Wait 'til I get hold of her!"

"There is one other possibility," said Thomas.

Myrtle let out her breath. "What is that?"

"There's a nice little art museum down in Chicago. It's owned by Ella Ellenwood. I stop there occasionally to see what she might have to sell or want to purchase. I told her what I was doing, and she said she'd be happy to hang it in one of the exhibit halls."

Myrtle relaxed. "She did, huh?"

"Yes. It would be on loan there—from you."

"From me?"

"I still want to give it to you, for it to be yours. I think the question is: where will it hang."

Myrtle took another sip of scotch. "We'll see."

"Ready to get back to work?" asked Thomas.

"I suppose," said Myrtle.

"Another hour and we'll call it for today."

*****

Myrtle sat on the front porch, sipping a cup of dandelion tea when she saw Daisy coming up the road from town.

"Hey, kiddo," said Daisy, as she reached the porch.

"Don't kiddo me," barked Myrtle.

Daisy stopped on the bottom step. "I'd say someone got out on the wrong side of the bed this morning, except it's four o'clock in the afternoon. What's got your goat?"

"You told Eddie about Thomas painting my portrait?"

"Uh . . . yeah. Why? Was it a secret?"

"Because Eddie told Thomas he'd be happy to hang it in the fire station."

Daisy doubled over with laughter. When she was finally able to stand upright, tears rolled down her cheeks.

"He did, did he?" said Daisy, wiping her eyes with her handkerchief.

"Yes, he did." Myrtle was still furious.

"Are you going to let him?"

Myrtle jumped up out of the rocker.

"What? Am I going to let him? Are you out of your mind? Of course, I'm not going to let him!"

"So what *are* you going to do with it? Hang it in the library?"

"No, it's not going in the library, either!"

"If it's real good, I bet you could sell it and get rich," said Daisy, grinning.

"Oh, shut up," growled Myrtle, heading into the house.

*****

Over the next two days, Myrtle took off each afternoon and met Thomas at the studio above J. P. Finnegan's Fancy Groceries and Fresh Meats store.

The routine followed much the same path as the first day's: Myrtle would pose for an hour while Thomas painted; then they'd stop for a short break and imbibe in some Johnny Walker Black Label scotch followed by another hour or two of work.

Afterward, Myrtle would return to the library, make sure everything was okay, then head home for the five o'clock meal.

All that time, she and Daisy had not spoken.

Following dinner—another sumptuous repast of chicken and dumplings, corn pudding, collard greens, sweet pickles and cherry pie—Myrtle retired to one of the rocking chairs on the front porch, intent on doing nothing more than sitting, while watching and listening to the birds and squirrels and chipmunks all celebrate the turning of winter into spring.

A few minutes later, Daisy, carrying two cups of tea, steam swirling up from their rims, joined her.

"Mrs. Darling was going to bring this out, but I asked her if I could," she said, handing a cup to Myrtle. "Mind if I join you?"

Myrtle didn't say anything but nodded her head toward the empty chair beside her. She took a sip of the tea.

"Yum–thimbleberry," she said.

"She tried to give me dandelion, but I told her I thought thimbleberry might be more to your liking."

"More to *my* liking, huh? Not yours?"

"Okay," said Daisy. "My liking, too."

After a minute, she added, "You spoke to me. Does this mean you're not mad at me anymore?"

"Yeah, I think I'm over it. I'm sorry."

"I'm sorry, too. I shouldn't have said anything to Eddie. Anyway, how's the painting coming?"

"Tomorrow's the last day. It won't be done, but he has to get back to New York. We'll finish it when he comes back."

"He's coming back?"

Myrtle brightened. "I hope so. After all this, I want to see what it looks like."

"You haven't seen it yet?"

"No, he won't let me until it's finished."

*****

Shortly after noon, Myrtle climbed the stairs to the studio, where she found Thomas waiting for her.

"So, this is our last day?" said Myrtle, disappearing behind the screen to change her clothes.

"I'm afraid so," said Thomas. "I have to catch the evening train to Houghton to make my connection to Chicago."

"I hoped we could have dinner," came Myrtle's voice from behind the screen.

"'Fraid not. I won't have time."

"Maybe some tea at Miss Madeline's after we finish?" asked Myrtle, returning to the room.

Thomas looked at her and drew in his breath. Her beauty almost overwhelmed him every time he saw her—especially this past week, in the gown she was wearing for the portrait.

"Maybe," he said. "Let's get to work."

True to form, an hour later he came out from behind the canvas. Myrtle sat up on the daybed but didn't get up. She watched as he prepared their drinks.

"You going to put your robe on?" asked Thomas, pouring scotch into the two glasses.

"No, I'm fine," said Myrtle. She didn't move.

"Your breast is showing."

She smiled at him. "I'm fine."

Thomas walked over and handed her the drink. Then he sat down next to her.

"How long will you be gone?" asked Myrtle.

"A month, maybe two. I'll be back just as soon as I can."

"I hope so. I'll miss you."

They sat and sipped their drinks in silence, both immersed in their own thoughts about Thomas's leaving.

"Ready to get back to work?" asked Thomas, getting up.

"We won't finish today, will we?" asked Myrtle, looking up at him.

"No, as I said, I'll finish it when I return. Then you can see it."

"I'm thinking, if we can't finish today, then let's not go any further right now."

"What do you mean?"

"Stop painting," said Myrtle, "and do something else with the time we have left—something more productive."

"Like what?"

Myrtle reached up, took Thomas's face in her hands, pulled him down and kissed him.

"We'll think of something," she said.

*****

"You didn't!"

Myrtle had caught Daisy that evening before the two of them went down for dinner. Although she hadn't meant to tell her about the delightfully unexpected afternoon she'd had, she couldn't restrain herself.

"You and Thomas? Again?" cried Daisy.

"Shhh. I don't want the whole household to hear."

"Okay, kiddo, tell me all about it. Okay, maybe not *all* about it, but tell me *something!*"

Myrtle settled down onto Daisy's bed.

"I'd forgotten what a good lover he was," she said. "I was laying there with nothing to do for an hour but remember what it had been like back in Paris. And every time he peeked his head around the canvas I saw those dark eyes; I knew it was going to happen."

"So when he made the move . . . ."

Myrtle smiled. "Well, *he* didn't actually make the move."

"You devil, you! So, are you going to see him tomorrow?"

Myrtle frowned. "No, he left earlier this evening. He has to get back to New York."

"When will he be back?" asked Daisy.

"He said maybe two months, maybe earlier . . . I'm hoping for earlier."

"I had lunch with Eddie today," said Daisy.

"Hmm," said Myrtle. "This sounds as though it's getting serious."

"Oh, pshaw," said Daisy. "We're good friends, that's all. But he said Electric Park is opening the first Sunday of next month, and he wants to take me. Wants you to go, too—with whoever you want to go with."

"Electric Park?"

"It's this terrific place over north of Hancock where they have dances and concerts and shows. Eddie wants to go over and spend the day: have a picnic and listen to a concert by the C and H Band."

"Sounds like fun," said Myrtle. "How much does it cost?"

"Oh, it's free," said Daisy. "It's a way for the trolley company to get people to use the trolley."

"Why not just drive there?"

"You could—if there were any roads to it."

"They built a park with no way to get to it except by trolley?" said Myrtle. "That's pretty dumb."

"Not if you're the trolley company," said Daisy. "That makes them pretty smart."

"Yeah, I guess you're right."

"Who are you going to ask?"

"I guess I'll go by myself," Myrtle replied.

Daisy shook her head. "Huh, uh, that's not how it works. Henri or George—take your pick."

"Henri or George? You think those are my only two choices?"

"Well, who else?"

"Perhaps I'll ask Andy Erickson."

Daisy's laughter could be heard all the way downstairs.

CHAPTER THIRTY-NINE

The previous year Myrtle had passed up the annual Decoration Day festivities.

"It's Sunday;" she'd replied when Daisy asked her to go with her, "my day off. I'm not even going to church today. I'm staying home in bed and reading this book I picked up yesterday from Paige."

This year the holiday fell on Monday.

"What's your excuse this year?" asked Daisy. "The library's not going to be open. Even if it was, you're the head librarian—you can take off anytime you want."

Myrtle sighed. "All right, I suppose I can't get out of it two years in a row."

"Wear comfortable shoes," said Daisy. "We'll be doing a lot of walking and standing."

*****

Monday morning's usual fare for breakfast at Mrs. Darling's consisted of sausage links, fried potatoes, applesauce, orange juice, coffee, and pancakes. Normally, the pancakes were served with real Michigan maple syrup. Today the plate-sized hotcakes were adorned with blueberries, thimbleberry jam, and whipped cream.

Myrtle smiled, thinking back to last year's Fourth of July, when Mrs. Darling served an identical patriotic repast—and remembering Mr. Pfrommer bypassing the new toppings for the usual maple syrup.

"What time does everything start?" she asked, digging into a sausage link.

"One o'clock;" said Henri, who had come back in after hanging an American flag from the front porch. "at the college."

"Dere'll be a parade from dere downtown to da cemeteries," said Mrs. Darling, who had come into the room, "where evergreen-covered crosses with da name of da dead soldier, will be put at da head of his grave. Den Mr. Koskinen will give a speech."

Myrtle looked at Henri. "The same Mr. Koskinen you told me about at the logging camp?"

"Yah," said Henri, "that's him. Then we head off to the park where we all sing *America* and *The Star-Spangled Banner* and listen to a concert by the band."

"Da one from da mine," said Mrs. Darling. "Dey're really good."

"Sounds like fun," said Myrtle, not at all sure it actually did.

*****

But Myrtle was glad she'd gone this year.

For perhaps the first time since she'd come to Booker Falls, she felt a real part of the community as she strolled down the road with Daisy, Pierre and a long line of other town folk, veterans, and relatives of the soldiers whose graves they were on their way to decorate.

Leading the parade was the Calumet and Hecla Band, playing patriotic music, Father Fabian, Reverend Albrecht, Fire Chief Eddie O'Halloran, and various town officials including Henri and George.

When they reached the township cemetery on the outskirts of town, the same cemetery where Mr. Pfrommer had been laid to rest, Myrtle watched as family members placed the crosses described by Mrs. Darling on the graves of their dead husbands, fathers, sons, and brothers. Then it was on to the Catholic cemetery in town, where the scene was repeated.

Another short stroll down the street to the courthouse, where a reviewing stand had been set up, brought the crowd to where Mr. Koskinen and another veteran would give their speeches.

The first speaker was young Theodore Simpson, twenty-one, a veteran of the war recently concluded, who described what it was like sailing into New York Harbor two years ago aboard the USS Ohioan along with sixteen hundred other soldiers returning from the conflict in Europe.

When he finished, he got a rousing round of applause.

Then it was Mr. Koskinen's turn.

Myrtle was impressed by the stately figure on the stage in front of her. It was hard to believe he was ninety-five years old.

"It was 1863," Mr. Koskinen began, "when Henry Feiser, Billy Fresise, William Tretheway and me headed down to Ypsilanti to join up. They was younger than me; I was turty-six. We got sworn into da Twenty-seventh Michigan Volunteer Infantry Regiment, Company C."

The old man went on to describe in detail the battles the company had been in: Vicksburg, The Battle of the Wilderness, Cold Harbor, Appomattox.

"We was lucky," he said as he neared the end of his speech. "The four of us—we was all lucky enough to get back home alive. A lot of fellers didn't. Dis is dere day—well, and Henry and Billy and William, too, 'cause dey ain't wit us no more, neither."

Then he turned and headed for his seat, amid a roaring round of applause, louder than his predecessor's.

"That was very interesting," Myrtle said, speaking to Daisy, who was standing next to her.

230 Paint the Librarian Dead

"Yeah," said a man close by, who'd heard what she said, "but not after seven or eight years of hearing da same ting."

*****

An hour later, the C and H Band concluded its concert with a rousing version of *Stars and Stripes Forever,* the final event of the afternoon.

"That's it," said Daisy. "Ready to head back home?"

"After a stop at the Polar Bear," said Myrtle.

"You don't have to twist my arm," said Daisy.

"Look," said Myrtle as they approached the ice cream shop, "there's Miss Vanderliet's motorcycle."

"It's a Harley;" said Daisy, stopping and looking the machine over, "an F-11. I'm guessing it's no more than six years old because that's when the three-speed transmission came out."

"How'd you know that?" asked Myrtle.

"A fellow I knew down in Traverse City had one, bought it new when it came out. It was just like this one. He told me all about it. It's got eleven horsepower, a sixty-cubic-inch F-head V-twin engine, front suspension. And look, it has electric lights in the front and on the back. He said you could even take the one off the back and use it as a service light."

"And you remembered all that? How good a friend *were* you with this fellow?"

Daisy grinned. "We might have gone out a few times."

They were surprised when they came through the door of the Polar Bear to find the place packed.

"I guess we weren't the only ones who had this idea in mind," said Myrtle.

"Wait. I see an empty booth over there," said Daisy, taking off.

They'd no sooner sat down when Ambrose Sherman sidled up to the table.

"Ladies," he said, tipping his derby.

"Doctor Sherman," said Myrtle. "How are you today?"

"I am fine, thank you. I wonder if it would be an imposition if I joined you. There do not seem to be any other seats available."

"Sure," said Daisy, scooting over. "You can sit right here."

"Much obliged," said Doctor Sherman, sliding into the booth.

"I haven't seen you around much," said Myrtle.

"Ah, that may be because there have not been any more murders in town for you to get involved in."

"I still can't get that vision out of my mind; Mr. Mitchell lying there on the floor, blood all over his face."

"On his neck, yes," said Doctor Sherman, "but not on his face: he had paint on his face."

"Oh, I know," said Myrtle. "I saw the paint; blue and yellow. But it's the blood I can't get out of my mind."

"Like I said, there was no blood on his face," said Doctor Sherman. "It was all paint: blue and yellow and red."

For a moment Myrtle was confused. "Mr. Mitchell had *red* paint on his face?"

"Why, yes," said the doctor. "Why? Does that seem unusual?"

"You bet it does," said Myrtle. "Mr. Mitchell never used red paint." She got up. "I'm going to use the ladies room. Daisy, order me a bananapalooza, will you?"

"A bananpalooza?" said Ambrose as Myrtle walked away.

"Bananas, chocolate ice cream with chocolate topping and vanilla ice cream with pineapple and strawberry topping," said Daisy.

"My, that does sound good," said Ambrose. "I believe I'll have one of those, too."

*****

Myrtle stopped short when she entered the ladies room.

Facing the mirror with her back to her was Kitty Vanderliet. The leather-fringed jacket she'd been wearing hung on a hook on the wall next to her.

It was not so much the state of Kitty's undress that caught Myrtle's attention, but the tattoo of a crucifix on Kitty's back, extending from the middle of her shoulder blades, disappearing under the camiknicker she had on.

That, and what Myrtle was sure was a healed gunshot wound in the woman's left shoulder.

"Oh, I'm sorry . . ." said Myrtle.

Kitty looked at Myrtle in the mirror. "Miss Tully. Oh, no, it's okay. I spilled some chocolate syrup, and I was trying to clean it up. Here," she said, moving away from the mirror, "I'm finished. It's all yours."

She took her jacket from the hook and slipped it on.

"You have a nice day, now," she said as she left the room.

Myrtle stood transfixed, a shocked look on her face.

*****

When Myrtle came back from the restroom, Daisy thought she had a funny look on her face.

You okay?" she asked.

Myrtle nodded. "I'm okay."

She eyed the banana split sitting in front of her, picked up a spoon and dug in.

*****

Later, out on the street, Myrtle pulled Daisy to one side.

"You won't believe what I just saw," said Myrtle.

She described her brief encounter with Kitty.

"A crucifix? And a gunshot wound?" said Daisy. "Are you sure. I guess you'd be sure about the crucifix—but the gunshot wound?"

"I'm sure about that, too," said Myrtle. "I saw enough soldiers in Europe who had been shot to know what a gunshot wound looks like."

"Are you going to say anything to Henri?"

"Not about Miss Vanderliet; but I am going to tell him what Doctor Ambrose said about the paint. Come on, let's check out some stores. I want to see if Paige has any new books in."

By the time they'd made their rounds of several stores offering Decoration Day bargains and walked the two miles to the boarding house, it was almost time for dinner.

Myrtle was anxious to talk with Henri about what she had discovered: that the painting Mr. Mitchell fell into couldn't have been one of his since it contained red paint. It must have belonged to someone else; possibly the killer's.

After a quick dash upstairs to wash her hands and face, she scurried back down and into the dining room. She stopped short when she saw who was seated there along with the others: Mr. Koskinen.

He stood as she approached, as did the other two men.

"Mr. Koskinen," said Henri, "I would like you to meet our other boarder, Miss Tully."

Mr. Koskinen gave a shy smile. "Miss Tully, I am honored to make your acquaintance."

"Mr. Koskinen," said Myrtle, giving a slight nod.

Pierre helped Myrtle into her seat and the three men sat down, joining the two women at the table.

"Mr. Koskinen is an old friend of Mrs. Darling's," said Henri.

"I see," said Myrtle.

234 *Paint the Librarian Dead*

"Yah," said Mr. Koskinen, "Eunice and I go back a long ways."

Henri, Daisy, and Myrtle looked at one another. Eunice? In all the time they had been living at the boarding house they had never known Mrs. Darling's first name.

"She and my kids, dey grew up togedder," said Mr. Koskinen. 'Course, all my kids, dey done moved away, and wit my wife dead and gone, rest her soul, dey's just me left here in town, eh?"

Mrs. Darling entered, carrying a bowl of steamed and buttered spinach.

"Ah, dearie, so you met Mr. Koskinen," she said.

"I did," said Myrtle. "I enjoyed your speech today," she added, turning to the old man.

"Me, too," said Daisy, digging into the spinach.

"And I'm looking forward to hearing more of what life was like at the logging camp," said Myrtle. "Henri took me out there one day last December."

"Yah, I'm sure he'll be ready to bend your ear on dat," said Mrs. Darling.

"I don't tink anyone wants to hear 'bout all dat old stuff," said Mr. Koskinen.

"Yes, we do," said Myrtle and Daisy in unison.

"Well, okay, den," said Mrs. Darling. "We'll have dessert in da parlor after dinner and he can tell you all about it."

CHAPTER FORTY

"Dere I was, yust nineteen years of age when I got off dat ship in New York."

They had barely settled into their places, with Mrs. Darling having served each a slice of pumpkin pie topped with heavy cream when Mr. Koskinen began to speak.

It was obvious that, in spite of his seeming reluctance at dinner, he loved to talk about the old days.

"I walked down da plank and stopped and looked around and den I tought—what now? I didn't speak English none too good, but I found me a map of da country, so I knowed where da Keweenaw was. I had a cousin who had gone dere to look for gold. He'd writ me, saying if I wanted to come, he'd put me up for a spell. So I set out walking—"

"You set out walking?" said Myrtle.

"Yah, well I didn't have no money, ya see, so I couldn't afford to buy no stage seat. So, like I said, I set out walking, and I got here 'bout a month later. 'Course, I had to sneak onto da ferry to get across da straights, ya know."

"Over at Mackinaw," said Daisy.

"Yah, dem. So, when I got here, dere was no sign of my cousin. Seemed he'd left to go on to Californiay to look for gold since he didn't find none in dese parts. But I warn't about to walk another two tousand miles, so I started lookin' for copper. Figgered if my cousin couldn't find gold, neither could I.

"Dat's when I run into Mr. Booker. We palled around for a bit, lookin' for copper; he had a claim, ya know. But we didn't find none. So he decides to sell his claim to da Joshua Mining Company and I figger, since I ain't findin' no copper neither, I might as well go get a job.

"I heard 'bout dis Mr. Amyx who was startin' a logging camp over around here, so I come over and got me a job. I'd done a little loggin' in Finland, ya see, 'fore I come to America, so I knowed a little bit about it. I worked at da camp for fifteen years, 'til we got all da timber cut. Dey was da best years of my life. I'd work out in da woods in da winter, den I'd get a job on one of da fishing boats in da summer."

"Tell us about life at the logging camp," said Myrtle.

"It was a hard one, dat's for sure, but a good one. Da foreman, he'd get us up 'bout an hour 'fore daybreak every morning—'cept Sundays; we got Sundays off, ya know. It was still real dark, and we'd all get dressed and troop over to da cookshack for breakfast. Dere was always real good food and lots of it: buckwheat pancakes wit blackstrap syrup, ham, eggs, cookies, hash, toast—and coffee—lots of coffee. We never talked while we ate—just ate."

"Why was that?" asked Pierre. "Why didn't you talk?"

"Don't know," said Mr. Koskinen. "Just never did. Anyways, once we finished eating we loaded into da wagon and da oxen would pull us out to where we was a'cuttin' dat day, and we'd get to work. I was a skidder."

"A skidder?" said Henri.

"Yah," said Mr. Koskinen. "After da choppers'd cut notches in da tree whichever way dey wanted dem to fall, and da sawers would cut 'em down with dere big long saws, den da choppers would cut off all da branches, and da sawers would move back in and cut dem up into logs, usually 'bout sixteen feet long. Dat's when I come in: me and da rest of my crew. Dere was seven of us; tree skidders, like me, tree deckers and da teamster. Us skidders, we'd lay pieces of timber down side by each, 'bout eight feet apart. We called dat da skidway. Den da swampers, dey'd trim da logs and make roads for da teamster so he can get da oxen to haul da logs, and den da deckers, dey'd roll da logs into a big pile on dat skidway, sometimes as high as ten feet."

"Only seven men worked at the camp?" asked Daisy.

"Oh, no. Dey was always 'bout fifty or sixty, sometimes more. We had different crews, ya see, and den dere was da ones what stayed in da camp; da foreman and da cook and da log scaler, da feller what run da store—dey was all dere, too.

"'Round noon, we'd break for lunch. We'd each get a sack when we left da cookshack. Dere'd be a couple of pasties, and another sandwich wit butter and jam."

Mr. Koskinen chuckled.

"Sometimes, I'd trade one of my pasties wit another feller for his butter and jam. Dey all tought I was crazy, but I really liked butter and jam. Anyways, along wit da pasties we always had either a piece of cake or some fruit. My favorite was when we got a orange.

"So den, it was back to work 'til dusk, when da wagon'd take us back to camp. It sure was nice to get back to da bunkhouse, 'cause dere was always a big fire a'roarin' in da fireplace. We'd take off our wet clothes and hang dem on dis rack dat ran along above da fireplace so dey'd dry.

"Den we'd wash up and get dressed for supper. If we had a few minutes before da gabreel blowed . . . ."

"The gabreel?" said Daisy.

"Yah, da gabreel. It's a big horn; you could hear it for two miles away. Anyways, if we had a few minutes, we'd play some cards or dominoes or fifteen-two."

"What's fifteen-two?" asked Pierre.

"Dat's cribbage," said Mrs. Darling. "Dat's what we call it up here. Go on, Mr. Koskinen."

"So," the old man continued, "when da gabreel blowed, we'd hustle off to da cookshack for supper. Dat's when we got da big meal of da day—man, dey fed us good: meat, potatoes, stew, always pork and beans, pie, cake, cookies. And we could put it away, too, I can tell you! Working out in dose woods for twelve hours, doing da work we did, we needed all dat food.

"I 'member one feller, Cooper McGonigal was his name, a big Irishman from County Sligo, as I recall; he was da biggest eater of all. I 'member one meal, he put away tree pork chops, two big slices of ham, and den finished all dat off wit a tee bone steak. Den he started on dessert."

"Makes me hungry again, just thinking about it," said Henri.

"Dere's more pie," said Mrs. Darling.

Henri shook his head. "No, thank you. Thinking about it is plenty for me right now."

"So logging was really hard work," said Daisy.

"Oh, yah, missy, it sure was; and cold, too. Sometimes it got down to twenty, tirty below."

"I'm not sure I could wear enough clothes to be out working in weather like that," said Myrtle.

"Well, we had good, warm clothes, dat's for sure. But working as hard as we did, we never got all dat cold. In fact, we'd even be sweatin'."

"Did you go to bed then, right after supper?" asked Daisy.

"Oh, no. Lights out weren't 'til nine o'clock. So we'd play some more cards and such. Some of da fellers was into checkers, too.

"Sundays was our day off. We didn't have to get up as early. We had a longer time for breakfast. Den we had da rest of da day off to do whatever we wanted. If da weather weren't too bad, we'd go outside and kick da ball around, or wrestle or have races. After I got married, I'd hitch a ride into town to see Ellie and den, later, my kids as they come along. Like I said, dose was da best years of my life."

"You were married?" said Myrtle.

"Yah, me and Ellie, we got hitched in fifty-two."

"Oh, of course," said Myrtle. "I forgot—you said Mrs. Darling played with your children when she was a little girl."

"Yah, my first two was born within two years after Ellie and me got married, and den da tird, Raymond, he come along the same year Eunice was born."

"What did you do when you quit logging?" asked Henri.

"So, den, I got to workin' on ships year 'round 'til da war broke out. I didn't go right away, 'cause Ellie tought I should stay home and take care of my family. But in sixty tree I told her I had to go: I felt it was my duty after what dis country did for me, taking me in and providin' me wit a living."

"And what did you do when the war was over?" asked Pierre.

Mr. Koskinen looked down, a sad look covering his face.

"Well, Ellie, she up and died 'bout tree months afore I got back. My kids was living wit Ellie's sister, Goldie. I tought maybe dat was da way it should be, so I went back to working on da lakes, fishing boats dis time."

"I'm sorry to hear about your wife," said Myrtle.

"Yah, well it was a long time ago, eh?"

"What was it like to work on a fishing boat?" asked Pierre.

Mr. Koskinen pulled out his pocket watch and looked at it, then put it back.

"Ah, lad, it's late, and I tink dat's maybe a story for another time."

*****

"Henri, I need to talk with you."

Henri had agreed to drive Mr. Koskinen back to his house. Everyone else had retired for the evening and Myrtle had waited in the parlor for Henri's return.

"What about?" he asked.

"Did you know Mr. Mitchell had red paint on his face?"

"Is this a joke? What do you mean, 'red paint on his face?'"

"When we found him there in his studio; he had red paint on his face, along with the blue and yellow. I thought it was blood, but I saw Doctor Sherman today, and he said it wasn't blood, it was paint."

"And?" Henri didn't know where she was going with this.

"Mr. Mitchell never used red paint in any of his paintings. He associated it with the Devil. And I don't think he ever used yellow, either. That paint must have come off the painting he fell into like the other paint did. The painting wasn't his; it belonged to someone else."

"What's your point?" asked Henri.

"I think it belonged to the killer!"

"And who might that be?"

"Who else do you know is an artist?"

"Your friend, Mr. Wickersham."

Myrtle was brought up short. She hadn't even considered Thomas.

"No, I'm sure it wasn't him," said Myrtle. "But there is Mr. Hutchinson."

"He was Frank's best friend. Why would he kill him?"

"I don't know," said Myrtle. "But I think it merits a discussion with him, don't you?"

"We'll see," said Henri, starting for the stairs. "Right now I'm going to bed. I'm exhausted."

"But aren't you . . . ?"

But Henri was gone, up the stairs.

*****

"Henri didn't think there was much to it?" said Daisy, somewhat groggily.

Myrtle had made a beeline up to Daisy's room and rousted her out of bed to vent her frustration with Henri's apparent lack of interest in what she had figured out.

"No," said Myrtle, fuming. "'We'll see'—that's what he said. He's such a nincompoop!"

"You think he will go talk with Mr. Hutchinson?" asked Daisy.

"I wouldn't hold my breath," said Myrtle.

CHAPTER FORTY-ONE

Myrtle decided since she'd told George she didn't play favorites when she asked him to go to the St. Patrick's Day Party with her, it was only right that Henri be the one she ask to accompany her and Daisy and Eddie to Electric Park.

He had said yes without any hesitation, and that he'd drive them to Houghton where they would catch the trolley. Mrs. Darling said she would pack them a proper picnic lunch.

After a filling breakfast of oatmeal, toast, poached eggs, bacon and coffee, and after picking Eddie up at the fire station, they headed out of town in Henri's Packard. Eddie sat up in front with Henri, while Daisy and Myrtle shared the back seat, the rattan picnic basket nestled between them.

"Henri, ring the bell, will you," said Daisy as they left Greytown and passed through a wooded area outside of town.

Befitting his role as the county constable, Henri had installed a twelve-inch high bell on the front of the hood that was rung using a chain that ran to a lever next to the steering wheel. The word "POLICE" painted on either side of the vehicle made it clear for what purpose the car was intended.

"That bell is solely for official police business," said Henri.

"Oh, come on, Henri, be a sport," said Myrtle.

A moment later, Henri reached up and pulled the cord attached to the bell, causing it to ring out.

"Oh, thank you," cried Daisy.

"Do it again," said Myrtle.

"Don't press your luck," said Henri.

Then he reached over and pulled the cord again.

*****

For the next half hour, the two women kept up a running conversation, while Henri and Eddie exchanged few words.

When they reached Houghton, Henri parked the car. Myrtle and Daisy decided they wanted to do a little shopping before starting out for the park.

"What are we supposed to do while you two are shopping?" asked Henri.

Myrtle shrugged, then headed off with Daisy. "We don't care. Use your imagination," she called back over her shoulder.

"Let's walk down to da lake," said Eddie. "Dere's a place down dere we can sit and watch da boaters."

"Okay, why not?" said Henri.

Myrtle and Daisy leisurely wended their way down Shelby Street, occasionally popping into a store, enticed by the goods displayed in the window. When they reached the bridge, Daisy spotted Yelps Confectionary Store.

"Oh, my God, Myrtle, look at that. Let's go there!" she said, making a beeline for the building.

"I think I've died and gone to Heaven," said Daisy as she and Myrtle stepped through the door and viewed the abundance of goodies that greeted them: Peach Blossoms, peppermint stick, Hershey's milk chocolate kisses, Goo Goo Clusters, Mary Janes, Turtles.

"What are these?" asked Myrtle, picking up a box labeled Jujyfruits.

"Dose come out last year," said Ted Yelps, the store owner. "Dey's gummy wit fruit flavors."

"Does the shape tell you what the flavor is?" asked Daisy.

"Hah! You'd tink so, but, no, it's da color what tells you da flavor. My favorite is licorice. Now, Sarah—dat's my wife—she likes da spearmint. Here, try one."

Mr. Yelps opened a box and held it out to the women. Myrtle reached in and withdrew a yellow piece in the shape of a banana, on which the name 'HEIDE' was stamped.

"Is this banana flavored?" she asked.

"Dat's lemon," said Mr. Yelps. "Not my favorite."

Daisy withdrew what looked like a bundle of red grapes.

"Raspberry," said Mr. Yelps. "Not bad—but not as good as licorice. Oh, and dey're pretty sticky, too."

Myrtle and Daisy each stuck a piece into their mouths and started chewing.

"You're right," said Myrtle, working with her tongue in a vain attempt to dislodge a chunk of candy stuck to her gums.

After much deliberation, Daisy decided on a pound of Brach's wrapped caramels.

"Dat will be twenty-seven cents," said Mr. Yelps, as he placed the caramels in a small brown paper bag.

"I'll save these until the trip back home," said Daisy, as she and Myrtle headed back down the street toward the car.

When they reached the Packard, they saw Henri and Eddie approaching from the opposite direction.

"What have you two been up to?" asked Daisy.

"We saw da North American head out to da big lake," said Eddie.

"The North American?" said Myrtle.

"It's a passenger ship that tours the Great Lakes," said Henri. "A sister ship to the SS South American, which does the same."

"You girls ready to get on da trolley?" asked Eddie.

"Yep," said Daisy. "Let's go."

They watched as the car glided to a stop and a few people disembarked. Then they boarded along with a dozen other passengers, many bound for Electric Park, as they were.

Eddie had brought the picnic basket from the car, and they all settled into their seats.

Minutes later, the conductor, Mr. Turja, who had been with the line almost since the beginning, passed by and collected the tickets the men had purchased at the desk inside the hotel for ten cents per person. He handed each of them a transfer.

Myrtle noticed he wore a revolver on his hip. When he passed by, she asked Henri about it.

"That's something new;" said Henri. "just started this year. After they went to one conductor instead of two, a lot of people were hitching free rides on the back of the cars."

"But they wouldn't shoot anyone just for doing that, would they?" asked Daisy.

"If they did, it wouldn't hurt much—they don't have real bullets, just blanks."

As the trolley rumbled over the bridge crossing the Portage River into Hancock, it passed a second car making its way south. Once in Hancock, the line ran through a sprawling commercial district.

Myrtle gazed out the open window as the buildings passed by.

"I'm glad we don't live here," she said. "This is too congested for me. I like our simple little town."

"Says the woman who was born and grew up in New Orleans," said Daisy.

"That was a lifetime ago," said Myrtle.

At the stop in Frenchtown a few people got off, but they were more than replaced by those getting on. The

246 Paint the Librarian Dead

conductor came and collected another forty cents from Eddie.

Four miles to Boston and another two further on through woods on one side and open fields on the other, the Electric Park's pavilion came into view.

"Oh, wow, that is big," said Myrtle, as the trolley rolled to a stop.

Above a covered porch that spanned the one hundred foot long façade was an equally impressive forty foot long electric sign with three-foot high letters that spelled out "ELECTRIC PARK."

"Wait 'til you get inside," said Eddie.

Along with everyone else except for three men traveling further north, the four of them disembarked and made their way across the wide wooden platform between the tracks and the park grounds.

"This way," said Eddie, as he headed for the picnic grounds, toting the basket of food Mrs. Darling had prepared. Swarms of people were already there, transported by the trolleys that left Houghton every half hour.

Within minutes, they found a large Weeping Willow tree that provided cover from a sun now starting to heat up the day.

Myrtle and Daisy spread out the tablecloth Mrs. Darling had so thoughtfully included and began setting out the dinnerware: plates, glasses, and cutlery.

"I'm not ready to eat yet," said Myrtle. "Is anybody else?"

"No," they all responded.

"Let's take a walk around so I can see the place," said Myrtle.

"Why don't you let Henri show you?" said Daisy. "He's been here; he knows the layout. I want to just sit and relax."

"Fine with me," said Henri.

After showing Myrtle the baseball park and the playground that contained swings, slides, teeter-totters and a small carousel, they headed for the pavilion.

"Wait," said Myrtle, "is that it? I thought there'd be rides for adults. You know, like a Ferris wheel or a roller coaster?"

"Nah, this park's not like that," said Henri. "The big attraction is the pavilion: the concerts, the vaudeville shows, the dances. You can ride the merry-go-round, though, if you want."

"Shoot," said Myrtle, disappointed.

"I think you'll still have fun," said Henri.

When they walked through the door into the pavilion, Myrtle had to admit it was impressive.

A hipped roof almost three stories high at its peak and featuring several dormers covered the five thousand square foot building. A narrow balcony ran around the entire room. Red, white and blue streamers hung from the ceiling, while dozens of American flags decorated the walls, providing a festive mood. Over seven hundred electric lights, including some designed as shields, anchors, and stars, provided more than sufficient illumination for nighttime events, such as dances and shows.

A stage sat at one end, facing a thirty-two hundred square foot dance floor capable of holding several hundred couples.

"Is this where the concert will be?" asked Myrtle.

"No," said Henri, "outside. The bandstand is outside."

"I'm glad it's not raining," said Myrtle.

"I think they move it inside when the weather's bad," said Henri. "I'm not sure."

"We'd best be getting back to Daisy and Eddie," said Myrtle. "I'm not sure we can trust those two alone anymore."

"You mean with the food?"

Myrtle looked at Henri and laughed. "Sure;" she said, taking off, "with the food."

When they got back to where they'd set up for the picnic, Daisy and Eddie were nowhere to be seen.

"I wonder where they went?" said Myrtle.

Henri looked toward the playground. "There they are," he said, pointing.

Myrtle looked and saw Daisy on a swing, Eddie pushing her.

"Looks like they're having fun," said Henri. "You want to go over?"

"No," said Myrtle, "I'm content to lie here and enjoy the fresh air."

Myrtle didn't know when she fell asleep, but she awoke when she heard her name being called.

She opened her eyes and saw Daisy's grinning face staring at her.

"What . . . what is it?" Myrtle asked, groggily.

Daisy held out her hand for Myrtle to see.

Myrtle struggled to adjust her eyes to the light. "What? What is it?"

"The ring, silly," said Daisy, still grinning. "Eddie proposed."

Myrtle sat upright. "What? He proposed?"

"Yes," said Daisy, giggling. "We're engaged." She dropped down and enveloped Myrtle in a bear hug.

Myrtle looked around and saw Eddie and Henri, grins on each of their faces.

"That's wonderful!" exclaimed Myrtle, wrapping her arms around Daisy. "I'm so happy for you."

Daisy explained that they were at the teeter-totters when Eddie got down on one knee and asked her to marry him, to which she had immediately shouted, "Yes, yes, yes!"

"This calls for a celebration," said Myrtle.

"Too bad we don't have no alcohol," said Eddie.

"Yah, unfortunately, they don't allow alcohol here, didn't even before the prohibition," said Henri. "But I can go to the refreshment stand and get us some cold lemonade."

"Do it," said Myrtle.

"I'll go wit you," said Eddie.

"Have you set a date?" asked Myrtle, after the men left.

"Oh, no, not yet. I'm still in a tizzy he even asked. We'll talk about that sometime, but for now, I'm just in seventh heaven."

By the time Henri and Eddie returned with the drinks, Myrtle and Daisy had set out the food: four pasties, two beef and two chicken; hard-boiled eggs; apples; homemade bread, cookies, and celery sticks.

An hour later, after wolfing down the meal and short naps for all of them, they were awakened by the voices of people passing by on their way to the bandstand.

"We'd better go get our places," said Eddie, sitting up.

They soon found themselves seated along with several hundred other park goers enjoying music by the Calumet and Hecla Band.

On the way home that evening, Myrtle found herself sitting up front with Henri while Eddie and Daisy shared the back seat.

By the time they got to the boarding house, Myrtle, exhausted, wanted nothing more than to go to sleep.

Daisy, however, was still too high and had other plans.

When one o'clock rolled around, she finally let Myrtle go to bed.

CHAPTER FORTY-TWO

It had been four weeks since Myrtle had taken her Model N out of winter storage. She'd been driving it around town, but now she was anxious to get in it and go somewhere—anywhere.

She'd already told Lydia she wouldn't be coming in to the library.

Daisy had convinced her she needed some new clothes, something more appropriate for her new position as head librarian at the Adelaide College Library.

She'd looked at the offerings at de Première Qualité Women's Wear but hadn't found anything appropriate she could afford. Daisy suggested Vertin's Department Store in Red Jacket. Myrtle liked the idea; it was the place where she had purchased the skunk fur coat her second day in town when she and Daisy had gone there to pick up a typewriter.

"I'll show you the house where George and I stayed New Year's Eve," she said when she asked Daisy after breakfast to go with her, "and the Hoatson Mansion across the street where the party was held."

It hadn't taken long at Vertin's for Myrtle to find exactly what she was looking for: two skirts, one blue and one black, both of which came down past her knees; four blouses—three plain white and one that was red with a white collar; for a change of pace, she'd said—and two pairs of shoes, one a satin lace-up heeled Oxford with a contrasting French binding, the other a somewhat more practical pair with black leather laced over the arch, two-inch wedge heels and ornamental piping.

"Come on," Myrtle said after the cashier had rung up her purchases and they were leaving the store. "I'll treat you to lunch. You bought me lunch the first time we came here. This time I'll return the favor."

They crossed the street to the Michigan House. Built eleven years earlier, it occupied the spot where a previous structure, a hotel and saloon, had been torn down.

As they settled into their seats, Myrtle pointed to the large ceiling mural that stretched above the enormous wooden bar, a rendering of a picnic, wherein a great amount of beer was being consumed.

"I love that mural," she said. "The people all look so happy and having a good time."

"They should," said Daisy. "They're probably all soused from drinking so much beer."

"What are you having?" asked Myrtle, studying the menu. "Remember, I'm buying, so don't be stingy."

"You know I love to eat," replied Daisy. "So don't say I didn't warn you."

Daisy was true to her word.

"I'll have the grilled lemon-dill salmon," she told the waitress when she arrived to take the order, "with a baked potato. And what's the vegetable?"

"Steamed kale."

"That sounds delicious," said Daisy, licking her lips. "And I'll have cold tea to drink."

"It comes with a salad and a breadstick, too," said the waitress.

"Better and better!" exclaimed Daisy.

"We got homemade apple dumpling for dessert," said the waitress.

Daisy looked at Myrtle.

252 Paint the Librarian Dead

"I don't care," said Myrtle, shaking her head and smiling. "Go for it."

"Okay," said Daisy. "Add that on."

"And you, miss?" asked the waitress.

"I think I'll have the beef and kidney bean chili," said Myrtle. "And a breadstick. And tea to drink."

The waitress nodded, turned and hurried off.

"You won't be able to eat dinner tonight," said Myrtle.

Daisy smiled. "Don't bet on it."

*****

They were almost to the car when Daisy stopped and grabbed Myrtle by the arm.

"Hey, let's go in here. I want to see how much this telescope in the window is."

Myrtle turned to see what Daisy was talking about. The sign on the window read "Macintosh's Pawn Shop."

"Oh, good," said Myrtle. "I love pawn shops."

Andy Macintosh's pawn shop was more than three times the size of Mr. Abramovitz's and held more than four times as many items.

"Look," said Daisy, handing the telescope to Myrtle, "It's only five dollars and sixty-five cents."

Before Myrtle could say anything, Daisy had picked up a pair of field glasses.

"Oooh, I like these," she said."

"How much are they?" asked Myrtle.

"Oh, my. They're more than twice as much as the telescope."

"Yes, but you'll be able to see twice as much," said Myrtle.

Daisy looked at her, confused.

"Two eyes instead of one," said Myrtle, laughing.

"Yeah, right," said Daisy. "That's a lot of money, though. I guess I can get by using the two good eyes God gave me."

A painting of an Indian hanging on one wall caught Myrtle's eye. He wore a white, collared shirt under a dark jacket. A red sash was at his throat, and an oval silver medal six or seven inches long hung around his neck.

"Mr. Macintosh, is this a painting of someone real?" she asked.

"Aye, lass, it is," replied the old man. "That's Red Jacket, Chief of the Seneca Tribe. See that medal around his neck?"

Myrtle nodded. It was hard to miss.

"Supposedly, that was given to him by President George Washington."

"Is the town named after him?" asked Myrtle.

"Aye, it is."

"He was from around here, then?"

"Nah, he was from New York. I don't know he ever stepped a foot in this part of the country."

"Then why is the town named after him?" asked Daisy.

"Haven't the slightest clue," said Mr. Macintosh.

"I see this place on the wall next to him where another painting used to hang. Was it of him, too?"

"Nah, that was a nice piece by one of the old masters. Don't remember who, now. Got stole a while back. Someone broke in one night and stole that piece and two others. I don't know why they didn't take old Red Jacket. Maybe they didn't like Indians. We've had a lot of robberies around here lately, paintings mostly."

While this conversation was going on, Daisy had been studying the array of pipes Mr. Macintosh had to offer, considering if she should buy one for Eddie, whose birthday, she knew, was coming up.

Myrtle moved to a large case that contained pendants, brooches, pins, and necklaces, debating if she wanted to spend any more money on this shopping trip. Daisy answered the question for her when she called her over to the pipe case.

Daisy pointed to a meerschaum pipe with a bowl sculpted in the shape of a bear.

"What do you think, Myrtle?" asked Daisy. "Do you think Eddie would like that?"

"Does he smoke a pipe?"

Daisy thought for a moment. "I don't know. But he should. I think I'll get it."

Myrtle rolled her eyes.

While Daisy paid for the pipe, Myrtle wandered to the back of the store where men's clothes were displayed. She stopped short in front of a blue greatcoat. Then she bent down, studying the buttons. Her mouth fell open.

"Daisy!" she called out. "Come here—quick!"

Daisy hurried to where Myrtle stood, still staring at the coat. "What? What is it?"

"These buttons," said Myrtle, fingering one of the buttons. "I've seen one like it before."

"Where?"

"In Mr. Mitchell's hand—when he was lying dead on the floor of his studio. Doctor Ambrose speculated he might have torn it off his killer's coat before he was stabbed to death."

"But it looks as if this coat still has all its buttons," said Daisy.

"Uh, huh, it does," said Myrtle. "But look here at the top button, at the collar."

Daisy bent down and looked, then stood back up. "It's not the same as the others. It's close, but not the same."

"No, it's not. All the other buttons have a 'C' on them. George thought it might have been an initial.

"But this has an "I"" said Daisy.

Myrtle nodded. "Yes, it does. You know, this coat might have belonged to the man who killed Mr. Mitchell."

"But Lars Jørgensen was already found guilty. He's over at the prison at Marquette right now."

"Like I've been saying all along, he didn't do it," said Myrtle. "The evidence didn't match up." She removed the coat from the dummy on which it was hanging and headed for the front of the store.

"What are you going to do?" asked Daisy.

"I want to ask Mr. Macintosh who he bought this from. Or who pawned it."

"Oh, yah," said Mr. Macintosh when Myrtle put her question to him. "I remember the fellow well. He was pretty desperate. Said he'd lost all his money in a poker game and didn't have any to get him back home."

"Did he say where home was?" asked Myrtle.

"Nah. Said he was takin' the train. I warn't too keen 'bout buying the coat, 'cause I could still see where the bloodstain had been washed off."

"Bloodstain?" said Daisy.

"Yah," said Mr. Macintosh, taking the coat from Myrtle's hand. "See right here?" He pointed out an area on the left breast. "Pretty good job, but not perfect. But I felt sorry for the bloke. I even gave him an old coat of mine I didn't wear no more 'cause it had gotten too small. It was still pretty cold out, and I was afraid he'd freeze to death."

"I noticed one of the buttons is different from the others," said Myrtle.

"Yah, that was another thing. That button was missing. I happened to have another one similar to it, so

I sewed it on. Coat'd be worth more if all the buttons was the same. But I didn't have a calvary button."

"Calvary?" said Daisy.

"Yah," said Mr. Macintosh, "you know—soldiers who ride horses?"

"You mean cavalry," said Myrtle.

"Yah, that's what I said: calvary."

"So the 'C' is not someone's initial," said Myrtle. "It stands for *cavalry*. And what does the 'I' stand for?"

"Infantry."

"Infantry," repeated Myrtle. "Do you have the man's name? The one you bought the coat from?"

"Oh, yah, sure. Always get a name. Let's see, now."

Mr. Macintosh opened a ledger lying on the counter and began thumbing through it.

"Okay, here it is. Joshua Logan. That was the feller's name—Joshua Logan."

"We don't know anyone by that name," said Daisy.

"No, but I'm betting that wasn't his real name," said Myrtle. "I'm thinking it was that Mr. Clearmont. Was the man who sold you this coat about your height?" Myrtle asked Mr. Macintosh, whom she took to be a few inches short of six feet.

"Are you joshing me?" asked Mr. Macintosh. "This is a pretty small coat. The fellow who sold it to me warn't as tall as you are, Missy."

Myrtle looked perplexed. "Smaller than me? Are you sure?"

"Oh, yah, I'm sure. And I remember now—he only had one hand, too; the left one. He said he'd lost his right one fighting Indians, eh?"

CHAPTER FORTY-THREE

When they returned home, Myrtle could hardly wait to tell Henri what she had discovered. When she turned the corner at the courthouse and saw the Packard parked in front of his office, she gave out a shriek of delight.

"Yes!"

She brought the car to a halt, grabbed the coat and hurried into Henri's office, Daisy hard on her heels.

"Here!" said Myrtle, dumping the coat onto his desk.

Henri looked up, startled. "What? What is this?"

"This is proof Herman Hutchinson killed Mr. Mitchell, not that poor Lars Jørgensen!"

Myrtle related to Henri everything Mr. Macintosh had told her about the man from whom he'd purchased the coat.

"It had to be him," she said. "Everything makes sense now. I told you the coat you found at Lars's home was too small to fit him. And remember when I told you about the painting that couldn't have been Mr. Mitchell's because it had red paint. And now that I think of it—the palette knives Thomas uses?—Mr. Hutchinson would use those also; he works with oil, like Thomas. Mr. Hutchinson killed Mr. Mitchell!"

"But what about the spade with the blood on it, not to mention Lars's fingerprints?" said Henri.

"And what was Herman's motive? He and Frank were old friends. Besides, Ambrose said the killer would have been as tall, or taller, than Frank, that he would have been behind him, and that he would probably have been right-handed."

"I don't know about the motive," said Myrtle, "but think about this: there's no way to know if the blood on the spade was Mr. Mitchell's or not. The one thing we know for sure is it was the same type. But a third of the population has that type. And the fingerprints? They would have been on it, just as I've said all along: Lars did gardening work for Mr. Mitchell—he would have handled that spade a lot."

"Herman wasn't as tall as Frank," said Henri. "And he isn't right-handed—he doesn't even have a right hand."

"Remember when I had you all stand up and demonstrate stabbing somebody? How it might have been possible Mr. Mitchell was stabbed from the front by someone shorter than he was—and who might have been left-handed?"

Henri didn't speak for a minute. Then: "Well, yah, I guess it could have happened like that."

Andy Erickson burst out from the back room that held the two cells.

"Damn right!" exclaimed Andy. "Ol' Herman must of done it—he kilt the libarian!"

Henri, Myrtle, and Daisy all jerked back in surprise at this unexpected appearance.

"Andy!" said Henri. "Shoot, I forgot you were back there sleeping it off."

Andy bolted for the door. "Wait'll the guys at Joker's hear this!"

Henri jumped up. "Andy, wait . . . ."

But Andy was already out the door.

"I have to stop him," said Henri, strapping on his gun. He reached for his coat. "And I don't want either one of you saying anything to anyone about this."

By the time Henri got outside, there was no sign of Andy.

He hurried across the street into Alton Woodruff's barbershop, which fronted Joker's illegal bar in the back room.

"Did Andy Erickson just come in here?" asked Henri.

"Nah," said Alton. "Ain't been around for a coupla days."

Henri turned to go.

"Hey," said Alton, "you hear 'bout Herman Hutchinson?"

Henri stopped. "What about him?"

"He's the one who killed Frank," said Roger Lampley, sitting in the barber chair waiting for Alton to finish cutting his hair.

Henri's brow furrowed. "How'd you hear that? I thought you said Andy hadn't been in here."

"He hadn't," said Alton. "It was Porgy—Porgy Plimpton. He come running in, spreading the word. He's back there now." Alton nodded toward the back room where Joker was dispensing drinks.

Henri shook his head. He was too late. Pretty soon everyone in town would have heard the news about Herman—including Herman. He bolted out the door, running in the direction of Miss Wasserman's Boarding House. It would be faster than going back and starting his car, he figured.

Minutes later, he knocked hard on the front door. When no one answered right away, he went on in and climbed the stairs to Herman's room.

No Herman.

Henri hurried back downstairs, through the kitchen and out the back door to the carriage house, where he knew Herman's studio to be on the upper floor. As with the bedroom, Herman was nowhere in sight.

260 *Paint the Librarian Dead*

Returning to the house, he found Miss Wasserman coming into the kitchen.

"Miss Wasserman, have you seen Herman?"

"Mr. Hutchinson? Why, no, not since dis morning when he left to go downtown, he said. 'Course, I don't always see him when he comes in or out. Did you check his room? His studio?"

"Both places—he wasn't there. Miss Wasserman, if he shows up, would you call me at the office at once? And if I'm not there, try the boarding house or Mayor Salmon's office."

"Yah, sure. What's happening? Why're you looking for Mr. Hutchinson?"

"I need to ask him some questions."

*****

"What now?" asked Daisy, after Henri had rushed from the office in pursuit of Andy.

"Let's go on home for now," said Myrtle. "I doubt if Henri was able to catch Andy in time to stop the news from spreading all over town. And as soon as it reaches Mr. Hutchinson, I have a feeling he'll be in the wind."

*****

"No sign of Herman?" asked George.

He was standing in Henri's office.

"I've looked everywhere I can think of," said Henri. "No sign of him. Miss Wasserman never called you?"

George shook his head.

"I've put a call into Leonard over in Marquette, and to Constable Simmons over in Houghton. He'll spread the word up the peninsula. And Leonard will get the word out to the whole state."

"What now?"

"Now I'm heading back to the boarding house. It's almost dinner time."

CHAPTER FORTY-FOUR

A month had passed since Myrtle had shown up in Henri's office with what they both now believed to be Herman's coat: evidence they felt proved he had indeed murdered Frank Mitchell.

During that time there had been no sign of Herman, himself.

Captain Wysocki had issued a statewide alert from the State Police Department in Marquette, but nothing had come of it.

Myrtle had pleaded with Judge Hurstbourne to authorize the release of Lars Jørgensen, even gathering ninety-seven signatures from the townsfolk on a petition asking that he be set free.

The judge had refused.

"Herman Hutchinson hasn't even gone to trial yet. Until he does and he's found guilty, we already have Frank's killer in jail."

The town of Booker Falls had settled back into its regular routine. Andy Erickson, unable to find a more suitable job, continued to keep the streets clear of horse droppings. Joker Mulhearn continued to fulfill the needs of most of the town's men—and a few of the women—through the operation of the illegal bar he ran in the room behind the barbershop. Most every Sunday afternoon Myrtle walked Penrod downtown, where they visited Mr. Abramovitz in his pawn shop.

Though he had never before smoked in his life, Eddie had started smoking the pipe Daisy gave him for his birthday. Mrs. Darling made weekly trips, sometimes accompanied by Myrtle, to visit Mr. Pfrommer's grave.

Reports continued to come into Henri's office of art thefts in neighboring towns, though not in Booker Falls.

Myrtle settled more comfortably into her position as head librarian of the Adelaide College Library. She'd been able to persuade Wilfred Forrester, president of the college, to budget additional funds for repairs, improvements, and new books.

This day she stood gazing up at the portrait of Betsy Hutchinson Amyx, wife of Louis Amyx, founder of the college, sister of Barnard P. Hutchinson, who built the library in her memory, and mother of Henry Hutchinson, whom Myrtle was now convinced had killed Mr. Mitchell.

The painting was displayed on the library's upper level above a large case at the top of the spiral staircase that wound its way up from the main floor. The case, some nine feet in length and four feet deep, held artifacts and ledgers about the founding of both the town and the college, and models of the first buildings on the campus.

How long, Myrtle wondered, *had it been since that picture had been cleaned?*

She headed back downstairs to find Claude, who had made a full recovery from the bear attack some four months before.

He was sweeping the floor in the stacks.

"Claude, I need you to do something for me."

"Yes, missus?" He set his broom up against the shelf.

"Is there a tall ladder someplace? At least ten feet?"

"Yes, missus, there's one over in da barn."

"Are there two?"

"Yes, missus."

"Come with me," said Myrtle.

She walked back out into the main room where a number of students were studying, preparing for final exams, and approached a table where four male students sat.

"Fellows," she said, "I need a favor. "Would three of you go with Claude to the barn to bring some ladders back here? Then set them up at the top of the stairs, so they lean over the display case toward Mrs. Hutchinson's picture, eh?"

All four boys jumped up.

"Elroy," said Myrtle, addressing one of the boys, "you stay here. Go on upstairs, and you can help pull the ladders up when the others get back."

Claude and the three boys took off.

As Myrtle climbed the stairs with Elroy ahead of her, the realization of the word she had just uttered struck her and she began to laugh: it was the first time she had ever said "eh" while speaking!

I guess I'm starting to become a native, she thought.

Fifteen minutes later, Claude and the others returned with two ladders and in minutes had them positioned as Myrtle had directed.

"Now," said Myrtle, "Claude if you'd go up one ladder . . . and Elmer . . ." Myrtle decided he looked to be the strongest of the four boys ". . . you go up the other one. Remove the painting and hand it down to Raul and Lawrence."

She hoped the painting was merely hanging, and not attached to the wall by screws.

A few minutes later, the painting leaned safely against one wall of the hallway.

"Now, Claude, if you and the boys could return the ladders I would appreciate it," said Myrtle. "We'll need them again, but not right away. But before you do, I need the painting taken down to my office. Lean it against a wall, with the back facing out so nothing can get on the front."

Myrtle followed the crew down the stairs, where she was approached by a female student.

"Miss Tully," she said, "Can you help me find this book?"

She handed Myrtle a slip of paper.

"I know where that is," said Myrtle. "I'll be right back."

Minutes later, Myrtle emerged from the vault that ran under the library the length of the building and handed the book over to the young woman.

When she reached her office, she opened the door and glanced at the painting leaning up against one wall, its back facing her. Then she looked again. She walked over, knelt down and strained to see what appeared to be a drawing.

"It's a layout of the library," she said to herself.

There, on the back of the painting, was a diagram of all three levels, including the vault from which Myrtle had come moments earlier.

But it was the drawing at the bottom that caught her attention.

It seemed to indicate a square room twenty feet by twenty feet—under the vault!

By its placement, Myrtle deduced it lay immediately under the four hundred square foot section of the vault that, unlike the rest of the floor, which was concrete, had a wooden covering.

She'd often wondered what the purpose of that wooden floor was from the first day Mr. Mitchell took her down to the vault on a tour of the building.

As odd as the existence of the room was, what was stranger was what appeared to be a tunnel that ran from the room to the grotto on the southwest side of the building!

Her thoughts went back to that night last December when she and Henri were returning from the logging camp and a man had run out of the library holding what they thought might have been a painting and then vanished at the edge of the frozen pond.

Was there a chance there might be an entrance to the room under the vault that could only be accessed through the grotto?

Myrtle walked to the window in her office that looked out over the garden, where two students sat at the picnic table, reading. Staring at the grotto at the far end, she wondered: *was this how the man managed to disappear?*

She took her cap off the hook on the wall and headed outside.

Once outside, she walked through the garden and around the pond to where it stopped at the grotto's entrance. A narrow strip of ground led around the edge, and she found herself inside the cavern. It was hard to see, as the only light was that which came from the entrance. She looked around, allowing her eyes to adjust to the dimness.

There was no opening that she could see.

She ran her hand along the wall until it came to rest at a protrusion, what felt like a lever.

Myrtle grasped the lever and turned it clockwise: nothing.

When she turned it counterclockwise, she felt a click and watched as a part of the wall swung back to reveal a passageway.

A shiver ran up her spine.

Stepping inside, she was engulfed in darkness. For just a moment she thought about returning to the library to get a lantern but decided against it.

She reached out her hand and felt a metal handrail on one side. Grasping it, she stepped forward—and felt herself start to fall.

Catching her balance, she felt with one foot and discovered a step going down. *Of course—the room is below the vault, which is below the main floor.* Gingerly, she took a step, then another and another, following the narrow staircase as it made a gradual turn downward in the direction of the library building, finally coming to a stop at the bottom.

Exploring the wall with both hands this time, she touched what seemed to be a wooden door. She found the handle, turned it and pushed: the door swung open easily on its hinges.

Myrtle stepped through the doorway and saw a sliver of light coming from a crack in the ceiling above.

That shouldn't be, she thought. The wooden floor in the vault was on top of the concrete floor which made up the rest of the room. *Where could the light be coming from?*

Again, allowing her eyes to adapt to the dark, she saw she was in a room. She noticed a cord next to her hanging down from the ceiling.

When she pulled the cord, light flooded the room. Myrtle gasped in amazement: paintings and a few other works of art—statues and sculptures, primarily—filled the place.

CHAPTER FORTY-FIVE

As she walked around the room, she recognized the names of some of the artists: Degas, Doré, Pissarro, Cassatt, Bierstadt, and more. Most were unknown to her. She stopped at a small bronze sculpture about eighteen inches tall depicting a young girl, meditating. Myrtle picked up the sculpture and read the artist's name on the back of the base: Camille Claudel.

A little further on, she stopped abruptly, and her hand flew to her mouth: before her was an exact reproduction of the Renoir that hung upstairs on the main floor of the library!

Myrtle studied the painting: she couldn't detect any difference in this work from the one upstairs.

"What are you doing here?"

Startled, Myrtle turned to find Herman Hutchinson standing at the entrance to the room.

"I said, what are you doing here?" Herman asked again.

"You . . . you killed Mr. Mitchell," Myrtle blurted out, her voice shaking.

Herman smirked. "Oh, yeah? What makes you think so?"

"Your coat. The one you wore the night you stabbed Mr. Mitchell. We found it in Red Jacket and brought it back to Henri. There was a button missing, just like the one we found in Mr. Mitchell's hand, the one he tore off when you killed him."

"Yeah, I heard about the coat. So you're the one who found it?"

"Yes. And I know you framed that poor Mr. Jørgensen. The coat they found in his shed was much too small for him. But it would fit you."

"Pretty smart of you to figure all that out. Yah, you're right—I killed Frank. Not that you'll ever be able to tell anyone."

Suddenly, Myrtle realized the precarious position in which she now found herself: in a room, underground, with only one way out, with a killer—and no one knew she was there.

Her mind started to churn. She needed to buy some time to think of how to get out of this situation in which she now found herself.

Keep talking.

"And these paintings—the artwork: they're the pieces that have been reported stolen all around here these past months."

"Right again. But I think we've talked long enough." Herman reached into his jacket pocket and pulled out a long slender object. When he pushed a button, a six-inch long blade sprang forth.

Myrtle's heart began to beat faster. She needed something—anything with which to protect herself. Her eye went to the Camille Claudel sculpture she'd been studying earlier.

Slowly she moved toward the piece, still trying to buy time.

"Wait. *Why* did you kill Mr. Mitchell?"

More time—she needed more time. She continued inching toward the statue.

"I thought you two were friends," she said

"We were," said Herman. "We were also in business together."

"Business?"

"Yes, I would steal—or have one of my associates steal—the paintings, sometimes sculptures and statues, and Frank would arrange purchasers for them."

"But the Renoir. Did you steal that? Is that a forgery upstairs?"

She was close enough now she could put her hand on the young girl's head.

Herman snorted. "Is that the forgery *upstairs*? No, *this* is the forgery, the one down here. I painted it. I haven't had the chance yet to make the exchange."

"*You* painted it?" Myrtle was both surprised—and impressed.

"That's what got Frank killed," said Herman. "I wanted to substitute it for the one upstairs like we did the Montague."

Thomas was right! That painting was *a forgery, as he'd said.*

"Frank said he couldn't go along with it;" Herman continued, "it being a Renoir and all. We argued, and I stabbed him. I didn't mean to—it just happened."

Myrtle wrapped her hand around the statue, ready to pick it up and use it.

"With a palette knife," said Myrtle. "The one you'd been using on *your* painting."

This time it was Herman's turn to be surprised.

"Very good. You really are good at this detective stuff. But now, we have talked much too long, and I've said too much but, as I said earlier, you're not going to have a chance to tell anyone."

"No, I think both of us will be able to say quite a bit, Myrtle and I."

Startled, Frank turned to see who had spoken: Myrtle's eyes darted to the doorway.

Kitty stood there, a gun pointed at Herman.

"Quite enough, actually," she said, "to put you away for a long time."

Herman made a move toward Kitty.

She shook her head.

"I wouldn't if I were you. I think you're smart enough to know a knife is no match against a gun. I could shoot you before you got within ten feet of me. Now, drop the knife and get down on the floor. And remember, this state doesn't have the death penalty, so life in prison sure beats a pine box in some cemetery around here."

Herman hesitated, then dropped his knife onto the floor.

"Kick it over to Myrtle," said Kitty.

Herman did as Kitty instructed him.

"Now," said Kitty, "on the floor."

Kitty walked over and handed her gun to Myrtle.

"You know how to use that, I'm sure."

Myrtle nodded, still confused by what was happening.

"Cover him while I handcuff him," said Kitty.

Then she laughed, realizing the futility of trying to handcuff someone who only had one hand. "As soon as I find something to handcuff him to. All right," she said to Herman, "get up and go over to that pipe."

Herman got to his feet and walked over to the wall. Kitty followed him and handcuffed him to the pipe.

She took the gun back from a still shaken Myrtle.

"Myrtle," she said, "would you go and call Henri and ask him to join us? You'll have to show him how to get down here."

*****

Myrtle, George, and Henri had gathered in the latter's office, Herman safely locked up in a cell in the other room.

"So Mr. Mitchell and Mr. Hutchinson were in cahoots," said Myrtle.

"Appears so," said Henri. "It was pretty common knowledge Frank was having money problems."

"That's why he borrowed money from Joker," said George.

"Yah," said Henri. "He hooked up with Hutchinson to run this scheme of stealing and selling artwork."

"Where Herman handled the stealing part," said Myrtle, "and Mr. Mitchell took care of selling the loot to purchasers."

"Loot?" said George, chuckling.

"Well," said Myrtle, a defensive tone to her voice, "isn't that what they call stolen goods?"

"Yah, it sure is—" said George, grinning, "—among other things."

"Anyway," said Henri, "Herman also painted a forgery of that . . . what was that painting, Myrtle?"

"*The Montague*. The one Thomas said was a forgery," said Myrtle. "And he was right."

Henri scowled. "Yah, okay, he was right."

"And Mr. Hutchinson wanted to do the same thing with the Renoir," said Myrtle, "but Mr. Mitchell said no, and that's what got him killed. Mr. Hutchinson stabbed him with a palette knife."

"And Frank took a step forward and fell right into the painting Herman was working on," said Henri.

"And that's how he got paint all over himself," said George.

"Including red paint," added Myrtle, "which Mr. Mitchell never used."

"Yah, red paint," said Henri. "Herman knew right away Frank was dying. He rolled him off the painting, packed up all his own stuff, including his painting, and was getting ready to leave when he noticed Frank's gold tooth. Not one to leave anything of value lying around, he picked it up and stuck it in his pocket.

"Then, when Herman decided he needed to frame someone else for the crime to make sure he'd be in the clear, he chose Lars. He really had seen him that evening as he left Frank's studio, so he was an easy mark.

"A few days later, he stopped by Lars's place with a bottle of whiskey. He got Lars drunk until he passed out and left the tooth where Lars would find it. He figured he'd try to sell it the first chance he'd get, which would probably be Mr. Abramavitz's pawn shop. And, he knew Mr. Abramovitz was honest, so he'd probably call me as soon as he got the tooth."

"What he hadn't counted on," said Myrtle, "was that Mr. Abramovitz didn't know about the tooth being missing."

"And if you hadn't stumbled on it, Lars might never have been a suspect," said George.

"Yes, I feel so bad about that," said Myrtle.

"Not your fault," said George. "It was an unfortunate consequence."

"The same day Hutchinson left the tooth," Henri continued, "he planted the spade and the coat in Lars's shed."

"I *knew* that coat couldn't have been Lars's," said Myrtle. "It was too small."

"Has he made a full confession?" asked George.

Henri nodded. "Yah, Jake convinced him the confession he made in front of Myrtle and Kitty would hold up in court."

"I'm confused about that room," said Myrtle. "Why is it there? And how did Mr. Hutchinson know about it? And where did that sliver of light come from, if the ceiling is all concrete?"

"First of all," said Henri, "according to Herman, his father, who built the library, designed that room as a safe place to keep valuable items. That part of the vault floor was to be wood, with an opening and a stairway down to the room. But the man who put the floor in didn't read the plans right. He made the entire floor concrete except for the stairway opening. When he found out he'd done it wrong, he got it wrong again and put a wooden floor over the whole thing, including the opening. The shaft of light you saw must have been from where the opening is under the wooden part.

"Mr. Hutchinson also planned for the tunnel to run from the grotto to the room as a second way to get in and out. The builder managed to get that right. Herman knew about the tunnel, because he inherited his father's estate when he died, including the blueprints for the library."

"Here's another thing," said Myrtle. "Who is this Kitty Vanderliet? I know she's no journalist. And how did she happen to show up in that room under the vault?"

"You're right; she's not a journalist. She works for Pinkerton; she's a Pinkerton agent," said Henri.

Myrtle's jaw dropped. "A Pinkerton agent?"

"Yah. Pinkerton was hired by the Eagle Insurance Company out of Superior, Wisconsin. They had an agent in this area who sold policies to hundreds of people, insuring their paintings and a lot of other things. Those were the houses being broken into and the items being stolen. Kitty was the agent assigned to the case. She let me know who she was when she first came to town but swore me to secrecy."

"You knew who she was all along," said Myrtle. The fact Henri had kept the information from her did not make her happy.

"Yah, but, like I said, I couldn't say. Anyway, she suspected the agent was involved in the thefts, and she found out he was friends with Herman. She tracked Herman here to Booker Falls, and she's been watching him, trying to catch him in the act. She also suspected Frank was involved, but she was surprised when he was murdered. She didn't know about the forgeries and had no idea Herman was involved in his death.

"After Herman disappeared, Kitty decided to stick around here. She knew he must have someplace where he stored his 'loot' as you referred to it, and she suspected it might be in the library.

"She was camped out in the woods across the road from the library, keeping an eye on the place when she saw you go into the grotto and disappear. A few minutes later, she saw Herman go in, and that's when she followed him."

"Lucky for me," said Myrtle.

"*Very* lucky for you," said Henri.

"What's the story with her tattoo?" asked Myrtle.

"You mean the one around her wrist?" said Henri.

"No, I mean the crucifix on her back."

Henri looked confused. "I didn't know she had a crucifix on her back. How would I know that?"

"Well, I just . . . no, I don't suppose you would," said Myrtle, embarrassed at what she might have thought about Henri's relationship with Kitty.

"So," she said, thinking it was time to change the subject, "all we have to do now is wait for the trial and for Mr. Hutchinson to be found guilty."

"I've already talked to Judge Hurstbourne about getting Lars released," said George. "He said it should happen in a few days. Now, Myrtle, about the Fourth of July picnic coming up . . . ."

"Uh, no," said Henri. "I'm planning on asking Myrtle to go to the picnic with me."

"I'm afraid you're too late," said George. "I had already planned . . . ."

"I guess you haven't heard," said Myrtle, as she got up and adjusted the cap on her head. "Thomas arrived back in town last night. I'm on my way over to his studio now."

A broad grin covered her face.

"He's finishing my portrait today," she said over her shoulder as she walked out the door.

THE END

ABOUT THE AUTHOR

 Kenn Grimes is both an author and a screenwriter, with two published books to his credit prior to the *Booker Falls Mystery* S*eries:* a collection of short stories, *Camptown: One Hundred and Fifty Years of Stories from Camptown, Kentucky,* published in 2005 by Arbutus Press (now out of print); and *The Other Side of Yesterday,* a time travel novel published in 2012 by Deer Lake Press.

A retired Lutheran minister who served congregations in Indiana, Kentucky, and Missouri, Kenn later owned and operated *Simply Married,* the largest wedding service on Maui, Hawaii. During his ministry he has officiated at over 4,200 ceremonies

He and his wife, Judy, also a retired minister, now split their time between their homes in Louisville, Kentucky, and Lower Northern Michigan, where they continue to do weddings.